B

NIGHTFALL AT LITTLE ACES

RALPH COTTON

THORNDIKE PRESS

A part of Gale, Cengage Learning

GALE
CENGAGE Learning™

Detroit • New York • San Francisco • New Haven, Conn • Waterville, Maine • London

GALE
CENGAGE Learning

Copyright © Ralph Cotton, 2008.
Thorndike Press, a part of Gale, Cengage Learning.

Thorndike Press® Large Print Western.
The text of this Large Print edition is unabridged.
Other aspects of the book may vary from the original edition.
Set in 16 pt. Plantin.
Printed on permanent paper.

LIBRARY OF CONGRESS CATALOGING-IN-PUBLICATION DATA

Cotton, Ralph W.
   Nightfall at Little Aces / by Ralph Cotton.
     p. cm. — (Thorndike Press large print western)
     ISBN-13: 978-1-4104-0923-2 (hardcover : alk. paper)
     ISBN-10: 1-4104-0923-6 (hardcover : alk. paper)
     1. Large type books. I. Title.
PS3553.O766N54 2008
813'.54—dc22   2008021104

Published in 2008 by arrangement with NAL Signet, a member of Penguin Group (USA) Inc.

Printed in the United States of America
1 2 3 4 5 6 7 12 11 10 09 08

NIGHTFALL AT LITTLE ACES

This Large Print Book carries the
Seal of Approval of N.A.V.H.

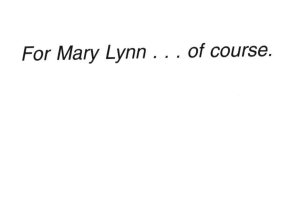

For Mary Lynn . . . of course.

PROLOGUE

Emma Vertrees stood in her backyard spreading a damp white bedsheet along the clothesline. She stopped what she was doing when she saw four armed riders move their horses at an easy gait along the alley toward the livery barn. Three of the four men did not seem to even see her as they passed by single file, no more than thirty feet away. But the last man turned his eyes to her and touched the brim of his hat. Emma stood rigid, giving no response.

There was nothing unusual about armed men riding into town. In fact, an *unarmed* man in Little Aces, New Mexico, would have been more of a rarity. But being the wife of a town sheriff for more than seven years had conditioned Emma to watch closely the comings and goings of armed men, especially those riding in off the southwestern badlands.

She had learned to intuitively read a man's

purpose by the manner in which he rode into town along the dirt street. It was a skill her husband, Dillard, had learned as a lawman; and while it was not something one person could teach another, having been made aware of it, Emma had learned it from him. She had gotten good at it too, she reminded herself, watching the four men stop their horses halfway up the dusty alley beside the livery barn.

These men rode into town with a purposefulness about them, yet she sensed no immediate danger. They were cowboys, she determined; and while cowboys could turn as dangerous and unpredictable as the wild broncs and range animals they lived among, they were for the most part not bad men.

But with cowboys you can expect most anything, she recalled Dillard telling her. She pictured him having said so while she'd touched a wet cloth to his most recently bruised, or sliced, or punctured flesh — battle scars acquired on the streets of Little Aces. *Enough of that . . . ,* she told herself, feeling bitterness slip into her thoughts.

She let the picture of her husband pass from her mind and watched the four dust-streaked young men saunter toward the battered wooden table where blind Curtis Clay sat, his sightless eyes aimed straight ahead.

"I keep hearing how fast you are with your big Remington, *blind man,*" said one of the four, a cowboy named Hank Lindley. As he spoke he lifted his Colt quietly from his holster. "I figure it's time I rode in and found out for myself."

Clay's ears piqued at the faintest sound of the gunmetal sliding up across holster leather. His were the only ears to detect the sound. Others might have heard it had they been listening for it, but blind Curtis Clay never missed such sounds. Nor did he take such sounds for granted. His ears distinguished in sound what his eyes could not see in the engulfing darkness that lay before them. He sat perfectly still behind the wooden table in front of his shack in the alley alongside the livery stables.

"My, my," came Clay's only response. His large black hands lay atop the table, the big Remington lying between them on an oilcloth, like some demon at rest. A silence passed as he smelled whiskey, beer, cigar smoke, horse, and sagebrush on the four young cowboys standing before him. Clay finally asked, "What kind of gun do you have pinted at me?"

Hank gave his friends a half smile, not even wondering how the blind man might know that the Colt was directed at his broad chest. "It's a Colt *pinted* at you," Hank said a bit mockingly. But he tipped the barrel upward. "Does that make any difference?"

Clay seemed to consider the question for a second, then said, "Naw-sir, I expect it don't."

"I ought to warn you, I'm fast," said Hank, the half smile still on his face. "I've been practicing ever since I heard about you."

"I thank you most kindly for telling me," said Curtis Clay. "But I take on all comers."

"What I'm saying is, I'm *danged* fast." As Hank spoke he looked at a tall hickory walking stick leaning against the table beside the blind man.

"Are you more than fifty cents fast?" Curtis asked respectfully.

"Oh, yes," Hank said confidently, "I'm more than fifty cents fast. I might be five dollars fast. Are you sure you want to try me?"

With no expression on his broad face, Curtis said flatly, "You're the one come looking."

Three of the four cowboys exchanged grins and nodded. "He got you there, Hank," Dennis Barnes said. "I expect you'll have to put up or shut up."

"Yeah," said Rupert Knowles, "I don't

10

mind telling you, I'm betting a dollar on the ni— I mean, *Mr.* Clay here," he corrected himself. "So get your money up and let's get on with it."

"Not so danged fast," said Hank, giving Rupert a stern look. "Before I put up any money, I ought to get some kind of idea to see what I'm up against."

The fourth cowboy, a serious-looking young man named Omar Wills, stood to the side, eyeing his companions and blind Curtis Clay with equal contempt. "What a waste of time," he grumbled to himself, hearing Hank Lindley begin to have second thoughts. "I'll be at Little Aces." He turned back to where he'd tied his horse alongside the others. "You can let me know who wins."

"Stick around a minute, Omar," Dennis Barnes called out. "This will be a hoot."

"I've got better things to do," Wills growled under his breath, snatching his horse's reins and flipping himself up into the saddle.

"Oh yeah? Like what?" Barnes countered.

Wills didn't bother answering. Instead, he jammed his spurs to his horse's sides and sent the animal bolting away in a hard run.

Standing at her clothesline, Emma Vertrees fanned the dust that had billowed behind the running horse and drifted across

11

her small backyard. As the young man had sped past her yard, he'd once again looked in her direction and touched his hat brim; once again she had ignored his gesture. Now she watched him rein his horse down to a halt at the end of the alley, where he turned the animal and sat gazing back toward her.

He nudged the horse forward at a walk back toward her yard. She looked away from him quickly, still hoping that ignoring him would send him on his way. But she was wrong. As she stooped slightly and picked up a damp pillowcase from her metal laundry tub, she watched through the corner of her eye as the horse drew nearer, sidling up to the weathered picket fence at the edge of her yard.

She wondered if it would be a good idea to simply walk away from her task and watch from inside her kitchen window until the young man left. *Yes,* she told herself, that would be the proper thing to do.

"Begging your pardon, ma'am," he said as she straightened and turned toward the back door. "That was most inconsiderate of me."

She stopped. *An apology . . . ?* She hadn't been expecting that. She wasn't sure what she had expected, but it certainly wasn't an apology. She tried to make herself walk on to the door, yet something in his voice compelled her to turn back toward him. As she did so she idly held a hand to the collar of her gingham dress. Her only response was a curt but tolerant nod, one that forgave yet dismissed him. That would be enough, she told herself. This was no rowdy drunken range hand. This one showed at least *some* signs of proper upbringing.

But as she once again started to turn away from him toward the door, he threw a leg over his saddle and slid down over her picket fence into her yard. Before she could object, he had twirled his horse's reins on the fence and come walking toward her. He took off his battered Stetson and held it respectfully at his chest.

"I hope my kicking up dust hasn't spoiled your whole wash," he said, coming closer and stopping seven feet from her. "I should have been paying more attention. I don't know where my mind was."

"That's — that's all right," Emma replied awkwardly, not knowing what else to say.

"No, ma'am, it's not all right," said Wills. As he spoke he looked down at the damp clothes wrung tightly and piled in the washtub. "A woman has enough to do without some dumb ole boy like me making more work for her." He gave her a wary smile — a nice smile, she thought. But his smile only brought her attention to his face, his eyes. Something in his eyes caught her and held her.

"It's no trouble, really," she said, realizing he was beginning to make too much of the matter. "We haven't had any rain. . . . It's got the ground so parched. . . ." Was she staring? Yes, of course she was. She knew it, yet she couldn't bring herself to look away. If she looked away now, it would be even more obvious.

"Where are my manners today?" the young man chastised himself. "I'm Omar Wills . . . one of Major Gentry's cattle hands." He took a step closer, as if somehow she'd given him permission. "And you, ma'am?" he asked politely. "That is, if I might be so forward?"

His question was forward indeed, she told herself. But for reasons she did not understand she answered him without hesitation, "I'm *Mrs.* Vertrees . . . wife of *Sheriff* Dillard Vertrees."

"Oh . . ." Her words caught Wills by surprise. He hadn't been in the high grasslands surrounding Little Aces for long, but he'd been here long enough to know that the sheriff in Little Aces was Vince Gale,

14

not Dillard Vertrees. Yet he recalled something about the name Vertrees. What was it? "Well then, *Mrs.* Vertrees," he said, realizing he would have to think about it later. Right now he needed to say something. "I'm honored to have made your acquaintance, even under these circumstances."

Her acquaintance . . . ? They had not been properly introduced. *How dare he?* Remaining composed, she said a bit sharply, "I must ask you to leave now, Mr. Wills." Before finishing her words she stooped to pick up the metal tub of damp clothes under the pretense of having to rerinse everything. "As you can see I have much work to do."

"Yes, ma'am, I understand," said Wills; but instead of turning away, he stepped in between her and the metal tub and picked it up before she could reach the handles. "First, allow me to take this for you," he said. He stood up holding the tub, his Stetson still in hand.

"No," said Emma, sounding more firm on the matter, "I will not *allow* it."

"Please, Mrs. Vertrees, it's the least I can do," said Wills, his voice respectful, innocent, a young man speaking to an older woman.

Emma relented, looking toward the

wooden washing machine standing on three legs beside the water trough nearer to the house. "That *is* courteous of you, Mr. Wills." She gestured toward the water trough as she stepped toward it. "If you will, please, set it down right there."

"Yes, ma'am," Wills replied. He set the tub beside the trough.

"Now, if you'll excuse me . . . ," Emma said curtly, walking toward the rear door.

"Allow me, ma'am," Wills said. Anticipating her move, he hurried ahead of her to the door and opened it for her.

Emma warily walked inside. She did not like the way she'd permitted him to put himself so close to her, to her home, her place of safety. Yet she had done so almost before realizing it.

As soon as she stepped through the door, she turned around quickly, expecting to have to stop him from inviting himself inside. "Look, Mr. Wills —" Her words stopped short as she saw him closing the door behind her.

Hearing her speak his name, Wills pulled the door open slightly. "Yes, ma'am?"

"Nothing . . . Thank you, Mr. Wills," Emma said, relieved, and at the same time feeling foolish. She noted that he had already placed his Stetson atop his head in preparation to leave. With a twinge of guilt, she said in reply to his earlier remark, "Likewise, it's good to make your acquaintance."

He smiled hopefully. "Yes, ma'am. I look forward to seeing you again soon."

Wait, no! Her words weren't meant to offer him encouragement. She wanted to explain that to him, but it was too late. The door closed quietly in her face. *What have you done?* she asked herself. She'd seen this type before. He'd be back, this one. . . .

Stepping away from the door, she ventured a guarded look out the kitchen window. "Omar Wills," she said cautiously, under her breath, as if to record his name in her memory. At the rear of the yard, she saw him hop up onto the picket fence, over it, and into his saddle. He was a handsome young man, she thought, but he had that lost and hungry look she had seen too many times in the past. Yes, he'd be back; she was certain. Was that what she wanted? she asked herself. *Of course not.* . . .

Beside the livery barn, Dennis Barnes gigged Rupert Knowles and gestured toward Wills riding away from Emma Vertrees' yard. "Look who's leaving the dead sheriff's house, Rupert," he said with a chuckle.

"What do you suppose Omar is up to with her?"

Rupert glanced at Wills for only a second, then shifted his attention back to the wooden table where Hank Lindley sat facing Curtis Clay. "I don't know Omar from a broken boot heel — I don't care what he's up to," said Rupert, irritated by Barnes' interruption. "I've got money bet here."

On the table in front of Lindley, his Colt lay disassembled on a one-foot-square oilcloth, the same as the cloth lying in front of Curtis Clay. The blind man's Remington pistol had been laid in pieces between his resting hands. At each man's elbow sat his wagering money. On Clay's five-dollar bill a bullet stood holding it down. Lindley's money consisted of three dollar bills held down by a handful of loose quarters.

Clay had heard mention of the *woman,* and he knew which woman Barnes referred to. He had heard Wills' horse leave moments ago, then heard it ride back a shorter distance — he knew where the young cowboy had been, and he'd also heard him leave. "Are we all set?" Clay asked, his face showing no expression, his cloudy blind eyes hidden behind a pair of dark-shaded spectacles.

"Yeah, I'm ready when you are," said

Lindley.

Clay put away his concern for Emma Vertrees and patted his hands gently on the parts of the Remington, getting a feel for their location. "Somebody say go," he said bluntly, his hands going back to the tabletop, relaxed yet poised.

Lindley grinned. "Just like that? You don't want them to say, *Get ready, get set* first?"

"If you need them to, they can," Clay said respectfully.

"No, I don't *need* for them to. I'm ready." The smile had left Lindley's face as he heard Rupert and Barnes stifle a laugh. With his eyes fixed on the blind man's face, Lindley said, "Barnes, say *go* for us."

Barnes stalled. "It don't seem natural, just saying *go,* without no warning or nothing else."

"Just say it, dang it to hell!" Lindley growled at him. "Let's get this over with."

"All right," said Barnes. A tense silence loomed for a second, until he said loudly, "Go!"

Clay's black hands worked deftly, almost in a blur, snatching piece after piece of the Remington from the tabletop and fitting them into place. Across from him Hank Lindley did the same. He worked fast, but not fast enough. Before his Colt had been

19

half assembled, he heard the spin of the big Remington's cylinder and heard Rupert say in awe, "Damn! He's done!"

Lindley let the cylinder to his Colt fall back onto the tabletop in defeat. He stared at the Remington looming before him in Clay's hand and said, "This is rigged. Nobody is that fast putting a gun together."

"Rigged? Rigged how?" Rupert asked. "You seen it with your own eyes. How could you rig something like this?"

"I don't know, but it's rigged, I'm telling you." As Lindley spoke, Clay heard the rustle of his shirtsleeve and the slightest jingle of coins as he reached over, picked up the five dollars in bills and coins, and set the money in front of him. "But I've never crawfished on a bet," Lindley added in disgust.

Relieved, Clay touched the money lightly with his fingertips, counting without giving the appearance of counting. "How close did you get?" he asked quietly. "I never heard your cylinder click."

"Not *very* danged close," Rupert laughed. He rubbed his finger and thumb together toward Lindley, reminding him of the dollar bet he'd made. His laughter was cut short as Lindley snatched a dollar from his shirt pocket and tossed it at him.

"Never mind how close I got," Lindley said grudgingly. "I'll be coming back. I'm going to try you again."

"I'm always here and you're always welcome," Clay said respectfully. This was what many of them said after he'd won their money. *I'm coming back. . . .* But they never did.

He sat silently as Lindley finished assembling his Colt, and then as the three cowboys mounted their horses and rode away toward the dirt street. When the dust had settled and he could no longer feel the gritty dryness of it in his nostrils, Clay stood up, shoved the Remington down into his waist behind his shirttail, and picked up the tall hickory walking stick leaning against the table.

"Come on out here, Little Dog," he said to a growth of weeds and debris on the other side of the alley. "Take me on over to the widow woman's fence. We best go see about her."

PART 1

CHAPTER 1

Arizona Ranger Sam Burrack had been tracking the Wheelers and their unknown accomplice for over a week when the three crossed over into New Mexico Territory. The Wheelers, Eddie and Dorsen, were not particularly smart, but they had the animal cunning that came with being lifelong criminals. They might not know that it was the ranger on their trail, but they knew instinctively that *someone* had taken up the chase. They were used to being hunted. Sam knew that slipping around by the skin of their necks came natural to them.

He'd been tracking three sets of prints ever since he got word of the killing of the sheriff in Whitehead. Two days into the hunt, a relay station attendant outside Peyton finally identified the two Wheeler brothers. The third man? He'd shrugged and said he had no idea. "But it was the Wheelers for dang sure," he'd said, holding a wet rag to the knot Dorsen Wheeler had left along the side of his head — his only payment for the three horses they'd taken from his corral.

After a week of tracking and gaining little ground, the ranger decided to play a hunch. He'd decided that if he were the Wheelers and headed in this direction rather than toward the Mexican border, his destination would be up into the Santo De Christo Mountains. He knew the Wheelers were Kansas boys and that sooner or later they would head there, but not straightaway. They needed to cool off first, Sam told himself.

Following his hunch, he'd spent the night riding his Appaloosa stallion, Black Pot, up a dark treacherous set of switchbacks. At first light, he sat under the branches of a sheltering pine, looking down onto stretches of woods broken up by grassy flatlands, seeing what those woods had to offer. If his hunch was wrong, he'd pick up the trail again, but it would cost him a day's ride without rest. Still, it was worth the gamble, he told himself — *Bring this hunt to an end.*

He'd decided to give himself only a few more minutes before scrapping his idea and picking up their trail once again. But no sooner had the thought entered his mind than he spotted the three men riding into sight from a stand of woodlands.

"Speak of the devil," he murmured to the stallion as the three riders slipped into sight above a rise of flatlands. He backed the horse a step even though the darkness beneath the big pine offered plenty of cover. Raising a battered field lens to his right eye, he homed in for a closer look. *Yep, Eddie and Dorsen Wheeler all right . . .* Now, moving the lens away from the Wheeler brothers' faces to the third man, he said quietly in surprise, "Warren Beck . . . ?"

Sam lowered the lens from his face and looked down with his naked eyes. "*Memphis* Warren Beck, I never figured a seasoned ole train robber like you to partner up with the likes of these two knot heads," he said under his breath.

Sam watched the three riders slip along warily toward the next cover of woodlands a thousand yards away. The Wheelers kept looking back over their shoulders, checking their back trail, but Memphis Beck stared straight ahead — a man with either nothing to fear, nothing to lose, or nothing to hide. . . .

We'll see, the ranger told himself. Knowing that his hunch had paid off, he collapsed the lens between his gloved hands, shoved it

27

inside his riding duster, and turned the stallion back to the narrow trail leading along the mountainside.

Once across the wide stretch of grasslands and back inside the shelter of towering pine and spruce, Dorsen Wheeler slowed his horse from beside his brother and sidled up to Memphis Beck riding behind them. "I expect we can breathe a little easier, now that we're out of the open."

Beck only turned a look to him. "Who's breathing hard?"

Dorsen looked a little embarrassed and said, "You know what I mean, though."

"Yeah," said Beck, "I know what you mean." He looked away.

Dorsen gigged his horse back up beside his brother and rode on in silence. His brother Eddie spat a stream of tobacco juice, shook his head slightly, and chuckled under his breath. "You have no winning ways about you, brother Dor. I always said so."

Dorsen offered no reply, but two miles deeper into the woodlands as the three stopped their horses alongside a wide shallow creek, he tried again. "I can't help but wonder, Memphis, what it's like up there with them ole boys in the Hole. An old hoss like you must've seen a lot of —"

"You'll have to go see for yourself," Memphis Beck replied quietly but rudely, cutting him off.

Again Eddie chuckled; again Dorsen's face reddened, this time with anger as much as embarrassment. "Are you being sharp with me, Memphis?" he asked. Standing beside his horse as it watered itself, he poised his hand near his holstered Colt. "Because I'm not known to take much guff or abuse off of any man."

Memphis' hand made no effort to draw itself any closer to the big bone-handled Dance Brothers pistol lying straight across his chest in a slim-jim holster. His horse also stood with its muzzle down in the cool water. Taking his time before answering, Memphis Beck took a step sidelong away from the watering animal, rubbing his hand along its side until he stood clear of it with nothing behind him but the woods.

"Sharp . . . ? No. I wouldn't say being *sharp*," he said in his easy Southern voice. Now his thumb had hooked loosely behind his belt, idly narrowing the distance between his hand and the big pistol, yet in a most natural way. "Had I meant to be *sharp*, we wouldn't be standing here right now . . . not both of us anyway." There was a threat

29

there, but it was spoken matter-of-factly, as if Dorsen Wheeler could make of it whatever suited him.

"Let it go, Brother," Eddie whispered cautiously to Dorsen, seeing him bristle a bit. "This is not the sort of man to get your bark on with."

"Oh, my bark is on, sure enough, Brother," said Dorsen. "And I allow it'll stay stuck tight until I get my concerns reconciled."

"Hole-in-the-wall is no different than any other place," Memphis Beck offered out of the blue, responding to Dorsen's earlier question. He stood relaxed, revealing nothing menacing in his eyes or demeanor. "Were you to ride in, you'd see that for yourself."

"Oh . . . ?" Dorsen was taken aback. He gave his brother a curious look, as if having a hard time understanding Memphis Beck, either in words or actions. Had he misread the man? He watched the famous train robber raise his gun hand, take off his hat, and run his fingers back through his graying hair. Was this Beck's way of easing a tense situation? Believing it was, Dorsen cooled down.

"See, Dorsen, that's all he meant," said Eddie. "Don't be so jackrabbit quick to jump ugly on a fellow."

Perhaps he had misread him. Dorsen eased up even more, letting his gun hand drop to his side. But Beck, having placed his hat back on his head, hooked his thumb back in place beneath his belly gun. Dorsen and Eddie didn't seem to notice.

"I reckon I have been stretched awfully tight of late," Dorsen said after a moment, seeming to forget all the other times Beck had short-answered or outright ignored him. "I might blame some of it on living *dirt-blanket* out here amongst the snakes and heathens." He offered a weak, tight smile to show his dark mood had begun to pass.

Seeing the worst of what could have become a bad situation pass, Eddie took the opportunity to change the subject. "I might never make it to see Hole-in-the-wall, but damned if I don't get the feeling the three of us are about to get ourselves *mightily fixed.*" He glanced back at Beck with a sly grin and a wink. "I bet you're as ready for that as we both are, eh, Memphis?"

Without changing his stoic expression, Memphis gave a slight nod and replied, "I'm always on the lookout to get mightily fixed."

"See?" Eddie said to Dorsen. "It goes to show you, we're all the same one scratch

31

under the surface." He turned his face toward the trail, he and his brother riding a few paces ahead of Memphis Beck.

Beck stared at their backs, picturing how easy it would be to slip his revolver from his holster and effortlessly put a bullet in their hearts. *Bang, bang, just like that,* he told himself. But then he smiled to himself and put the notion out of his mind. There had been a time though . . .

But that time had been long ago, back before he came to realize that the lives of men like these two were truly not worth the price of a bullet, let alone worth shattering the silence of a peaceful trail and filling the air with the smell of burnt powder. Besides, he reminded himself, it wouldn't be long. He looked warily forward and along both sides of the trail. Surely whoever was dogging them would have taken a higher trail and been up there watching them cross the grasslands.

Nudging his horse, Beck offered himself a faint grin as he felt the trail slant upward beneath his horse's hooves. He had a strong feeling the Wheelers were about to get themselves *"mightily fixed"* for good.

The ranger sat at the top of the thin trail, knowing how difficult it would be for the

Wheelers to spread out or make a fast turnaround and get away. This would be it, he was certain. They would be too, he thought, once they rounded the steep turn and found him waiting. He'd tucked his right glove behind his belt. His rifle stood propped up on his thigh, his thumb over the hammer. His pearl gray sombrero lay back off his head, on his shoulders, held there by a thin loop of rawhide. He sat quietly, resolved to facing whatever outcome lay in store. Beneath him the stallion stood as still as stone — no newcomer to this grave and deadly situation.

Sam listened to the sound of quiet banter and approaching clop of hoof on stone as the horses walked into sight. Upon seeing him facing them midtrail, the Wheelers reined their horses back hard, in surprise. Behind them, Memphis Beck stopped and backed his horse calmly. He had not yet rounded the turn. Had the ranger seen him? He didn't think so.

"Dorsen and Eddie Wheeler," the ranger called out as a matter of form, "I'm Arizona Ranger Sam Burrack. You are both under arrest for murder. Throw down your guns."

"Like hell!" Dorsen blurted out, his hand going for his gun even as his horse reared slightly against the tightened reins. "Kill him, Brother!" he bellowed.

But beside him Eddie shouted, "Wait!" as if it would only be fair and sporting of both the ranger and his brother, Dorsen, to give him a second to settle his spooked horse before making a grab for his pistol.

But neither man offered him a sporting chance. Before Dorsen's gun leveled toward the ranger, the ranger's rifle snapped upward from his thigh and fired. The shot nailed Dorsen midchest and sent him flying backward as his revolver fired wild and flew from his hands. In that split second it dawned on Eddie Wheeler for the first time just how truly fast his brother had been with a gun — fast, but not fast enough.

"Don't try it," the ranger warned. But even as he'd spoken the words, his right hand levered a fresh round into the rifle. Eddie Wheeler barely got his gun barrel above holster level. As he made his play, he let out an enraged scream, as if that would somehow work to his advantage. It didn't.

From his position out of sight, Beck heard the second rifle shot and shook his head. No surprise there, he told himself, and backed his horse slowly out of sight behind a large boulder at the turn of the trail. He'd begun to turn the horse on the narrow trail. But he stopped when he heard the ranger call out, "Warren Beck . . . throw out your guns and come forward."

Beck stopped and took a deep breath. "So you recognized me, huh?" He eyed the narrow trail and weighed his chances of getting down it alive, the ranger right on his heels.

"Throw them out, Beck," Sam warned him. "We'll talk more afterwards."

Beck ran things through his mind. It had been a long time since he'd ridden on a job with the Hole-in-the-wall Gang. The railroad detectives had been quiet lately. The fact was, nobody had ever linked him to the gang with any witnesses, or any solid proof. He wasn't wanted by the regular law for anything in Arizona Territory, New Mexico, either; he was certain. Still . . .

"What's the charge, Ranger?" he asked calmly as he slipped the big Dance Brothers from his belly holster, checked it, and cocked it, just in case.

"*None* as far as I'm concerned," said Sam, his rifle ready at his shoulder. "But I don't like thinking you're sitting there out of sight, ready to throw down on me. The longer you put me off, the more I'm going to convince myself that you were partnered up with the Wheelers, not just making a trail with them."

"What if I just ride away, Ranger?" Beck asked.

"You know that's not the way it works, Beck," Sam said.

"You're right, I was just making a trail with these two." He smiled to himself. "A man never knows when he might come upon some hostiles in this high country. It pays to have something to feed to them."

"That's what I thought," said Sam. "But unless I see some iron on the dirt, you'll be riding with them facedown, partners or not."

Memphis Beck considered it a moment longer, knowing that the ranger meant every word he said.

Sam held his rifle at ready. After almost a full minute of silence, he watched a hand reach out from around the edge of his rock cover and toss a rifle into the dirt.

"That's a good start," Sam said flatly.

The hand pitched the big Dance Brothers to the dirt with a soft plop. "I don't carry a hideaway gun," Beck called out.

"And I don't tolerate liars," Sam replied. "Let's not get off on the wrong foot here."

Another short silence passed; then a short-barreled .38-caliber pistol plopped softly beside the big Dance Brothers. "I almost forgot this one," Beck said matter-of-factly.

"I bet. Now step out here, slow and easy," Sam said.

Beck stepped into sight and calmly walked toward him, saying as he drew nearer, "This is a waste of your time and mine, Ranger." He looked hesitant and said, "Unless you have a deal with the railroad, I'm clean all around these parts." He kept his hands chest high.

"I don't work with the railroads," said Sam. "I figure you must be clean, else you would never have given up your guns without a fight."

"You got that right," Beck said, looking around at the Wheelers lying dead in the dirt. "One of us would be dead right now." He sounded insincere, as if he'd heard so many threats and so much tough talk that he took none of it serious anymore.

"I expect that's so." Sam looked the infamous outlaw up and down. "We'll know for sure how clean you are once we get to town. If the law in New Mexico Territory doesn't want you, you'll be free to ride away."

"I'm always clean, so let's get it done, Ranger," Beck said, holding his wrists out. "The sooner we get to town, the sooner I can be on my way." He grinned. "Next time I'll be more careful of the company I keep."

"That's always a wise policy," Sam replied. As he spoke he stepped around Beck and ran his hands up and down his sides, searching for any other weapons. "You can lower your hands. I'm not going to cuff you unless you cause me trouble."

"Oh, you're going to trust a member of the Hole-in-the-wall Gang, Ranger?" Beck lowered his hands and hooked a thumb into his belt, beneath his empty holster. Sam took note of it.

"No, I don't trust you, Beck," Sam said flatly, not allowing himself to get too sociable. He stepped back and picked up the rifle and the two pistols from the dirt. "I'm keeping you in front of me at all times, the way you kept those two in front." He stuck the big pistol into his belt, the smaller one into his rawhide vest, and held the rifle under his arm.

"I ought to take offense at that remark, Ranger," Beck said with a smile, "comparing me to a couple of small-time thieves like the Wheelers."

"You're a thief and an outlaw, Warren Beck," Sam said. "I consider you and your Hole-in-the-wall pals no different than the Wheelers. You boys are bigger thieves than the Wheelers. In my book that's nothing to be proud of." He gestured toward the two bodies. "Now help me get these two across their saddles and we'll get moving. You and I don't want to spend any more time together than we have to."

"Well," said Beck, turning to the bodies, "I see that a man knows right off where he stands with you."

"I'm a lawman, Beck," said Sam. "Keep that in mind and we'll get along just fine until our trails part. Maybe you've always been too slick to get charged with anything, but that doesn't make you a hero in my book."

"Understood, Ranger," said Beck. "Now then, what town are we headed to anyway?"

Sam looked off toward a distant line of low-stretching hills as if considering it. "Nickels is less than a day's ride. They've got a telegraph office and sheriff."

"Then Nickels it is," said Beck, as if he had any say in the matter. "If there's no detectives snooping around, I might just stay a day or two, rest my tired old bones and my cayouse too before heading north. Think there'll be any objections?"

"That'll be up to the town sheriff," Sam replied. "I'll have no say in the matter."

"You might mention to him how I came along with you without putting up a fight," said Beck.

"He'll know that as soon as he sees you sitting upright in your saddle," the ranger answered.

"You sure have a way of making yourself clear, Ranger." Beck chuckled, walking toward the bodies on the ground.

CHAPTER 2

The ranger sipped tepid water from a canteen and stood beside Black Pot while Beck finished tying the Wheelers' bodies down over their saddles. He watched Beck step back with the two horses' reins in hand and slap dust from his shirt with his flat-crowned hat. Sam had to admit, Beck had a disarming way about him. The aging outlaw hadn't stopped his line of friendly banter since he'd begun loading the bodies.

That was all right, the ranger told himself. This wasn't the first smooth-talking thief he'd ever come upon. Sam wasn't taken in by him. ". . . And don't forget, the law has never successfully tied me to the Hole-in-the-wall Gang," Beck said, as if Sam's attention had been hanging on his every word.

"Oh, I know what you're thinking, Ranger," said Beck, not realizing the ranger had only been half listening to him. Sam had been more interested in watching his actions than hearing his words. "You're thinking, good schooling, good Mormon, Christian upbringing, how in the world does a man like this end up a train robber? Not admitting that I *really am,* of course."

But the ranger didn't tell him he hadn't even been listening. Instead he said, "Whatever you've done, you must've figured out a way to justify it by now."

"Justify it?" Beck seemed to consider it for a moment, then said, "No, I'm not justifying anything I've ever done. I don't have to." He grinned knowingly. "I'm just making barroom conversation." He put his hat back atop his head. "Usually after a drink or two a buddy will get around to asking me *why* a man like me would choose the owl-hoot trail. I was just obliging you, Ranger."

"This is no barroom, we're not drinking buddies, and I don't really care," Sam said bluntly. He nodded him toward his waiting horse as he capped the canteen. "Let's get some saddle time in before dark."

"Whoa, Ranger," Beck said with a friendly laugh, stepping forward toward him with what Sam took to be deliberation. "Don't I get a swig of water first? This trail has been as dry on me as it has you."

"That's close enough, Beck," Sam said firmly.

Beck stopped and shrugged. "Sorry, Ranger, didn't mean to make you so touchy. Do I need to ask your permission before I take a step in any direction?"

There it was, Sam told himself — Beck making it appear as if the ranger were unreasonable, being overcautious with him. "Yes, you do." Sam gave him a hard stare, letting him know right off where he stood. "If I have to tell you again, I'll cuff you."

"Would you feel better if I'm cuffed, Ranger?" Beck asked, playing the part of a reasonable man trying his best to get along with some hard-bitten lawman. Again he held his wrists out as if willing to go along with whatever the ranger asked of him.

"Get on your horse," Sam said, ignoring the gesture as he took a hold of his saddle horn to swing up.

"No," Beck said just as firmly, taking a stand. "Not until you tell me what it's going to take to get along with you."

Sam halted. He gave Beck a closer look. Was this man playing out a role? Was this his way of getting the ranger in close so he could make a move on him? Sam studied his eyes for a moment. *Whatever it is, you're good at it, Memphis Beck. . . .*

"No, I mean it, Ranger," Beck said, shaking his head with determination, seeing the resolve in the lawman's eyes. "I'm not under arrest. I've gone along with everything you've asked of me. Now it's time I know where I stand." He took a step forward with his hands spread.

"Get back, Beck," Sam said, his hand going around the butt of his big Colt.

Beck stopped, but he appeared on the verge of taking another step. The reins to the two horses fell from his hands. "Or what, you'll shoot me? An *unarmed* man? For *no reason?* You're not known for that!"

Before Sam could speak, a voice said from atop the rock above them, "If he won't, I will."

The Ranger's Colt streaked instinctively from his holster and cocked. He stood poised, looking at the rifle pointing down at him from thirty feet.

"Easy, Ranger Burrack," said the rifleman, "I know who you are. I don't want to kill you."

His words kept the ranger from firing, but only for a second. "You might know me, but do I know you?" Sam said.

"Ranger, that's Lightning Jack Strap," Beck cut in, his hand going back up chest high. "He *is* known for shooting unarmed

44

men . . . women, kids, pigeons."

"Keep running your mouth, Memphis," said the rifleman. "You'll make my job so much easier."

"If you're Jack Strap, I've heard of you too," Sam said, not lowering his Colt. He took a slow step sidelong, ready to jump off the trail for cover if need be. "Now, why is your rifle pointed at me?"

"It's not pointed at you, Ranger," said Strap. "It's pointed at Beck. I see you've got your hands full with this jake."

"He's not a prisoner, Strap," Sam offered. "I found him riding with the Wheelers." He nodded toward the bodies draped over their saddles. "I'm riding into town with him, see where he stands with the law hereabouts."

"Then we're both in luck, Ranger," Strap called down to him. "We're obliged to take him off your hands."

We're? Sam glanced around, and saw a second rifleman step into sight from around the base of the rock. "I'm not looking for anybody to take him off my hands," he replied, moving the barrel of his Colt back and forth between the man above and the one on the ground. Were there more waiting behind cover?

From atop the rock, Strap called down to the other man, "Vlak, keep an eye on Beck

45

while I walk down from here and talk closer up with Ranger Burrack." He backed away out of sight, in order to climb down to the trail.

Without reply the second rifleman walked forward warily, his rifle barrel leading his way, leveled at Memphis Beck.

"That's Vlaktor Blesko — *Bloody Vlak*," Beck said under his breath. "He once rolled heads for the czar of Russia. I'd rather have you shoot me in the heart right now instead of turning me over to these two. Their biggest reason for *living* is to see *me dead*."

In spite of Beck's cool, calm manner, Sam noted a trace of apprehension in his voice. He gave Beck a look and said quietly, "Who mentioned turning you over to these two? Stay where you are and keep your hands in sight."

"My hands?" Beck held his hands in front of him and turned them back and forth. "Ranger, I don't know what it is you think I can do. Look at me, I'm old enough to be —"

"Keep your mouth shut for starters," said Sam, "before I change my mind and feed you to them."

Beck nodded. He managed to keep silent until Vlaktor Blesko walked up closer and stopped, the tip of his rifle inches from

46

Beck's belly. A thin smile of satisfaction creased his stony face.

"Hello, *Bloody* Vlak," Beck said quietly. "This must be a big day for you."

The Romanian's expression didn't change. He leered at Beck as if the ranger weren't even there. Sam stood with his Colt cocked as Jack Strap walked into sight from around the edge of the large rock. When Strap drew closer and stopped less than six feet from the ranger, he looked Beck up and down, then said to Sam, "Pardon me if I sounded a little pushy, Ranger. The truth is we've been tracking this man and the rest of his bunch longer than I like to admit."

"We?" Sam asked, his pistol ready as he looked around again.

"Vlaktor and I are scouts for Colonel Dan Elgin's Railroad Security Alliance. I know you're bound to have heard of Colonel Elgin . . . of the Great Western Railroad Posse?"

"I have," said Sam, looking the two over closely. He'd heard of several railroads pooling their resources and hiring a posse of professional manhunters to bring down gangs like Hole-in-the-wall. This was the first time he'd met any of them face-to-face.

Noting that the ranger was not as impressed as Strap had hoped he would be,

Strap said with a slight shrug, "All right, I understand. You're the one who captured Beck. I'll see to it you get an ample reward. I'll even give you a receipt saying so, if that's wh—"

"I didn't *capture* him," Sam said, cutting him off, "and I don't accept reward money."

"Then what is going on here?" Strap gave both the ranger and Beck a curious look.

"I tracked the Wheeler brothers down." Sam nodded at the bodies on horseback. "Beck here just happened to be riding with them. Now he's agreed to ride into Nickels with me, just to see where he stands with the local law."

"Sort of doing my civic duty," Beck cut in.

"The local law?" Strap looked Beck up and down with contempt. "This snake is too slick for any *local law* to handle. We're doing you a favor taking him off your hands." As he spoke his grip grew tighter around his rifle stock.

"That's the second time you've mentioned taking him off my hands," said Sam. "If that's all you've got to say, it's time you and your partner here take leave." His hand held the big Colt steady.

"I've been about as reasonable as I know how to be, Ranger," Strap said, his attitude turning dark. "He's wanted by the railroad and I'm taking him in. Stay out of my way." Without another look at Sam, Strap said to Beck, "All right, outlaw, let's get going." He nodded toward Beck's horse.

Hesitating, Beck gave the ranger a look. Sam only watched in silence, his expression offering no clue to what was going through his mind.

"You heard me, Beck," said Strap. "You can ride straight up or facedown. It makes me no difference one way or the other."

The Romanian stepped in closer, helping Strap seize the situation.

Glancing at Sam, Strap said confidently, "As for you, Ranger. The best thing for you to do is —"

His words never made it out of his mouth. The barrel of the ranger's Colt swung fast and hard. Strap hit the ground with a long red welt along the side of his head. His rifle flew from his hands as Sam's Colt leveled toward Bloody Vlak.

"Drop it," Sam warned as the Romanian jerked his rifle away from Beck and pointed it toward him. There would be no time to crack this one in the head, Sam knew instinctively as he started to pull the trigger. But before he could, he saw Beck's right forearm come around fast and knock the rifle barrel to the side. Then, as quick as a whip, Beck spun in a circle, faster than a man half his age. His left leg shot upward into a roundhouse kick to the Romanian's jaw.

Vlaktor turned a crazy flip sideways and landed with a thud, knocked cold. The side of Beck's boot heel left an impression on his broad jaw.

Sam kept his surprise from showing, yet he couldn't help but wonder if this was what Beck had in mind trying to get in closer to him before the two railroad detectives showed up.

"I learned that years ago along the Barbary Coast. I'm surprised I even remembered it," Beck said. As he spoke, he took a step toward Vlaktor's rifle lying in the dirt.

"I'll take that." Sam stepped around him, and picked up the rifle, his Colt still in hand. On the ground, Jack Strap moaned and tried to struggle upward. As Beck backed away with a shrug, Sam picked up each man's rifle and unloaded them into the dirt. He slipped Strap's pistol from its holster and unloaded it as well. Then he took the half-conscious detective by his hand and pulled him to his feet.

"Pick up those bullets," Sam said to Beck. To Strap he said, "We'll leave your horses three miles up the trail. Don't let me catch you dogging us the rest of the way to Nickels, Detective."

"You — you've cracked my damn head," Strap managed to say in disbelief, his gloved hand to the welt above his ear.

"You're lucky I didn't put a bullet through your foot," Sam said. "You should know better than to interfere with a lawman doing his job." With his free hand, he helped Strap steady himself for a moment until the bleary-eyed detective gained his balance.

"Ranger, don't leave us out here afoot," Strap said. "We're forward scouts. This is going to make us look like a couple of fools!"

"You did this to yourself, Strap," Sam said quietly.

"You better hope and pray our trails don't cross again, Ranger," Strap said, cupping his throbbing head. "And you," he said to Beck. "I ever run across you again, next time I'll kill you quicker than you can turn around."

"You hear him threatening me, don't you, Ranger?" said Beck. "See? If they can prove something, they put a fellow in jail. If they *can't* prove anything, they just kill a man straight out."

"Let's go, Beck," Sam said, seeing Beck

ready to take a step toward the wobbly detective.

Strap stood over the unloaded guns lying in the dirt until he watched the ranger and Beck ride away, Sam leading the Wheelers, their dead arms dangling loosely. Beside him Beck looked back with a grin, leading the detectives' horses around the large rock to the winding trail.

No sooner had the two gotten out of sight than Strap hurriedly punched bullets from his holster belt and loaded his revolver. "Wake up, Vlak!" he shouted at the limp figure on the ground and kicked him roughly on his leg.

Vlaktor groaned, shook his head, and struggled against the ground. Strap cursed under his breath and helped the Romanian to his feet. "Vat dids he hit me vith?" Vlak asked in a slurred voice.

"His foot, you idiot," Strap said sharply, drumming his fingers on the butt of his holstered revolver. "He gave you a Chinese roundhouse. You should have seen it coming!"

"How vould I see it . . . ?" Vlaktor batted his bleary eyes and cupped his stiff, throbbing jaw.

Looking toward the trail, Strap said, "Come on, shake yourself off and let's get going. Maybe we can get to the horses and retrieve them before the colonel and the others catch up to us. I've been humiliated enough for one day."

The pair struck out along the narrow trail, their unloaded rifles under their arms. But before they had walked a thousand yards, they looked back and stopped. Colonel Elgin, in his long black duster and derby hat, led the posse toward them.

"Damn it, he's seen us," said Strap. "I could kill that ranger for this."

Moments later the colonel brought the seven-man posse to a halt, circling Strap and the Romanian. "I hope there is some good reason why you two are walking," the colonel said briskly. He jerked a pair of dust goggles from his eyes and let them hang from his neck on a strip of black rubber as he looked all around, as if searching for their horses.

"It's Memphis Beck, Colonel," said Strap. "Him and an Arizona ranger caught us unawares and took off with our horses."

"Caught you *unawares?*" said the colonel, his voice growing more gruff. "What kind of scouts get caught unaware?"

"I — I don't know what to say, Colonel," Strap replied.

But the colonel didn't even pause for an

answer. Instead he asked angrily, "What in *blazing hades* is an Arizona ranger doing riding with an outlaw like Memphis Beck?"

"He's taking Beck to Nickels to see if he's wanted by any local law —"

"Local law, my *virgin aunt!*" said Colonel Elgin, cutting him off. "If these local lawmen could handle this bunch of thieves, the railroad wouldn't need us out here in the first place!" He contemplated things, then said, "He's headed for Nickels, eh? How far ahead are they?"

"Twenty, thirty minutes at the most, Colonel," said Strap. "Soon as we can get mounted, we can catch right up to —"

Cutting him off again, Elgin called back over his shoulder, "Bobby, you and Roundhead get up here! You're scouting ahead for us. You too, Skimmer."

"But, Colonel," Strap said, "me and Vlak are your scouts."

"Not anymore, you're not," said the colonel as Bobby Vane and Roundhead Mitchell slid their horses to a halt and waited anxiously. "I need scouts on *horseback!* You two are without transportation. We have no spare horses for you. I never thought any man of mine would be left without one."

"But our horses will be waiting along the trail, Colonel," said Strap. "Ranger Burrack said he'd leave them waiting for us."

"Good, then," said Elgin, "As soon as you reach your horses, you can hurry along and catch up to us." His stare remained on Strap and the Romanian as he gestured the three newly appointed scouts ahead with his gloved fingers.

"Yes, sir," said Strap. He noted the smile on Bobby Vane's face as he, Roundhead, and Skimmer heeled their horses out ahead of the rest of the posse.

As if on second thought, the colonel's gaze turned curious. "Did you say *Ranger Burrack?*"

"I did, Colonel," said Strap.

"Siding against a railroad detective with Memphis Beck?" Elgin stared off in disbelief for a moment. Then he said, "Once you reach us, I'll expect to hear the full account of what happened here. Is that clear?"

"Yes, sir," said Strap as the colonel jerked his horse and heeled it away before hearing his reply.

"Vat ve do now?" Vlak asked as the posse rumbled away along the trail.

"What do you think *ve* do *now?*" Strap said mockingly. "We get our horses and catch up. I've got to settle with that ranger if I'm ever going to show my face again." As he spoke his fingers drummed on his gun butt. "I've got to kill him . . . there's no other way."

CHAPTER 3

No sooner had the ranger and Memphis Beck ridden around the rock and out of Strap's sight than they heeled their horses up into a brisk pace. They kept the horses moving quickly, stopping only long enough to tie off the detectives' animals alongside the trail. Their next stop came when they'd reached a fork leading down to their left over a rise of rock. "We're going down this way," Sam said, gesturing a gloved hand.

"That won't take us to Nickels," Beck said confidently.

"I know," said Sam. "But now that the railroad detectives know we're heading to Nickels, I thought it best if we head someplace else."

Beck smiled. "I like your thinking, Ranger." He nudged his horse ahead of the ranger, leading the Wheelers behind him. "Where does this take us?"

"To Little Aces," said Sam. "Ever heard of it?"

"No, can't say that I have," Beck said over his shoulder. "But if it's got no railroad dicks hanging around, it suits me."

"I doubt if we threw the railroad posse off for long," Sam said. "I'm counting on us getting to Little Aces to see the sheriff by early morning, before the colonel and his men figure out what we've done and come riding in on us."

"So, once you see that I'm not wanted, I'll be on my way before they get too hot on my trail," Beck concluded. "I'm obliged to you for that, Ranger Burrack. The railroad is not known for fair play."

"Don't be obliged to me, Beck," Sam said. "I don't work for the railroad. If you have nothing hanging over you with the law here, you're on your way. That's what I agreed to and that's what I'll do, plain and simple."

"Yes, but you could have gone on to Nickels and turned me loose with the posse breathing down my shirt."

"Not if I wanted to feel right about what I gave my word to," Sam said.

"Oh? Even though you gave that word to a *suspected* outlaw like me?" Beck asked, knowing Sam's low opinion of him.

"It makes no difference. I knew what you

are when I gave it," Sam replied.

Beck nodded, thinking about it. "But some people like seeing a good fox and hounds chase," he said without looking back at Sam, "and not everybody takes giving their word so serious these days."

Sam didn't reply. He knew that everything he said was being scrutinized by Beck — an outlaw's way of trying to get inside a lawman's mind and hopefully gain an advantage on him should the need ever arise. But this was a game that two could play, Sam reminded himself, and what Beck didn't seem to realize was that he himself had been doing most of the talking. The ranger smiled to himself and rode on.

An hour later the two rode back onto a wider trail and followed it around the side of a steep hillside. Stopping as they reached a clear view of a valley below, Sam nodded downward and said, "There's Little Aces."

They had come upon sight of the town so quickly, Beck, riding in front of the ranger, looked surprised and commented, "The place sort of jumps right up out of nowhere."

"I suppose so," said Sam, nudging his Appaloosa forward behind Beck and the two dead outlaws, "if you're not expecting it."

"I hope the sheriff there has no bones to

pick with the boys from Hole-in-the-wall," Beck said. "If he does I could still end up with Colonel Elgin's railroad posse down my shirt."

Sam didn't answer.

"Who *is* the sheriff?" Beck asked, seeing that Sam wasn't going to offer the sheriff's name otherwise.

"Vince Gale." Sam offered nothing more.

Beck sighed to himself and shook his head slightly, realizing how the ranger was putting him off. "Do you know this sheriff? Would you *mind* telling me what kind of fellow he is?"

"I never met him, don't know much about him," said Sam. "He only took the job a year ago, after their elected sheriff got killed breaking up a street brawl among a bunch of rowdy cowhands. *His* name was Dillard Vertrees."

"Dillard Vertrees," said Beck. "That's a name I recognize."

"You've heard of him?" Sam noted a change of some sort in the outlaw's voice. He wasn't sure what it was. Beck seemed to catch himself and cover up quickly.

"Aw, you know how it is, Ranger," he said. "In this business you keep an ear to the wind, listening to who's who among lawmen."

But there was more to it than that, Sam thought. The name had struck a chord, he was certain. But before he could find out more, the sound of voices, laughter, and hooves came toward them around the turn twenty feet ahead. Beck looked back to him for direction. Sam said, "Stop here, let them pass."

Stepping his Appaloosa up beside Beck, Sam watched as three young men dressed in range clothes came into sight and stopped short at the sight of the two bodies lying over the saddles. "Holy moly!" said the one closest. "Look at this!"

Another young man, seeing the badge on Sam's chest, nudged his horse a step forward and said to Sam, "Pay Rupert here no mind, Marshal. We don't see many lawmen traveling through here. I'm Dennis Barnes. Ma pals here are Hank Lindley and Rupert —"

"He's not a *marshal,* fool," said Lindley, cutting the introduction short. "He's a ranger. Arizona Territory, I take it?" he asked Sam expectantly.

"That's right — Arizona ranger." Sam realized that these were cattle hands from one of the nearby grassland spreads. "I'm Sam Burrack." He nodded toward Beck, wondering if he should say his name and get the word spread among the ranchers that a famous outlaw had arrived in Little Aces. But before he could say anything one way or the other, Beck cut in and said with a tip of his hat, "I'm David Hite . . . just helping the ranger deliver these men."

But the cowhands hadn't seemed to hear him. "What'd they do?" Barnes asked, no longer interested in introductions.

"You faced them both down and shot them?" asked Rupert Knowles.

Lindley sat staring at Sam as if in awe. "Jeez," he said, "you're the territory ranger who killed the Lake Gang . . . Junior, his pa, the whole bunch?"

"Yes," Sam said modestly. He touched his gloved fingers to the brim of his sombrero. "Now, we need to be moving along. I need to see the sheriff in Little Aces."

The three accommodated him quickly, moving their horses to the inside of the trail, so the ranger, Beck, and the dead outlaws could pass. "Obliged," Sam said, giving them a nod as he stepped Black Pot past them, following Beck and the bodies.

"Holy moly!" Rupert repeated under his breath as the ranger and Beck and their gruesome cargo moved around the turn in the trail.

"Stop saying that, Rupert," Lindley demanded. "You sound like an *idiot.* It makes *us* look stupid too."

"Am I still drunk, or did we just run smack into the ranger everybody is always talking about?" Barnes asked, a little bleary and red-eyed from three days and nights in Little Aces.

"That was him all right," said Rupert Knowles. "I recognized that Appaloosa stallion right off. It's the one ole Outrider Saze rode up until Junior Lake and his gang killed him."

"Yeah, that's the ranger, but who do you suppose this David Hite fellow is?" Lindley asked.

Rupert shrugged. "I don't know, some other lawman or citizen volunteer, I expect."

"Wrong," said Lindley with a sly and confident grin, staring at the turn in the trail. "He's no lawman — no volunteer either, I can tell you both that much."

"Then who is he?" Rupert asked.

Lindley didn't answer. Instead he gave the other two a knowing look, turned his horse to the trail, and nudged it forward.

"Don't pay attention to him," Barnes said to Rupert under his breath. "He don't know near as much as he likes to put on that he does."

"Well, neither do we," said Rupert. He

looked toward the turn in the trail. "I'd give anything if we was just getting here instead of just leaving." He called out to Lindley, "Hank, do you suppose we could —"

"Don't even think about it," Lindley replied without looking back at him. "We're supposed to be back this evening. We've got cattle to deliver all the way to Spurrier come morning. Bad enough we've got to tell the ramrod that Omar quit short on us."

"Dang it!" said Barnes, jerking his horse's reins to the trail and nudging the animal forward to catch up with Lindley, Rupert right beside him. "Just when things start to look interesting. What do you suppose made Omar do a thing like that anyway? Who's going to hire a cowhand that quit short?"

"I don't know," said Lindley, "but Omar told me he was just marking his time. He's no cowhand, I saw that plain enough."

"I'll say one thing for Omar Wills," Rupert commented, looking back almost longingly in the direction of Little Aces. "Anything the ranger does there, Omar gets to see it firsthand."

"Good for Omar," said Lindley. "We've got cattle needs tending."

Emma had been right about the young cowhand. He did come back, she reflected, looking at Omar's bare shoulder as he lay sleeping beneath the quilt on her feather bed.

She'd seen him lingering near the back fence later that first afternoon, his horse's reins in hand — standing there in the evening gloom, staring toward her door. She had ignored him and closed the window curtains. Moments later when she'd let her hair down and brushed it, she'd returned to the window and opened the curtains with a bold sweep of her hand. But when she looked out this time, he was gone.

Good . . . , she'd resolved, after searching back and forth the length of the darkening deserted alleyway. But was that the last of him? She didn't think so. Did she want that to be *the last of him?* She wasn't sure.

Later, when she'd dressed for bed and idly walked past the window with a glowing candle lamp in hand, she'd heard a tapping sound and looked out through the curtains into the last waning vestiges of purple light. But instead of seeing the young cowhand, she'd seen the blind man, Curtis Clay, and his spotted dog walking along her fence toward his shack behind the livery barn.

She'd watched man and dog move along like ghosts, Clay's walking stick probing its way along the picket fence. She'd smiled to herself, recalling how Clay had stood at her fence earlier after Wills had left for the first time. Clay had turned his expressionless face back and forth, his head slightly tilted, as if distinguishing what scent loomed in the air and what that scent might reveal to him.

But then the quiet tapping had stopped as man and dog reached the end of the fence and moved away into the darkness, to do whatever a blind man did in the impartiality of night. Closing the curtains slowly, Emma had stepped over and put her hand on the door bolt in order to lock it overnight. But instead of locking it, she'd stopped and stared at her fingers on the bolt. *One year, four months, and six days . . .*

Without admitting to herself what she was about to do, she'd taken her hand away from the open bolt and walked away.

In her bedroom, she'd set the candle lamp on a nightstand, taken off her night robe, and slipped beneath the covers on her feather bed.

Out front on the darkened dirt street, Omar had stepped forward when he saw the candlelight go out and murmured to himself, "It's about damned time. . . ."

That had been three nights ago. Now it was time for him to leave, Emma told herself, wrapping her robe around herself and sitting down on the side of the bed. Before daylight the morning after their first night together, she'd insisted that he go move his horse somewhere besides the hitch rail across the street from her house. He'd done so reluctantly. But when he returned he'd slipped in through the back door carrying his saddlebags, and told her he wouldn't be going back to the ranch with his friends. *Be that as it may . . .*

"Wake up, Omar," she said quietly, shaking him gently by his shoulder. "It's almost sunup. Time for you to get dressed and go."

When he didn't stir, she shook him more firmly. "Omar, please, it's time to get up. I have things to do. You must leave now."

Omar groaned and rolled onto his back. He batted sleep from his eyes and looked up at her. "Go where?" he said blurrily, rubbing a hand over his face, his black beard stubble.

"Anywhere," Emma said, reaching down and brushing his hair from his eyes. "You've been here three days. It's time to go."

Omar stared at her in silence, his expression hard for her to read. Finally he stifled a yawn, ran a hand inside her robe, and cupped her warm breast. "Hey, settle down and stop being so nervous. What are you worried about?"

She didn't move his hand; she didn't want to move his hand. She gasped slightly at the feel of it on her skin. But she said, "I'm not nervous. But it won't be long. Folks will know you're here. It's not proper."

"Hang what's proper," said Omar. "Those folks can all kiss my —"

"I'm still in mourning," Emma said, cutting him off. "I'm not ready to take up with a man."

"It's been well over a year," said Omar with a playful grin. "I did some snooping around and found out after I left here the other day. You made it sound like your husband's still alive, I found out he's been dead a long time."

"A year, four months, and ten days," she quoted from the running calendar in her mind. She didn't like hearing him say *your husband,* here in the room where Dillard Vertrees and she had slept — here in this most private place.

"That's a *long* time." Omar grinned. His hand left her breast and traveled down the length of her stomach, into the warmth of her lap. "Besides, I've got no place to go right now. I'm staying here until my plans start working out."

She stared at him, wondering if he honestly thought he could move in here. "That can't be," she said more firmly, lifting his hand from under her robe.

"Like hell, it can't." He shoved his hand back inside her robe in a way that dared her to try pulling it away again. "I need a clean place to lay up awhile. I'm sick of dirty shacks and bunkhouses. I'd rather sleep with a woman any day."

"I'm almost old enough to be your mother, Omar," Emma said. "I'm glad you came here. But this is not something that can go on —"

"*Almost* old enough doesn't cut ice with me. You're sweeter than a ripe peach, being so long without a man to cool you down," Omar said. "But if you were old enough to be my ma, so what? I like what you do to me." He smiled. "The two of us under this quilt, nothing on, just your bare skin against mine." He relaxed his hand and rubbed it up and down her side. "If you tell me you don't like it too" — he smiled — "you know you'd be lying."

"All right, yes, I enjoyed it," she admitted with a smile, liking the feel of his hand on her. "But I have things that I must go about doing —"

"Shhh," he said, placing his free hand over her lips, a bit strongly, she thought. "What you've got to go about doing right now," he said, smiling playfully, but gripping her firmly beneath the robe, "is fixing me up a big ole breakfast . . . after wearing me out all night."

She sat staring at him until he lowered his hand from her mouth and released his grip on her and drew his hand from inside her robe. "I'll — I'll have to go to the store. I'll need to get some things first."

"Sure, you do that, *sweetheart*," Omar said, scooting up and resting against a pillow, putting his hands behind his head. "I'll be right here waiting. Oh," he added, raising a finger and pointing at her breasts, "be sure and get some canned peaches. I love sweet peaches after a big meal."

She backed away from the bed and looked around at his boots on the floor, one standing, one lying on its side. A crust of dirt had broken loose from a heel and crumbled onto her clean bedroom floor. *My God, Dillard,* she said to herself, *what have I done . . . ?*

CHAPTER 4

Town Sheriff Vince Gale stood on the boardwalk out in front of his office and searched the morning shadows still lingering beneath the deep wooden overhang. He'd made his early rounds while coffee cooked on the potbellied stove; his shotgun still hung under his arm. He held a steaming cup of coffee in his gloved hand, the collar of his wool plaid coat standing against the crisp morning air.

When he saw Emma Vertrees step onto the boardwalk at the far end of the street and walk toward him, he set his coffee on the windowsill behind him and headed her way. He took his time, looking into shops just opening for the day, and tipping his broad-brimmed hat at proprietors through wavy window glass. He did not want to appear as if he'd deliberately set out to meet Emma, although he had.

Seeing the sheriff, Emma felt her first

impulse was to cross the street and avoid him. But he had seen her coming and knew that she had seen him as well. All right, she told herself, she had nothing to be ashamed of. Still, she felt a twinge of guilt, as if Sheriff Gale somehow *knew,* as he drew closer and looked into her eyes.

"Morning, Miss Emma," Gale said, touching his hat brim with his gloved fingers. "I hope you've had a pleasant night?"

She looked into his eyes in return. Did he know or suspect something? Maybe he'd seen Omar's horse across the street, in front of the saloon. *Nonsense. Why would he think anything of that?* "Yes, Sheriff, thank you," she replied, collecting herself, averting her eyes from his for only a second. "And I hope you did, as well."

"Yes, ma'am, most pleasant," Gale said. He turned beside her as she continued on along the boardwalk. "May I accompany you?"

"Yes, you may." She smiled, knowing he'd suspected nothing. More often than not, she would find him strolling along the boardwalk making early business rounds when she came to shop. Sometimes they met purely by chance. But other times she was certain he watched for her and timed his rounds in order to happen upon her.

He reached out, offering to carry her straw shopping basket for her. "May I?"

She relinquished the basket to him and the two walked along at an easy pace. "You know I haven't seen much of you the past few days," he probed gently. "I hope all is well with you."

"Yes, Sheriff, quite well, thank you," Emma said, smiling, looking ahead.

"Please, call me Vince, Miss Emma," he reminded her a bit awkwardly. He had asked her to call him by name several times in the past.

"I prefer addressing you by your title, *Sheriff,*" she replied cordially yet firmly.

They walked on, and after a short pause, Sheriff Gale ventured, "It's been a while since I invited you out to dinner. I had hoped to hear your answer by now."

"Yes, you're right, Sheriff Gale, I should have replied before now. That was impolite of me. Please forgive me," Emma said.

"Oh, ma'am, it's all right," Gale said. "I know you've been in mourning. I don't want to seem pushy. But I do think you know how highly I think of you."

"Yes, I do," said Emma almost before he'd finished his words. "But having given it thought, my answer is *no.* I'm sorry, but I think it's best that we don't begin socializing, Sheriff."

"Miss Emma, I don't know what to say," Gale replied. "I've tried to be as respectful to you as a man can be. There's nothing I wouldn't do for you. What is wrong with me? What have I failed to do?"

Almost cutting him off, she said, "There is nothing wrong with you, Sheriff. It's just that I remember too much about Mr. Vertrees' years as a lawman . . . and, of course, how they ended." Her voice softened in vulnerable reflection. "I will never allow myself to be put through something like that again."

"What happened to Dillard Vertrees was terrible, Miss Emma," Gale said, stopping on the boardwalk, still holding her shopping basket. "But because it happened to him doesn't mean it will ever happen to me."

"That's true, Sheriff Gale," Emma said firmly, reaching out and putting her hand on the basket handle. "Nor does it mean that it *won't*. But I'm not taking that chance. Now, if you'll excuse me." She tugged gently on the basket handle.

But Sheriff Gale held it tight in the crook of his arm. "Why is it you never allow me to finish a conversation with you?" He sounded on the verge of turning testy with her. "Just once I wish I could speak my mind with you. I want to do right by you, Miss Emma. You're a widow . . . I'm a man not without prospects and a respectable future."

"Meaning what, Sheriff, that I could do a lot worse than you?" she said, not releasing her grip on the basket handle.

"I didn't say that," said Gale, "but the fact is, this is no country for a woman on her own, especially a . . . well . . ." He hesitated, then said, "A *mature* woman, who's already had a man, and who is —"

"But you are willing to overlook all of that and take care of me?" Emma said harshly.

"You're taking this the wrong way, Miss Emma," the sheriff said.

"I'm taking it the very way you intended it, Sheriff Gale," Emma said stiffly. She jerked the basket handle sharply. "Now, will you please let go of my shopping basket?"

"Yes, ma'am." Gale turned the basket loose and glanced around to see if anyone had been listening. He saw a horseman riding in from the hill country leading two horses with bodies draped over their saddles. In front of the rider a man on foot led his limping horse along the street.

Emma saw the approaching horseman and took note of the two bodies as she freed her basket and started to turn and leave. Lowering her voice, she said coolly, "Well, Sheriff, it looks like this is another conversation you won't be finishing."

"What do we have here . . . ?" Gale said more to himself than to Emma Vertrees. He gazed toward the newcomers as they entered Little Aces from the far end of town. Emma had started to leave, but she hesitated for a moment, unable to take her eyes off the man on foot. As the party drew closer, recognition struck her and she raised a hand to her face as if to hide.

"Oh my!" she gasped.

"Something wrong, Emma?" Sheriff Gale asked, turning to her for only a second, then back to the horseman. He noted the glimmer of a badge on the man's chest, showing from inside the open lapels of his riding duster.

"No," Emma said, recovering quickly. "It always disturbs me seeing the dead treated in such a coarse manner."

"Why? They don't feel a thing," Gale commented matter-of-factly. He turned his attention back to the grisly scene. Emma stood back quietly, having ascertained for herself that this was *indeed* Warren Beck walking toward her. He looked a little older, his beard stubble the color of wood ash, his lean stature slightly bent, but he still looked ready and capable, moving with the grace of a seasoned and wary mountain cat.

When he stopped a few feet from her in the dirt street and looked at her and tipped his hat, he made no sign of recognizing her. Was that intentional? She watched silently as the ranger stepped down from his big Appaloosa. He touched the brim of his sombrero toward her courteously, saying, "Morning, ma'am," then turned to Sheriff Gale. "Howdy, Sheriff."

Eyeing the ranger badge, the pearl gray sombrero, and the Appaloosa stallion, Gale said, "Ranger Burrack?"

"I am." Sam had intended to introduce himself, but seeing it wasn't necessary he stopped himself and said instead, "Sheriff Vince Gale?"

Gale tipped his hat. "Yes, that's me." His eyes slid over Beck. He gestured a hand toward Emma Vertrees and said, "This is the late Sheriff Dillard Vertrees' widow, Mrs. Emma Vertrees."

"Ma'am," Sam said in a softened tone, lifting his sombrero from atop his head. "I had the honor of knowing your husband. He was a fine lawman. You have my condolences."

"Thank you, Ranger Burrack," said Emma. "Sheriff Vertrees spoke highly of you."

Sam only nodded, holding his sombrero at his side. Before he could introduce Beck to the sheriff, he saw Beck and Emma exchange a glance. It was quick and fleeting, yet Sam caught something there, enough to summon his interest.

"You look familiar," Sheriff Gale said to Beck, eying the outlaw closely. "Have I seen you somewhere before?" When Beck only stared at him, he turned his question to Sam.

"This is Memphis Warren Beck, Sheriff," said Sam.

"Oh?" Sheriff Gale's look hardened a bit. "Then I've probably seen your face on wanted posters?"

"It's not likely," Beck offered in an offhand manner. As soon as he answered Gale, he looked at Emma and said, "My condolences as well, ma'am."

"You're one of that bunch of rogues from Wyoming," Gale said with a harsh tone.

"*Alleged* to be," Beck said firmly, giving the harsh attitude right back to the lawman.

"*Alleged!*" Gale said skeptically. A nerve twitched in his chiseled jaw. "Everybody knows about that wild bunch of thugs."

Sam cut in before the sheriff could say more on the matter. "Beck isn't wanted for anything in my territory, Sheriff. I found him riding with the Wheelers." He gestured a hand toward the bodies. "I thought it would be a good idea to come here and see if New Mexico had anything on him."

Gale stared fiercely at Beck for a moment as if in contemplation, trying hard to come up with something against him. But finally he gave up, let out a breath, and said, "No, not that I can think of, he's not wanted for anything here. He should be, though."

Sam noted how Beck and the woman had given each other a guarded look.

Gale continued. "The territorial governor has been conferring with other governors over these outlaws committing crimes and then hightailing it across territorial lines and getting away free as birds." He looked at Sam, then back to Beck. "Their spree will come to a halt one of these days. I can't wait to see it."

"Meanwhile, Sheriff," Beck said, letting the sheriff's words run off him, "my horse picked up a stone bruise back along the trail. Any chance you'll allow me to stay here long enough for him to heal up?"

"You've got some nerve, Memphis Beck," Gale said, stepping down to the horse as he spoke.

"Far as I know, this *cayouse* of mine hasn't broken any law," Beck said. He gave the woman another glance, not realizing the ranger saw it. He patted a gloved hand on the horse's muzzle.

"I expect I can't blame the horse for what he has to carry around," Gale said. He stepped in close and raised the horse's favored hoof without asking Beck's permission. But Beck let it pass and watched as the sheriff looked the hoof over and ran his hands up the horse's foreleg.

"The horse would be obliged, Sheriff," Beck said. Again a looked passed between him and Emma Vertrees; again the ranger saw it.

Setting the horse's hoof back down gently onto the ground, Sheriff Gale dusted his hands together and said to Beck, "He's bruised sure enough. Lucky for this animal it happened close to town. A few more miles on a bad hoof would have laid him up for a month." His look at Beck seemed to soften just a little. "Good thing you're not the kind who'll ride a bruised horse."

"I wouldn't think of it, Sheriff," said Beck, rubbing the horse's muzzle. "I don't suppose you might have a horse doctor here in Little Aces?" He allowed himself another brief look at the woman as he spoke.

Emma replied before the sheriff could. "No, we don't have an animal doctor. But we do have Curtis Clay. Nobody is better than him when it comes to horses —"

Sheriff Gale cut her off with a narrowed gaze, then turned that same narrowed gaze to Beck, as if not liking the idea of Beck talking to the woman. "Curtis Clay is a blind Negro who's handy treating horses. He lives over beside the livery barn." He pointed at the weathered tin roof looming above a row of dust-streaked clapboard cottages. "If you ask him to, he'll have your horse trail-worthy before you know it."

"Sheriff, I'm obliged," said Beck. He deliberately averted his eyes from the woman.

"Don't be obliged to me, Memphis Beck," said Sheriff Gale. "I'm doing this for the horse, not for the likes of you."

Beck, having to stop himself from making a sharp reply, let out a patient breath and said, "I understand, Sheriff."

Beck looked at Sam. "I can't say it was a pleasure riding with you, Ranger . . . but it wasn't too bad either. Now, if there's nothing else required of me, I'll ask your permission to take my leave and go have this horse attended to."

"On your way, Beck," Sam said with a nod. "I'm glad you're not wanted for anything here. New Mexico could be a good place for a man to make a new start."

"Thank you, Ranger," said Beck. "If I was looking for a new start, I'd consider it." He gave Emma a tip of his hat and a quick glance that revealed nothing between them, Sam thought, watching closely.

Sam stood beside the sheriff watching Beck turn and walk his horse toward the livery barn. Beside them, Emma said, "Gentlemen, if you'll both excuse me, I'll be about my shopping this morning."

Both lawmen tipped their hats to her. "May I see you later today and finish up what we were talking about?" Gale asked quietly.

"Another time, Sheriff," Emma said coolly. "I'm awfully busy."

"Wait, please." Gale looked embarrassed when she just walked away; and as soon as she walked a few yards, he avoided Sam's eyes and looked toward the outlaw, who was turning the corner toward the livery barn. Getting back to the subject of Beck, he said to Sam, "I didn't feel I had a right to chase him out of here, his horse injured and all. Soon as the animal is better, I'll let him know his welcome is worn out."

"I expect he knows it already, Sheriff," said Sam. "The fact is he won't be in Little Aces any longer than he needs to. He's got a railroad posse on his tail right now."

"Oh?" said Gale. "You mean Colonel Elgin's *Great Western Railroad Posse?*"

"Yep," said Sam, "that's the one. I had a run-in with a couple of the colonel's scouts along the trail. We might have thrown them off for a while. But I expect they'll figure it out and be coming this way."

"I'd just as soon they didn't come here," said Gale, staring up the street after Beck had already walked out of sight. "Those detectives and hired gunmen get drunk, they can get as rank and mean as any outlaws."

"They've got rewards for anybody who helps them capture one of these big-name outlaws," Sam said. He wanted to know where the lawman stood on such matters.

"Yeah," said Gale, "I heard Elgin even has a photographer who travels with him, takes *photographs,* so they can prove the outlaw is dead." Sheriff Gale spat in the dirt, as if to get a bad taste from his mouth. "It don't matter to me. I don't take railroad money, Ranger Burrack. Never have, never will."

Sam nodded, liking what he heard. "That's good to know, Sheriff . . . neither do I."

CHAPTER 5

When Emma left the two lawmen standing out in front of the sheriff's office, she'd walked on toward the mercantile. But instead of going inside, she'd looked back to make sure Gale wasn't watching, then stepped down from the boardwalk into an alley. She followed the alley to the rear of the row of buildings and hurried back toward the livery barn.

Standing beside the barn, she saw Curtis Clay reach down and lift the injured horse's foreleg and inspect its hoof and tendons with his fingertips. Beck stood watching. Emma stayed back behind the crumbling remnants of an adobe wall, looking for a chance to get Beck's attention. At the same time she carefully kept an eye on the picket fence behind her house, and on the house itself, making sure Wills wasn't looking out the kitchen window.

"It's not bruised deep, yet," Clay said, setting the animal's hoof down gently. He dusted his hands together and straightened up. "Were it my horse, I'd rub it good with witch hazel and wrap it in an herb and cactus poultice for a few days."

Reaching into his pocket, Beck pulled out three gold coins and jingled them together for the blind man to hear. "Treat him like he *is* your horse, until he's ready to travel," Beck said. He took a step forward to give Clay the coins. On the ground the spotted dog sat observing the two men closely, his head turning back and forth between them as they spoke.

Hearing Beck's single footstep on the dirt, Clay also took a step forward. With a wide aimless smile he held his hand out for the coins. "I treats every horse like it's mine . . . it *is mine* so long as my hand tends it."

"Obliged," said Beck, dropping the coins into Clay's expectant palm.

Taking the horse's reins, Clay turned to the rear livery barn door and said, "Come on, Little Dog." To Beck he said, "I'll get this horse into a stall and shuck his saddle."

The dog flipped quickly to its feet and hurried into its task, walking in front of Clay while the sightless man turned the horse toward the barn door.

"I'll come in and get my saddlebags," said

Beck, stepping in behind the horse. "If I need to rent a horse while I'm waiting, do you have any?"

"We've got three to pick from," said Clay. "Two are out in the corral, and there's the roan over there in a stall. He's the best, far as I'm concerned."

"I'll keep him in mind," said Beck.

"If you want him and nobody is here, leave the money on his stall post," Clay said.

"Obliged," said Beck.

As Clay took a step forward, he caught the scent of the woman — the familiar scent he'd grown used to when he followed her fence and heard her in the yard hanging clothes or tending her modest garden. He expected her to call out a greeting, as she did on occasion. But after a second of pause he realized she had no greeting for him this morning.

Instead Clay heard Beck say behind him, "I'll be along in a minute," and he heard the man turn away and walk a few steps toward the crumbling adobe wall.

Clay followed the dog to an empty stall door where he stopped and spun the horse's reins around a post. "Shhh," he said down to the dog, causing the animal to stop as if frozen in place.

For a moment Clay stood in complete

silence, listening intently into the blackness between himself and the open barn door. The woman was out there, he knew it. He had caught her scent — now he sifted through the musky smells inside the barn and searched for the scent of her again. What had he detected in her scent? Something different, he thought. *Fear? Tension? Excitement? A little of each?* he asked himself.

It was not something he could have explained to people with sight, but he knew that each person carried his own scent. With that personal scent came certain distinct variations and changes, dependent on the state of mind and emotional condition. Clay had learned intuitively how to identify the underlying scent of fear, tension, anger, even grief and sorrow. He wasn't sure how it worked or what brought it about, but he'd learned to depend on scent to identify in people what his blind eyes could not see in their faces.

Hoping to find the woman's scent again and try to better identify what he'd detected inside it, Clay felt his way along the stalls, walking stick in hand, until he stopped at the inside plank wall beside the open door and listened closely as his nostrils searched for her. Through the faint drifting smell of crumbling adobe, Memphis Beck's trail clothes, dried sweat, and riding duster, he found the scent of her again. As he breathed in the smell of her, he listened to traces of their two voices speaking, judging by the sound just how close they stood to each other.

"My goodness, look at you," Beck said, having followed her gesture and joined her at the adobe wall. "I never thought I'd see you again." They had embraced when he had crossed the alley to the wall. Now he held her at arm's length and looked into her eyes. "You're as beautiful as always," he said softly, caressing her cheek. "Just the way I remember you."

Emma smiled, closed her eyes, and cupped his hand on her cheek for a moment. But then she pulled his hand away and squeezed it in mock anger. "I shouldn't even be speaking to you, Memphis Beck!" she said, yet without turning loose his hand. "I wrote to you after Dillard's death . . . you never answered me."

"Emma, I never received a letter," Beck said with a look of regret. "I found out about Dillard from the ranger on our way here. Believe me, if I had only known, I would've been here first thing. Nothing could've kept me away."

"You're forgiven," Emma said in a bit of a playful tone, clasping his hand in both of hers. "I had already decided you must not have gotten the mail. I sent the letter to the post office in Casper."

"I haven't been to Casper in almost three years," said Beck. "Things got hot for all of us in Wyoming . . . even up in the Hole." He considered the bad news about her husband and shook his head. "Ole Dillard, dead. I hated hearing it . . . especially from a stranger."

"I — I made him happy, Memphis," Emma said. "I mean, you and the others said we'd never make a go of it, but we did." She looked into Beck's eyes. "I loved him, you know?"

"That's good, Emma," Beck said. "I would never have made you for a lawman's wife, but what did I know?" He shrugged and offered a smile. "When you said you were putting the life behind you, you meant it." Now he clasped her hand in his. "Good for you."

"He — that is, Dillard knew about you, Memphis," Emma said. "I felt I had to tell him."

"Oh, you did?" Beck's smile went away. "Why did you have to go do something like that?"

"I wanted to be honest," Emma said.

Beck looked a little annoyed and shook a finger for emphasis. "See? That always worried me, that honesty thing you carry around on your shoulders. You never got over that? You still have spells of it?"

"Not as often, but yes, I'm still cursed with it," she replied. They both smiled at their humor.

"How did Dillard take it, about us?" Beck asked.

"Much better than you would ever have taken it if I told you I'd spent those years with a *lawman*," Emma pointed out.

"All right, maybe I shouldn't have asked," Beck said. He turned loose her hands and looked into her eyes. "When can we see each other?" He looked all around. "Where do you live? Take me home with you."

"I can't right now," said Emma, thinking of Wills lying sprawled on her bed when she'd left. "There's things I have to do first." She looked away as she spoke.

"Really?" Beck bent his head to look her squarely in the eyes. "You're with somebody?"

"Only recently," said Emma. "I've been in mourning over the past year. Only the other day I met —"

"Wait, stop right there," said Beck, only

half jokingly. "I don't want to know. Just tell me if it's serious. If it is, I'll walk away, no hard feelings."

"No, it's nothing serious," said Emma, shaking her head. "I've just got to break away from him."

"Get rid of him, then," said Beck.

"I will, but it's going to take a day or two." She'd been wondering how to go about easing Wills out of her house and her life before he made himself any more deeply entrenched.

"I'm not here for long, Emma," Beck said. As much as anything he told her this to keep her from building any expectations. "I've got a posse on my back trail," he added flatly. "They could be here any day."

"But your horse," said Emma. "You're leaving it with Curtis, aren't you?"

"Yes, for as long as I can," said Beck. "I hope it gets healed up before I have to leave in a hurry. I can't wait around for a lame horse, Emma. You know me better than that. There's too many good horses standing around. If I have to I'll take one and go."

Emma shook her head slowly. "Nothing has changed for you, I see."

"I still try to keep things simple," Beck said. "I still travel fast and light."

"Don't worry, Memphis," said Emma, realizing his reason for saying all this, "I'm not about to expect anything from you. I know how the life is, remember? No strings?" She looked into his eyes, summoning up conversations on the matter from years past. "It was always that way with us, wasn't it?"

They stood in silence for a moment; then as if something had just occurred to Beck, he said, "Hey, wait a minute. This is not Sheriff Gale you're hooked up with, is it?"

"Hooked up with," she repeated. "What a romantic way of putting it."

"Is it?" Beck asked. "Because if it is —"

"No, no, it's not Vince Gale," said Emma with certainty, shaking her head. "But it's not because he hasn't been trying." She found that in spite of the time and distance between the two of them, being with Memphis Beck brought something youthful and restless out of her — a wildness she had kept suppressed inside herself for a long time. Her words surprised her.

"Then who is it?" Beck said, getting more curious about it now.

"Stop it, Memphis," she giggled, shoving him back as he pressed closer to her. "It's nobody. Let's just say I made a foolish mistake, and now I need to correct it before

I can go on and do what I want to do." Was this her talking? she asked herself.

"I hope that means spending some time with me?" Beck asked.

"*Some time* with you? You're hopeless!" Emma laughed and shook her head. "Be careful you don't pin yourself down to anything."

"You know what I mean, Emma," Beck said, looking embarrassed. "If there ever was one woman I wanted above all the others, it's you. I just can't bring myself to say anything that sounds permanent. I'm afraid if I did, I would jinx everything."

"I'm not asking you for anything, Memphis. I never did," said Emma. "I just want to be with you. Let me get things settled first." She couldn't believe she stood here talking this way.

"I won't rush you, Emma, posse or no posse," said Beck. "I'll take a room at the hotel. You'll find me there or else at —"

"At the saloon," Emma finished for him. "I know where to look." She took a step back and gathered her shawl across her shoulders against the crisp morning air. In reflection she said, "Remember how we each always swore that the other was a bad influence?"

"Yeah, I remember." Memphis Beck smiled.

She reached out and rubbed a hand down the front of his leather coat. "I've only been with you a few minutes, and I already feel like doing something bad."

"Keep that thought in mind," Beck said. "Now go get rid of your beau and come find me. . . ."

Inside the livery barn, Curtis Clay stood close to the plank wall listening to only faint murmurs of conversation from across the alleyway. From the other end of the barn, he heard soft footsteps on the straw-covered dirt floor and turned in time to catch the sour scent of whiskey and tobacco juice waft through the front door.

"Clay, what the hell are you doing hanging around in here in the dark?" said the harsh voice of Bland Woolard, the livery manager and town councilman.

"Dark don't mean a thing to me, Mr. Woolard," Clay replied. He stepped away from the plank wall and felt his way along the stall rail until he put a hand on Beck's horse standing at the empty stall. "You can see I've got me a horse needs tending. Town council said I can come here anytime, take care of an ill horse."

"Don't tell me what the town council says,

boy," said Woolard. "I am the town council, don't forget." He thumbed himself on his chest in spite of the fact that Clay couldn't see the gesture. "One word from me, you won't come in here again, not without somebody watching, making sure nothing's missing when you leave."

Clay's nostrils flared, but he held his rage in check. "You know me, Mr. Woolard, sir, I never steal nothing."

"You've never been caught at it, let's put it that way," said Woolard idly, stepping forward. He brushed Little Dog aside with his boot as he looked the horse over good. The dog moped away a few steps, turned around, and sat down on the floor, watching Clay.

"Say, this is some fine-looking animal you have here, Curtis," Woolard said admiringly. "What's the problem with him?"

"Stone bruise, is all," said Curtis, "not too deep. He didn't walk much on it. His owner was wise to get off him as soon as he felt him limp."

"Who is his owner?" Woolard asked, still looking the horse up and down. "I'm always on the lookout for good horseflesh. He might want to trade this one."

"I never asked his name," said Clay. "I figure he'd tell me if he thought it was

95

important I know." He felt his way to the animal's side and deftly uncinched its saddle and lifted it, blanket and all. Woolard watched him toss the saddle over the rail no differently than a man with two good eyes would do.

"It always amazes me," said Woolard, "seeing how you can go about doing things. And that trick you pull with the old revolver. You should be traveling with a carnival. Folks would pay to see what you can do."

Clay let the remark about the trick with the gun go. It was no trick. And he disregarded the remark about the carnival — folks paying to see what he did. He was no freak to be singled out and stared at as something miscast by nature.

"It's not so hard, what I do here. I know the layout of everything, Mr. Woolard," Clay said as he stepped along the horse, felt its muzzle, loosened its bridle, and dropped its bit from its mouth. "Besides, I always got Little Dog pinting my way for me if I need him to."

"Little Dog, eh?" Woolard stared down at the spotted cur. "This old runt isn't worth an ounce of what it leaves behind itself."

"He's worth lots to me, Mr. Woolard," Curtis said firmly. "He takes me anywhere I want to go, anytime I need to go there."

"Bull." Woolard laughed a little. "I've watched that old dog, he doesn't do anything but walk along in front of you. How does that help you any?"

"I hear him walk. I can feel him with my walking stick if I need to," said Clay. "If he stops all of a sudden, I run into him and know to stop myself. Nobody realizes what a good dog is worth to a blind man." He reached a hand down and searched around until Little Dog stood, walked over, stepped under his hand, and licked it.

"Yeah, whatever you say, Curtis," said Woolard skeptically. Dismissing the matter, he turned toward the front door. "When the owner of that dun comes back, tell him where to find me. I'm in a trading mood today."

"Yes, sir, Mr. Woolard, I'll tell the man, sure enough," said Clay, rubbing Little Dog's bristly muzzle. When Woolard had walked out of sight, Clay turned his cloudy eyes toward the rear barn door, knowing intuitively that the man and woman had left the adobe ruins. "I hope she knows what she's doing, Little Dog. We worry ourselves about her, don't we?" The dog sat quietly on the dirt floor against his master's ankle.

CHAPTER 6

No sooner had Emma left her house to find what she'd need to prepare her guest a hearty breakfast, than Omar slipped from the warm feather bed and into his trousers. He'd padded barefoot throughout the small cottage checking inside every drawer, cabinet, or covered bowl that might contain anything of value. Some things he'd already gone through while she had slept during the night. He'd found a coin purse in the pocket of her coat hanging on a coat tree in the corner by the front door. There had to be more money around here somewhere, he was sure of it. . . .

By the time Emma had finally stepped inside the mercantile store, she'd almost forgotten what had brought her there. Seeing Memphis Beck after all these years had caused something to change inside her. She didn't realize how lonely and isolated from the world around her she'd become since her husband's death. There had been times when she could not have said with certainty what part of her day-to-day living was real, and what part was some sort of dream that had seeped out into her waking hours.

Now, after seeing Beck, feeling his arms around her as he'd hugged her by the crumbling adobe wall, there was no doubt: this had been real; this was no dream. This was reality as she remembered it to be, alive and exciting with her back at the center of it. Yet this was a feeling that she knew had slipped further and further away from her over her years with Dillard Vertrees. But Dillard had nothing to do with it, she knew.

As she reached for a jar of peaches on a shelf, she realized that Memphis Beck had kindled to life a part of herself that had died long before her husband's death. Perhaps *died* was not the right word, because she felt it alive inside her now. Perhaps it was something she'd lost only for a while, or that had slipped further and further away from her until she only saw it now through some distant and fading veil.

Well, whatever the case, she had a feeling all that was about to change. She had no idea what she had meant, giving herself to the likes of Omar Wills, some young, ignorant ruffian whose only redeeming feature had been his good manners — which as it turned out were false, she reminded herself, laying the peaches into her shopping basket. She drifted along a row of shelves and a locker of dried meat. She remained caught up in her thoughts about her and Memphis Beck until she'd made her way to the long polished wooden counter.

What she felt come alive inside her at the adobe wall had been *live by the moment,* she told herself, one moment at a time, because any particular moment might be the end of it. Beck had pointed that out to her long ago, the two of them lying naked on a blanket beside some cool and nameless stream, high up among drifting pieces of low white clouds in an endless stretch of hill country. . . .

"Will that be all, Mrs. Vertrees?" asked Fred Gunderson, the mercantile owner, taking the canned peaches, a bag of dried beans, and a hand-six slab of jowl bacon from the basket she'd set absently on the counter.

"Yes, Mr. Gunderson, thank you," Emma said, snapping out of her preoccupation. She reached inside her coat pocket, took out her small coin purse, and unsnapped it. As she fished inside it with her fingers, to her surprise she found the purse empty. "I — I'm sorry, I seem to have no money this morning," she said. Odd, money *should* have been inside the purse. Embarrassed, she said at length, "Will you please —"

"Put this on charge for you," Gunderson said, anticipating her words. "Of course, anytime." He efficiently placed the items back into the shopping basket and stepped back from the counter. "Anything else you need, you feel free to point it out to me." He grinned.

"That will be all, thank you," Emma said, still wondering what might have happened to the coins in her change purse as she picked up the basket and turned to the door.

Stepping onto the boardwalk, she saw Sheriff Gale walking toward her, saying, "There you are. I didn't know what had happened to you. I — I can't wait to talk to you later. I felt like I owed you an apology, not so much for what I said, but for how you took it."

"You mean an apology that is not an apology at all?" Emma said a bit curtly.

"No, that's not what I meant," said Gale. "I felt like we were starting to talk to each other for the first time back there . . . maybe coming to an understanding of some sort. I wanted to pursue it — I'd like to pursue it right now if it's all the same with you." As he spoke he stepped in closer and reached out, offering to carry her shopping basket.

But with Memphis Beck having walked back into her life and Omar Wills seeming to think he had some sort of hold on her, Emma suddenly felt crowded. "No, it's not all the same with me," she said harshly. Clutching the basket to her bosom, she stepped wide around the sheriff and walked off briskly along the boardwalk, saying over her shoulder in a chilled tone, "If you will *excuse* me."

Through the dusty window of Little Aces' telegraph office across the thinly peopled street, Sam stood watching Emma and the sheriff. Behind Sam a bushy-haired young clerk wrote down an incoming reply to the message Sam had just had him wire to the badlands ranger outpost regarding Memphis Warren Beck.

A question had nagged at Sam ever since his encounter with the railroad detectives. He wondered, why were so many men searching for Memphis Beck in this part of the country when every lawman knew that Wyoming was the gang's stomping grounds?

Curious . . . Sam watched Emma Vertrees leave the sheriff standing with his hands spread. As Sam watched he asked himself again what the connection might have been between the lawman's widow and Memphis Warren Beck.

"Here's your reply, Ranger Burrack," said the telegraph clerk, laying his pencil down.

But Sam's attention lingered for a moment longer on Emma as she disappeared around the far corner of the boardwalk. Had he been reading her and Beck both wrong? Had this woman simply been stricken by Beck's charm? Had Beck only been responding to her the way any outlaw of his caliber would? Sam knew that a man like Beck stayed on a constant lookout for someone he could dupe into helping him should the opportunity ever present itself. Was that it? Or did they know each other? That was more the way it had struck him, Sam thought, picturing their expressions, the way their eyes had met. He'd have to give it some more thought. . . .

Turning to the clerk standing behind the counter, he said, "Obliged, young man," and took the telegraph from his outreached hand.

"You're welcome, Ranger. Please feel free to call me Rodney," the clerk replied.

"Thank you, I will. Tell me, Rodney," Sam said, looking down at the telegraph as he spoke, "how long did Sheriff Vertrees and his wife live here in Little Aces before he was killed?"

"Oh, it must have been six or seven years," Rodney said, rubbing a wisp of a reddish goatee as he thought about it. "I was just a young boy when Sheriff Vertrees took over. His wife joined him shortly afterward."

"She fitted right in here, did she?" the ranger probed effortlessly. "Sometimes it takes a woman a while to get used to a place where her husband has taken a new job."

Rodney glanced out through the dusty window as if the street might reveal more information to him. "It seems like it took her a long while to fit comfortable here," he said in reflection. "She was shy, never left the house much at first."

"I see." Sam turned his attention to the letter, not wanting to appear too nosy about the sheriff's widow. "But after a while she began to fit right in," he said idly.

Rodney shrugged. "Yeah, that's how it was."

Sam fished a coin from his vest pocket and laid it on the counter. "Keep the change, Rodney. I'm much obliged for your help."

"Thank you, Ranger." He slid the coin off the counter and into a wooden cash drawer.

Sam turned toward the window reading the ranger outpost's reply to his telegraph.

No current charges against Memphis Warren Beck in any western territories at this time, Sam read to himself. Just as he'd suspected. But as he read the next line, his senses piqued. *Three members of the Hole-in-the-wall Gang sighted and identified by stagecoach driver seven days ago near Lobo Lupo Springs, headed east toward New Mexico Territory . . .* He paused at that point.

That made sense, he decided, beginning to understand why the Western Posse were hot on Beck's trail. They were acting on information about more than one member of the gang being here. Memphis Beck just happened to be the one whose trail they found first.

Reading on across the three names, he murmured each one as if to implant it more clearly in his mind. "Collin 'the Blade' Hedgepeth . . . Bennie Drew . . . Thomas 'Cat' Weaver." Not only did this explain the big posse being so far off their graze, he told himself, but two of these three names were on his wanted list.

Bennie Drew and Tom Cat Weaver had been wanted for murder long before they'd taken shelter in Hole-in-the-wall. It was about time they decided to show their faces, he thought. Folding the telegraph, Sam shoved it down into his shirt pocket and looked back across the street where Sheriff Gale had taken off his hat and stood scratching his lowered head.

Put her out of your mind, Sheriff, Sam said to himself. He had a feeling things were about to get busy in Little Aces.

Emma returned home determined to stay cool and calm and go about easing Omar Wills out of her house and out of her life quietly without any problems, and without causing a scene. She could do it, she told herself, entering through the back door and setting the basket on the kitchen table.

"I'm back," she called out through the house toward the bedroom where she'd left Omar still lounging naked beneath the covers. Omar, not having heard her come into the house, had been busily riffling through an oaken dish cabinet when her voice caught him by surprise.

Emma heard the sound of his bare feet hurrying across the wooden floor. "Omar?" she said, stepping into the other room curiously. Looking around, she saw a door on the dish cabinet swing open slowly, and she knew without a doubt what the young cowboy had been up to. *All right, stay calm, pretend not to have noticed anything,* she told herself, stepping over and closing the cabinet door quietly.

She walked into the bedroom and saw him lying beneath the covers, pretending to be asleep. *A big stupid child,* she thought, looking down at him. She noted to herself that his trousers were no longer hanging over the chair back by the wall. "I'm back," she said, raising her voice enough to penetrate his feigned sleep.

Omar opened his eyes groggily and stifled a waking yawn with his hand. "Oh, you're back. I must've fell back to sleep."

"I see. . . ." Not wanting to play along with his deceitful game, Emma said flatly, "I'll have your breakfast on the table in a few minutes."

In the kitchen she tied a white apron around her waist and began working coolly in spite of a burning rage that had begun to boil inside her chest. She had no doubt now of what had happened to the gold coins in her change purse. Wills had robbed her. He was nothing more than a sneak thief — a low-life penny-ante purse robber. Whipping her biscuit batter into a frenzy, she said under her breath, "To think that you *gave yourself* to such an animal."

Later, when the smell of warm biscuits drew Omar into the kitchen still buttoning his shirt, Emma had set out a plate, a cloth napkin, and knife and fork. Beside the plate sat a cup of steaming coffee she'd poured as she'd heard him walking through the house.

"Aw, this smells like heaven to me," Omar said. Grinning, he stepped behind her, wrapped his arms around her, and hugged her against him, his hands managing to cover both of her breasts. "After I eat, if everything is to my liking, we might just roll back in that feather bed and I'll show you the kind of morning any woman wants to wake up to."

"Please, this is hot," said Emma, holding the tin pan of hot biscuits with a thick kitchen cloth. Her skin crawled at the feel of him against her. But she kept calm, wrenched herself away from him, set the pan of hot biscuits on the table, and said, "There, sit down . . . let me get your eggs and bacon for you."

"Yes, ma'am, I'm all set to dig in!" Omar said, rubbing his hands together.

After she'd set the food before him, Emma pulled a chair out across the table from him and seated herself with a hot cup of coffee of her own. She watched him eat for a moment, then said, "After breakfast, I think it would be a good idea if you leave."

Omar stared at her blankly as he chewed a mouthful of food and swallowed it. "I hope you didn't forget the peaches." He gave his wide grin. "I love peaches after a good meal."

"Yes, I remembered the peaches," Emma replied, keeping her temper in control in spite of wanting to scream out that she knew he'd stolen her coins and searched her house while she was gone. "See?" she said evenly, nodding toward the jar of golden peaches sitting on a shelf on the wall.

Omar nodded and continued eating.

"Did you hear me, Omar?" Emma asked quietly, sipping her coffee.

"Yeah, I heard," said Omar. But he forked more egg into his mouth and ate in silence for a moment longer, putting her off, she decided. Finally he said, "I've been thinking. You don't really want me to go." He offered a knowing smile and added, "Not after last night." He winked suggestively. "You're just playing a little hard to get. But that's all right — an older woman like you. I figure you need to go that extra step to make sure a man is interested."

Emma just stared at him, her finger crooked in the coffee cup handle. She couldn't believe only three days ago she'd been so starved for affection. . . . *Forget it,* she told herself. *What's done is done.* Now to get rid of him . . .

"Omar, I hope you will take this the right way, but I just don't want a man in my life right now. You see, after losing my —"

"The right way?" He wiped his mouth, using his sleeve instead of the napkin she'd laid out for him. "Let me tell you something about the *right way*. Running your mouth while a man is trying to eat his breakfast is not the *right way*. Keep that in mind." He pointed his finger at her. "Keep this in mind too. You might not have wanted a man, but you've got one. I know you've been on your own for over a year, so it's going to take you a day or two to get used to me being here. But now you best get used to having a man tell you the way things are going to be from now on."

Emma turned loose her coffee cup. "Omar, leave. This is *my home*. You are not welcome here."

"Hmmmph." Omar forked another mouthful of eggs, chuckling at her as he chewed. "I'm not going no-damn-where. I'm the man of this house now." He thumbed himself on his chest. "Now shut up and get those peaches."

Emma felt herself about to lose control. She held on, clenching her jaw, and said in a tone that was little more than a growl, "Get them yourself." She started to rise from her chair.

But Omar came half up from his chair quickly. His powerful hand swung sharply, backhanding her across her face. She flew sideways from the overturned chair and lay half conscious for a few seconds shaking her throbbing head.

"See? That's what sassing me will get you every time," Omar said, settling back into the chair and casually swabbing a biscuit around on his plate as if nothing had happened. "That was just a little slap — sort of an attention getter, because you didn't know any better. So, now, let's try it again. Get those peaches for me."

Emma shook off the hard slap, struggled to her feet, walked to the shelf, and took down the jar of peaches. Without a word, she set the jar on the table. Seeing the harsh look in Omar's eyes, she picked up the jar, lifted the sealing wire, and twisted the lid off.

Omar smiled. "That's more like it. I'll say one thing, you older women catch on fast, having been with a man before."

As she turned and left the kitchen, she heard him say behind her, "It might be that you're one of them who can't get the day started without a good slapping — sort of an eye-opener," he chuckled. "Hell, maybe you're one of them that like it rough. Are you? Because I don't mind accommodating a woman's peculiar needs."

Emma didn't answer. She walked silently into the bedroom and returned with the gun Omar had left in its holster hanging from a bedpost. Omar looked at the gun and gave her a short laugh. "What are you going to do, shoot me?"

"Yes," Emma said with resolve. She struggled at trying to cock the hammer.

Omar watched, taking a bite of biscuit and chewing it slowly as he shook his head. "Use two hands, fool," he said. Then as if speaking to himself he said, "This is why a woman should never be allowed to carry a gun." He swallowed his food, took a sip of coffee, and watched unconcerned as she continued to struggle with the heavy gun. "Here, want me to cock it for you?" he asked.

But as soon as he said it, Omar heard the hammer click back and saw Emma raise the gun barrel toward his head.

"All right, put it down now before I have to slap you again . . . this is how folks get hurt."

The single shot hit him in the center of his forehead and sent his chair toppling backward. As the contents of his skull streaked up the wall ten feet behind him, he hit the floor still seated perfectly, a stunned look on his face, eyes and mouth open wide, arms outstretched on the floor.

"There's that," Emma said aloud, her voice calm and even. "You had no idea who you were messing with, cowboy."

With the heavy gun still smoking in her hand, she stepped around the table and looked down at Omar, wondering what to do next.

CHAPTER 7

Sheriff Gale had returned to his office; but after considering Emma's sharp attitude for a few minutes, he'd decided that whether she liked it or not, he needed to speak his mind to her. He still felt if she'd only listen to him he could convince her of just how perfect they were for each other. He a sheriff, she the widow of a sheriff. *What could be better . . . ?* He rehearsed the conversation in his mind.

Closing the office door behind him, Gale had started walking along the boardwalk in the direction of the Vertrees cottage when he'd heard the single muffled gunshot. At that time a few heads along the boardwalk turned toward the sound, but only in reflex. A raised hand from the sheriff let the townsfolk know he had matters in hand.

Since the gunshot came from the same direction in which he was headed anyway, Sheriff Gale hastened his step a little, knowing that it never hurt for townsfolk to see how seriously he took his job. Besides, he reminded himself, loosening his Colt in its holster, with a man like Memphis Beck in town, who knew what sort of trouble Beck might have conjured up?

But the closer Gale drew to the Vertrees cottage, the more he began to realize the possibility that the shot could have come from there. "Easy now . . ." he cautioned himself. Stopping out front and looking the cottage over for a few seconds, he continued forward quietly, stepped onto the front porch, and sidled up to a window instead of knocking on the front door.

Peeping inside the house, he saw the gray haze of gun smoke drifting lazily into the parlor from the next room. That gave him every right and reason to slip inside and see what was going on without announcing himself and putting his life in danger. *Here goes.* . . . He crept over to the front door, turned the knob silently, and, finding the door unlocked, slipped inside, his Colt out of its holster, cocked and ready for anything.

In the kitchen, Emma had wasted no time. She'd gone to a closet and brought back two blankets and a ball of heavy twine. From a kitchen drawer she'd taken out a long, sharp butcher knife. As Sheriff Gale eased into the doorway behind her, she stood over Wills' body, rolling up her dress sleeves.

"Oh my God, Emma!" Sheriff Gale said in a hushed tone, staring at the body.

Emma spun toward him, startled, her knife coming up in a defensive position until she saw the Sheriff's Colt raised and cocked. Then she lowered the knife and said in a tearful voice, "Oh, Sheriff, thank God you're here! I was afraid no one had heard the gunshot. I didn't know what to do!"

"You — you did this?" Gale asked, stepping sideways for a better look at the body, Wills' boot soles facing him from the back-turned chair.

"Yes, I did, I had to, Sheriff!" Emma said with a trapped look in her eyes. Yet, even as she spoke, she began getting herself collected, ready to say whatever it took to keep herself from going to jail. "He — he came in here while I was gone shopping! He stole money from my purse." She pointed at the spread-armed corpse. "Look in his pocket, you'll find it there! He went through my things, stealing whatever he —"

"Take it easy, Emma," Sheriff Gale said, cutting her off. "Are you saying he's a *burglar?*" His voice sounded skeptical.

Hearing the sheriff's dubious tone, Emma

said, "Yes. Maybe. Why, don't you believe me?"

"I don't know what to believe, Emma," Gale said. "Most burglars don't stay for breakfast." With a wag of his pistol barrel Gale gestured for her to lower the butcher knife and lay it on the table. As she did so, he kept a close watch on the pistol already lying there.

When she stepped away from the table, the sheriff looked relieved and continued. "Are you saying he *forced* you to fix his breakfast? Because, if you are, that sounds a lot more believable."

"He did force me to fix breakfast for him," Emma said quickly. "It was terrible. He — he threatened me!" She grasped for what to say next. "Look at my face, where he slapped me! I was afraid he was going to kill me."

Gale looked closely at her swollen red cheek. "How did you get his gun from him?"

Emma froze for a moment, not wanting to say that the gun and holster hung from her bedpost. "It's all so confusing," she said finally, holding her hand to her forehead. "But it *was* self-defense. You do believe it was self-defense, don't you, Sheriff?" She gave him a look of desperation.

"I'm trying *hard* to believe you, Miss

Emma," said the sheriff, looking back at the body on the floor, then letting his eyes follow the streak of blood and brain matter up the wall. "I know how things can happen. But whether or not a jury would believe —"

"A jury!" She looked stunned. "Oh no, please, you're not going to arrest me for killing him, are you?"

"Arrest you, no," said the sheriff. "But any time something like this happens and there's no witnesses, I have to take a full statement from you and turn it over to the circuit court judge. He decides what to do, if anything."

"Please, Sheriff Gale," Emma said, "I don't want to go before a judge, or a jury, or anybody else. Can't you help me?" Tears welled in her eyes. "I'm the victim, please don't treat me like a criminal!"

The sheriff looked into her eyes, contemplating the matter. After a pause he pulled a clean handkerchief from his pocket and handed it to her. "I was on my way here, you know, when I heard the gunshot."

"You were?" Emma said, taking the handkerchief and touching it to her eyes.

"I was," said Gale. "I wanted to try *one more time* to see if I could get through to you about how I feel." He gave her a patient smile. "After the way you cut off so fast this morning, I felt like I needed to say something on my own behalf."

"I'm sorry, Sheriff," Emma replied. "I haven't been myself of late."

"Please, call me Vince," the sheriff said, more insistently than he had ever said it before.

Emma began to see a way out of her predicament. "Yes, I will . . . thank you, Vince. I know you might not believe this, but I had been thinking about you all the way home. That may have been what caused me to walk in unsuspecting on this man."

"Oh, thinking about me?" Sheriff Gale's eyes brightened with hope.

"Yes," said Emma, "it's true. I realized how rude I've been with you these past weeks. You must think me a terrible person, *Vince.*"

"No, Emma," said the sheriff, his Colt sliding down into his holster. "You put that thought out of your head. I could never think anything bad about you." He swept his tall Stetson from atop his head. "Sometimes it takes something terrible like this to make two people realize how much they *need* each other."

"You are so kind, Vince," Emma said, feeling less trapped than before. "I don't know what I'd do without you here, helping me, being strong for me. I —"

"Shhh, wait a minute," Gale said, cutting her off as he turned toward the sound of a voice coming from the fence out back. Stepping over and opening the back door, he looked out to Bland Woolard, who had heard the gunshot while walking to his buggy out in front of the livery barn.

"Everything all right in there, Sheriff?" Woolard called out. Trailing along the fence behind Woolard, Sheriff Gale saw, Curtis Clay was tapping along with his walking stick, Little Dog walking along in front of him.

"Everything is all right here, Councilman," Gale called out. "One of the late sheriff's guns accidentally discharged in the wardrobe. No harm done."

Hearing the sheriff, Emma breathed easier.

"I understand, Sheriff." Bland Woolard nodded, waved a hand, and turned and walked way. "You heard him, Curtis," he said as the blind man walked toward him along the fence, "everything is all right . . . just an accident."

"Yes, sir, I heard him," said Curtis, stopping, turning his blank eyes in the direction of the Vertrees cottage. "I'm glad to hear it." But Curtis knew from the sound of the sheriff's voice that something wasn't *all right* in there. What had he heard in the sheriff's voice, tension, a slight deceptiveness? He wasn't sure, and he wanted to hear more.

Continuing along the fence, Curtis stopped at a point where his shoe touched a small rock he'd placed there weeks ago. Seeing Clay stop on that spot and turn facing straight through the yard to the rear door, Sheriff Gale said quietly over his shoulder to Emma, "Woolard's gone. But Curtis Clay is standing back there. I swear, sometimes I believe that ole Negro can see as well as the next fellow."

"Can I do anything for you, Sheriff?" Clay called out, just to get to hear the sheriff's voice again and further analyze it.

"Obliged, Curtis," Gale replied, "but everything is all right. I've got everything *under control.*" He smiled to himself with satisfaction, realizing how quickly his standing with Emma Vertrees had changed.

"I hear you, Sheriff Gale," said Curtis, raising a hand. "If you or Mrs. Vertrees need anything I can do, you holler for me."

"Will do, Curtis," said the sheriff, watching Little Dog turn around with a gentle tap of the walking stick on his rump and head back toward the shack. Curtis walked along behind him. "I don't know who leads and who follows with those two," Gale commented offhandedly as he turned back to Emma and the body lying with its boot soles facing him.

"Sheriff, what will we do with his body?" Emma asked quickly, not wanting to give Gale time to reconsider helping her cover up her act.

The sheriff shook his head slowly, looking down at the corpse with uncertainty. "What were you going to do before I got here?" he asked, looking at the blankets, the ball of twine, and the butcher knife.

"I was going to cut him into pieces and haul the pieces out into the wilds," she replied matter-of-factly. "Is that the best thing to do?" She wanted to get his involvement in whatever happened from here on in the matter.

"You were going to butcher him like a steer?" The sheriff stared at her with a look of shocked disbelief.

Seeing his expression, Emma said, "Oh, of course not. I must have been out of my head with fear. I could never have done something like that. I'm still horrified at having shot him."

"I know you are. A gentle lovely woman like you shouldn't have to face this ugliness alone," Gale said sympathetically. "Leave it to me, I'll get rid of this rascal. You clean up here and try to put this whole terrible mess out of your mind."

"Vince, I — I can't tell you how grateful I am," said Emma. "I hope you will allow me to thank you properly after we're through with all this."

"Oh, I feel properly thanked just being able to look at you and see that you're finally smiling back at me, Emma." Sheriff Gale smiled himself. "Now, I'll go get a pack mule and be right back. We'll wait until tonight when it's dark and I'll haul him away from here."

"Oh, wait, Sheriff," said Emma. "I just remembered, he has a horse."

"A horse." Gale stared at her. "How would you know that?"

Thinking fast, Emma said, "He told me he had one. He said he'd left it at a hitch rail across the street, out in front of the Little Aces Saloon, so no one would see it while I was out."

"All right, I can believe that." Gale nodded, finding it plausible. Seeing the look in her eyes, he quickly said, "I mean, of course *I believe it.* I'm just wondering if anybody else would."

"Why wouldn't they?" Emma asked coolly. "It's the truth."

"They *would*," Gale replied. "Isn't that what I just said?" He spread his hands, showing her how much he agreed with her. Then he changed the subject and said, "It could take a while to find his horse this time of day with the town so busy. I'll look for it later. I better go get the pack mule now, and make sure we'll have it when we need it tonight."

Inside the livery barn, Curtis Clay caught the scent of the sheriff as soon as the lawman stepped into the doorway. With the midmorning sunlight at Gale's back, Curtis could make out the lawman's dark shadowy image, but nothing more. "Yes, sir, Sheriff Gale?" he said, standing up from pouring water into a tin pan for Little Dog. "You thought of something I could do for you after all?"

"Well, in a manner of speaking, yes, Curtis," said Gale. "I'm going to need that pack mule, Delilah, that the town keeps here. Is she available?"

"She sure is, Sheriff," said Clay. "Delilah is the most available gal in town." He grinned. "Want me to go fetch her for you? Tell me how you want her rigged, pack frame, saddle, or cart harness?"

"Obliged, Curtis," said Gale, "but don't

trouble yourself. I'll handle her. You go ahead and look after Little Dog." He didn't want to reveal any more to Clay than he had to. The blind man had a way of putting things together with only a small amount of information.

"It's no trouble, Sheriff," said Curtis.

"No, please, I've got her," said Gale. He stepped past the blind man toward the corral where the pack mule would be this time of morning.

"All right, Sheriff," said Curtis, staring blindly at the ceiling as the sheriff headed out the side door. "The pack frame is hanging over the grain bin where I been keeping it."

"Obliged, Curtis," said Gale.

Curtis smiled faintly, noting to himself how the sheriff's voice revealed a high level of tension. The fact that the lawman tried hard to keep from sounding tense and nervous only made his condition more clear to Curtis's sharp hearing. Whatever Sheriff Gale needed Delilah for, the blind man was certain the lawman had no need for a pack frame.

When Gale returned to Emma's cottage, leading the pack mule, Emma had stepped out onto the back porch and down into the yard to meet him. While he'd been gone, she had done little to clean up the bloody mess on the wall and floor, but had used the time alone to change the sheets and pillowcases, straighten up the bedroom, and get rid of any signs of the young cowboy.

Stepping close to him, she looked the mule up and down and asked, "How did it go?"

"It went fine. Why wouldn't it?" said Gale. "It's the town's livery operation. I'm the sheriff." He smiled at her. "You just try to relax and let me take care of you, Emma. You're in good hands now."

Emma put a hand on his muscular arm and squeezed admiringly. "I know that, Vince," she said softly.

"How is it going, cleaning up in there?" Gale asked, nodding toward the kitchen.

"It's terrible," said Emma. "I start shaking when I try to do anything. That horrible scene keeps coming back to my mind." She touched her wrist to her forehead. "But I will get it done, eventually, I'm certain."

"You leave it alone," Gale said gallantly. "I ought to be ashamed of myself, expecting you to do all that. Why don't you fix us a pot of coffee? I'll clean his brains off the wall."

"I can't let you do that, Vince," Emma protested weakly. But she only stood back

126

and watched as he hitched the pack mule
and started into the house, rolling up his
shirtsleeves.

CHAPTER 8

In the darkened shade of a white oak in the alleyway behind Emma's cottage, Beck stood watching her house out of curiosity, deciding to see if he could get a look at the man Emma had told him about.

When the kitchen door began to open, he watched from around the thick tree trunk as Sheriff Gale stepped out onto the porch, Emma right behind him. At the porch steps the sheriff turned, and Beck watched a smiling Emma place a hand affectionately on the lawman's broad chest.

So it *was* the sheriff after all. He watched the two standing close, Gale speaking to her upturned face, his head bowed. Why had she lied to him? Beck had to ask himself. It would have made no difference to him that she was involved with a lawman.

"You could have told me, Emma," Beck murmured in disappointment, watching Gale roll his sleeves down and button his cuffs. At a hitch rail in the shade beside the porch, he saw the pack mule and the sheriff's horse standing side by side. Gale picked up a bag of oats from the porch, stepped down, and walk toward the animals.

Well, tough break . . . , Beck told himself. Letting out a breath, he stepped back and leaned against the tree trunk for a moment before walking away. He wasn't sure why Emma would lie about her and the sheriff, but he'd seen enough to know what was going on. A person can change a lot over seven years' time, he reminded himself with regret.

As soon as he saw the sheriff out making his rounds tonight, he'd come back. He needed to hear what she had to say on the matter. He owed her that much, he told himself, riding out along a thin path that led away from the alley.

On an out-of-the-way path as he walked along toward the wide dirt street, he suddenly ducked down at the sight of three riders slowing their horses from a brisk pace to a walk as they reached the town limits.

"Uh oh, detectives!" Beck said to himself, recognizing Roundhead Mitchell's grim moon face beneath a dusty bowler that looked much too small for his large head. Without hesitation, Beck ran crouched down along the path into the cover of brush and woods. He only stopped for a moment to consider his situation; then he hurried to a spot where he could observe the livery barn without being seen.

For twenty minutes he forced himself to be patient as Curtis Clay sat at the wooden table outside his shack beside the livery barn. The blind man took his time cleaning his big revolver. "Come on, Clay, get out of this heat," Beck said to himself. He kept a wary eye toward the alley leading to the dirt street, watching for the three detectives who might bring their horses to the livery any minute.

Finally, the blind man shoved the revolver into his belt, wiped his forehead with a gray handkerchief, and stood up and tapped the side of his shoe gently against Little Dog, who lay sleeping against his foot. "It's about time. . . ." Beck breathed a sigh of relief, watching the man and the dog walk inside the shack, the revolver stuck down inside his belt.

As soon as man and dog were inside the shack, Beck slipped wide around the barn and inside through a side door. He walked straight to one of the rental horse stalls and took out the big red roan he'd eyed earlier in case such an emergency as this should arise. As Clay had instructed, he left a gold coin on the roan's stall to cover the rental, saddled it, walked it out, and rode away quietly.

Atop the roan, Beck heeled it out through a stretch of wild grass, onto a path through a stretch of tangled brush, then onto a wooded hillside north of Little Aces. A mile into the shelter of trees, Beck finally stopped and looked back. Beck patted the roan's neck. As if the horse could understand him, he said, "I'm not hightailing out of here yet. *Forewarned is forearmed,*" He smiled, staring in the direction of town. Now that he knew the detectives were there, all he had to do was avoid them. *Or, better yet, leave,* he warned himself.

"I won't leave until I've looked into her eyes and asked her why she didn't think she could be on the level with me," he said quietly to the surrounding woods. Then he said to the roan, "Looks like you're stuck with me until I can slip in and get my horse back from the blind man. . . ."

On the busy street running through Little Aces, the three detectives rode their horses along at a walk. A few feet ahead of the other two, Bobby Vane looked back and forth at the pedestrians along the boardwalks lining both sides of the street. "I always find it peculiar why a mud hole like

131

this turns into a town," he said over his shoulder.

Behind him, Roundhead Mitchell rode with a sawed-off shotgun lying across his lap, his broad hand resting on the cut-down stock that he'd wrapped with rawhide, fashioning a pistol grip. "Maybe it wasn't a mud hole until it turned into a town," he replied.

"Maybe." Vane shrugged, not liking the idea of Roundhead questioning what he'd said. "There's some places that were mud holes before anybody showed up. Some turned mud holes afterward, I expect."

Eyes along the street turned warily toward Roundhead's shotgun. Roundhead tipped his too-small bowler with a grim expression and said to Vane, "That's all Chicago *ever* was, a big stinking mud hole, where trappers got together just to smell one another's stink. Damned trappers." He spat and stared straight ahead. "This whole frontier country is one big *mud hole,* far as I'm concerned. Washington is the same way, nothing but a big nasty mud hole. I hate that place."

"I've never been there," said Vane, still scrutinizing the town as they rode toward a large flat wooden whiskey bottle hanging by chains from an iron frame. The giant bottle was tipped slightly toward the street. Beneath the bottle another sign read, LITTLE ACES #1 SALOON."

"You haven't missed anything," Roundhead offered, the three of them veering their horses toward a long iron hitch rail out in front of the saloon.

But as they drew closer to the hitch rail, behind them, Frank Skimmer, who had ridden in silence, suddenly jumped his horse ahead of them and said, "This is my kid brother's horse!" He jumped down from atop his horse and took a closer look at the dusty black gelding standing reined between two other horses. "Yep, that's his saddle all right," Skimmer said.

Looking the gelding over, Roundhead said, "You better tell your kid brother that *live* horses require feed and water. This one looks like a pile of hide stretched over a washboard."

"I expect my brother knows how to take care of a horse as much as the next man," said Skimmer, taking on a gruff tone. Yet even as he spoke he fanned away a snarling cloud of flies looming above a pile of excrement at the horse's rear hooves.

"Suit yourself," said Roundhead, also noting the excrement and the horse's neglected condition. He and Vane looked at each other and nudged their horses to the rail.

"Touchy about his kin, ain't he?" Vane said under his breath as the two swung down from their saddles and hitched their reins.

"All big gunmen like him are crazy," Roundhead commented quietly. "I've never seen one yet that wasn't cat-screaming *loco,* have you?"

Bobby Vane didn't answer. He stood staring as Skimmer bounded up onto the boardwalk and through the batwing doors. "I hope he ain't forgot that we're here on business."

"By business, I hope you're not getting ready to tell me we can't be drinking on the job, cut some of this dust out of our gullets."

"No drinking on *the job?*" Vane repeated with a wry grin. "I don't know where you get these strange notions of yours, Roundhead. I never saw a job that didn't *require* a certain amount of drinking."

They walked inside to the saloon in time to see Frank Skimmer grab a drinker by the front of his shirt and raise him onto his toes. "What do you mean, he's not even been here? His damn horse is out there, looks like it's been in one spot long enough to draw buzzards!"

"Whoa, Mr. Skimmer, please!" said the

drinker, not daring to reach for the gun on his hip. "I didn't say he's not been here! I said *if* he's been here I haven't seen him!"

Skimmer turned him loose with a rough shove and turned to the rest of the men and the saloon girls lined along the bar. "Everybody listen like your life depended on it. You all know me. You've all heard how quick-triggered I am and how quick-tempered I can get. I'm looking for my brother, Omar Wills. His horse is that black rack of bones standing in a pile of its own leavings." He pointed toward the hitch rail beyond the batwing doors. "Anybody knows where he is better loosen their jaw and start talking. The longer I wait the more apt I am to go killing wild."

"A quick question, Mr. Skimmer," a tall, broad-shouldered surveyor asked innocently, raising a finger for emphasis. "If he's your brother, how come his name is Wills and yours is Skimmer?"

"Oh, hell, here we go," Roundhead said to Bobby Vane, seeing Skimmer jerk the big man from his feet by his belt and the nape of his neck. At the bar the rest of the four-man surveyor crew stood in stunned disbelief and watched their comrade struggle wildly as Skimmer crossed the plank floor. Behind the bar the saloon owner shouted,

"No, please! For God sakes!"

Out front on the wide street, pedestrians ducked and fled as the big surveyor shot headlong through the large window in a spray of broken glass and splintered window frame. A team of wagon horses reared as the man bounced off the iron hitch as if it were a leaf spring and landed into the middle of the street, causing both buggy and saddle traffic to come to a sudden halt.

Half-conscious, hatless, and with a long shard of glass embedded in the tip of his thick nose, the surveyor staggered to his feet and tried to walk away as if he had no idea what had happened to him. But as he zigzagged back and forth on wobbly legs, Frank Skimmer walked from the saloon with determination, carrying a long, two-handed, seasoned oak bat he'd snatched from behind the bar.

At the saloon doors the other two detectives backed out with the surveyors pressing angrily toward them, in spite of Roundhead's sawed-off shotgun and Vane's drawn Colt.

Stepping up behind the staggering man in the street, Skimmer took a stance and braced himself as if preparing to hit a baseball. But before he took his swing, two pistol shots exploded into the air from

Sheriff Gale's Starr revolver.

Skimmer froze in his batting stance, looking back at the sheriff over his shoulder. Onlookers hurried out of the way, horse traffic backed and turned and jammed up in both directions. "Drop the shillelagh, mister, the fight's over," Gale called out, his revolver out at arm's length pointed at Skimmer.

Skimmer only lowered the club an inch, but he kept it cocked back, ready for a swing. "He had it coming, Sheriff, he insulted my family!" He started to step toward the wandering surveyor.

"I said, *it's over!*" Gale said more firmly, causing the detective to stop, this time realizing that the sheriff meant business. "Drop the club."

"All right, there," said Skimmer. "It's dropped." But as the club hit the ground, Skimmer's Colt streaked up from his holster, cocked and aimed. His move was so fast, it caught Gale off guard. Skimmer grinned slyly. "Aw, now what do you have to say, Sheriff?" He took a slow step forward. "You had no idea you were crowding one of the fastest guns in this territory, did you?" His confidence swelled. "I'm Frank Skimmer, detective for the Great Western

Railroad Posse. I'll wager you've heard of me."

"I've heard of you," Gale said flatly. "Lower the gun, Mr. Skimmer," he added, realizing Skimmer had him cold, but also knowing that as sheriff he had to make a stand.

"As one lawman to another," said Skimmer, in no hurry, taking his time, taunting the outclassed town sheriff, "I can't help but ask myself, if I were you, what would I do about now? What would be going through my mind, knowing I was facing a dangerous man like me?"

"I'm not telling you again, Mr. Skimmer," Gale said, his voice steady, but with an expression of fear tightening around his eyes.

"Or *what?*" Skimmer gave a short dark chuckle, his thumb poised across the cocked hammer.

"Or I'll empty your belly all over the street," a voice replied coolly. Sam Burrack stepped sidelong from the edge of the gathered crowd. He answered before Gale got the chance to. Just the sight of the ranger and the shotgun caused Gale's tight chest to ease down. But this thing wasn't defused yet.

Cutting a glance to the ranger, Skimmer

said in a calm tone, "Well, well, Ranger Burrack, I bet. Now, what do you suppose you are going to —"

"Drop it or use it, Skimmer," Sam said, cutting him off. "I'm not here to talk."

There was iron in the ranger's words. Skimmer shut up, knowing that his next word would likely draw a blast from Sam's shotgun. Before giving in and dropping his gun, he cut a glance toward Vane and Roundhead, who stood only fifteen feet to the ranger's left. "Don't look to them, Skimmer," Sam said. "They're dead too."

Roundhead shouted, "Drop the damn gun, Skimmer. Are you crazy?" As he spoke his own shotgun fell from his hand as if it were red hot.

"You heard him, Frank, drop the gun!" said Vane. Both men raised their hands chest high even though the ranger hadn't told them to.

Skimmer grimaced, but let the hammer down under his thumb and let the gun roll from his fingertips. "I've never dropped a gun in my life," he said, sneering.

"Today was a good day to start," Sam said. As he walked forward, slowly, Gale felt a heavy weight lifted from his shoulders. He turned his Starr toward Roundhead and Vane.

"I'm a lawman too, Ranger, a bona fide detective," Skimmer said harshly, "in case you don't know it."

"Then shame on you, threatening a fellow lawman," Sam said. The butt of the shotgun snapped upward in a hard jab to the center of Skimmer's chest, sending him off his feet and backward onto the dirt.

"You had no call to do that," Skimmer growled, holding his right hand to his chest.

"It kept your hand out of your vest," Sam said, "and it kept me from having to kill you." As he spoke he stepped over, reached down, and pulled a hideout pistol from behind Skimmer's black vest. Skimmer glared at him. "On your best day, you can't kill me, Ranger. Toss that scattergun away and let's throw down. I'll show you who you're messing with."

Sam stepped back, stooped down, and picked up the gun he'd made Skimmer drop in the dirt. "You've showed me enough for one day," he said. Then he said to Gale, who walked closer, still keeping an eye on the other detectives, "Are you arresting him?"

"You bet I am," said Gale. "Any man makes me look down his gun barrel goes to jail."

"I work for the railroad!" Skimmer protested. "We're in the midst of a manhunt!

I'll have your badge yanked off when the colonel gets here."

"On your feet," said Gale, disregarding the detective's threats.

"My brother's missing. I can't find him if I'm in jail," Skimmer growled. "What's the law going to do to find him?"

"Who is he? How long has he been missing?" Gale asked matter-of-factly, taking Skimmer's two guns as Sam held them out to him.

"His name is Omar Wills, and that's his horse." As he stood, dusting his sleeve, he pointed at the skinny horse standing out in front of the saloon. "I've got a feeling something bad's happened to him. None of the drinkers or whores have seen him."

Sam noted a flicker of something in Gale's eyes as Skimmer mentioned his missing brother. But his observance was quickly interrupted by the bloody surveyor who had staggered back to them, the glass missing from his nose and replaced by a short stream of blood. "Ask him . . . why his brother and him . . . have different last names, Ranger," the surveyor said haltingly.

Skimmer cut in, "We don't, you idiot! His name is Omar Wills Skimmer!"

Gale asked the surveyor, "Do you feel up to filing a complaint for him throwing you through the window?"

"Who?" the surveyor asked in confusion. "What window?"

"Never mind," said Gale. "Come see me when you're feeling better." He gave Skimmer a shove toward the jail. As the detective walked forward grudgingly, Gale said to Sam under his breath, "Ranger, I'm obliged. I owe you one."

Sam only nodded and watched him and his prisoner walk away. In the street the surveying crew stopped their friend from wandering away and steered him in the right direction.

CHAPTER 9

The crowd dispersed and the traffic thinned as Vince Gale escorted Frank Skimmer across the street and through the door to the sheriff's office. The surveyor and his pals drifted off along the boardwalk grumbling among themselves. Sam walked over to Roundhead and Bobby Vane with the shotgun draped over his forearm. Stooping, he picked up Roundhead's pistol-grip shotgun, unloaded it, and handed it to the big moon-faced detective butt first. He handed him the shotgun shell.

"You're not arresting us, Ranger?" Vane asked, his hands still chest high.

"No, I'm not," said Sam. "You two didn't do anything. I saw that you were with Skimmer, I just didn't want you turning the odds in his favor."

Vane lowered his hands. "I've got news for you, Burrack," he said stiffly. "Frank Skimmer doesn't need anybody stacking his odds for him. You're lucky to be alive."

"Aren't we all?" Sam said quietly. He looked at Roundhead Mitchell, seeing the shotgun shell in his thick hand, and said as the detective started to break open the gun to load it, "I'd appreciate it if you'd leave it empty right now."

"Oh, all right," said Roundhead, stopping immediately and putting the shotgun shell in his pocket.

"What was Skimmer talking about, his brother being missing?" Sam asked them both.

"Yeah, he's been talking about his brother catching up to us and going to work for the colonel," said Vane, easing his attitude a little. "He spotted his horse when we rode in. But nobody in the saloon has seen him. The horse looks ready to fall over."

"I'll take him over to the livery barn, get him tended to," Sam said. "Skimmer can claim him when he gets out of jail. Or maybe his brother will have shown up by then," he added.

"Frank Skimmer won't be in jail long enough to have to change socks," said Roundhead. "Soon as the rest of the posse catches up to us, the colonel will pay whatever it costs to get his top gunman back on the job."

"I hope you're not thinking anything is over between you and Frank, Ranger," Vane put in. "He ain't likely to forget what happened here."

"It's over," Sam said with finality.

"No, it's not." Vane grinned and continued. "It ain't over between you and Jack Strap and Bloody Vlak either, for you taking their horses and shaming them in the eyes of the posse."

"That's over too," Sam said, "as far as I'm concerned."

Vane chuckled and shook his head. "What you want doesn't cut any ice with these men. The colonel and all of us have a mad-on at you anyway, for not cooperating and giving us Memphis Beck when you had him by the tail feathers."

Roundhead asked curiously, "Yeah, what is it with you anyway, Ranger? We're all lawmen. You with the territorial court, us with the railroad. You could help yourself a lot, getting on the colonel's side in this Hole-in-the-wall crackdown."

"I don't work that way. If Beck is guilty, I need to hear it from a territorial judge before I go on the prod for him."

"Meaning you've got no respect for the railroad's judgment?" Vane asked.

"Not enough for me to go dogging a man

on just their say-so," Sam replied. "As soon as Beck gets himself on my wanted list, I'll hound him like I would anybody else. But not until somebody can prove he was involved in a crime."

"Nobody ever comes up with hard evidence against a man like Beck," said Roundhead.

"Then he'll never have to worry about me," Sam replied. "I don't take the law into my own hands."

"Not ever?" Vane grinned. "Because I've heard tales that say otherwise."

Sam ignored him.

Roundhead asked, looking back and forth along the street, "Where is Memphis Beck now, Ranger? You'll tell us that, won't you?"

"I haven't seen Warren Beck since I arrived in Little Aces," Sam said truthfully.

"And if you had, would you have told us so?" Vane asked pointedly.

The ranger didn't answer. Instead he said, "I expect you two will want to be getting on back along the trail and telling the colonel what happened here." He touched the brim of his sombrero toward them, turned, and walked away. He was through in Little Aces as far as Memphis Beck was concerned. He felt no need to tell these two his plans, but it was time for him to get on the trail. He hoped he could take down Bennie Drew and Tom Cat Weaver before the railroad posse caught up with them.

"So, that's the man who killed Junior Lake and his gang?" Roundhead said quietly.

"Yeah, can you believe that?" Vane replied. "He don't look like all that much to me."

"Really?" Roundhead looked at him.

"Yeah, really," said Vane with a testy snap to his voice. "For two cents I'd be tempted to take him on myself."

Roundhead said flatly, "If Skimmer had known that, I bet he'd have given you the *two cents.*"

"Meaning what, Roundhead?" Vane asked with a sharp stare. "Are you trying to say that I'm afraid of that ranger?"

"Yeah, I suppose I am," Roundhead said, returning the stare.

Vane turned his eyes away from the big man and spat and cursed under his breath. "There's no sense in us arguing the point. When Skimmer gets the chance, he'll eat that ranger alive." He grinned thinking about it. "That is, if he beats Jack Strap and the Romanian to him." He spat again and wiped a sleeve across his lips. "I think we ought to get ourselves properly liquored before we ride back and tell the colonel."

"I can't argue with you on that," said

Roundhead, turning toward the batwing doors. On the boardwalk a bartender had already started cleaning up broken glass with a broom and shovel.

Inside the sheriff's office, Sam looked back along a bleak hallway at three jail cells. A ray of afternoon sunlight shone through barred windows and lay in stripes on the dusty floor. The iron-barred cell doors stood wide open on two of the empty cells. In the third cell stood Frank Skimmer, only his hands visible, his fists wrapped around the bars of the locked door.

Speaking in a lowered voice to keep Skimmer from hearing him, Sam said, "The surveyors headed out of town. The two detectives were going back into the saloon when I looked back."

"Obliged, Ranger," said Gale. "I expect that's that, at least until the railroad posse gets here." He looked closer at Sam and asked, "Have you seen Beck around anywhere? If the detectives run into him on the street, there'll be hell to pay."

"I haven't seen him since he walked his horse to the livery barn," said Sam. "I'll take Skimmer's brother's horse to the livery and check on Beck's horse while I'm there."

Having heard their voices but not the

content of their conversation, Frank Skimmer called out from his cell, "I want my brother found, Sheriff! Do you hear me out there? And if I find he's met with foul play, I want the man who done it."

"I hear you," Gale called out in reply. Then in a lowered voice he said to the ranger, "I don't know what to tell him about his brother. I'll ask around at the saloon first chance I get. What else can I do?"

"Want me to ask around some before I leave town?" Sam asked.

"No, no, that's all right, Ranger," Gale said quickly, maybe *too* quickly, Sam thought. "It'll keep for a while. He might have gotten dog drunk and crawled up under something, for all we know."

"You're right," Sam said. "I thought I'd make the offer."

"Obliged again, Ranger," said Gale. "You've been a great help. But you've done enough."

Sam noted that the sheriff suddenly appeared distracted. He watched Gale open a drawer, then idly pick up Skimmer's revolver from where he'd laid it atop the desk. But instead of putting the gun in the desk drawer, he shoved it back down behind his belt.

"Everything all right, Sheriff?" Sam asked.

"What? Oh yeah," said Gale, catching himself, seeing the ranger glance down at the pistol. "I expect it might have rattled me some, a man like Frank Skimmer pointing a gun at me." He took Skimmer's pistol from his belt once again; this time he put it in the desk drawer and closed the drawer quickly.

Sam considered his words. He'd watched Gale out in the street. He'd seen fear in his eyes, yet no more than normal for a man taking a stand and staring down death. But *rattled?* He didn't think so. There was something else concerning the sheriff. *What is it?* he asked himself.

Seeing the look on the ranger's face, Gale seemed to take exception. He stiffened a bit and asked, "Haven't you ever been rattled?"

"I understand," Sam said, dismissing it without further question. Changing the subject, he said, "If you need me to stay for a while, I will. Otherwise, there's still three good hours of riding before dark. I'll get back up on the high trails."

"I'm all right, Ranger," said Gale. "I suppose when the posse gets here, the colonel will manage to throw around enough weight to get Skimmer out of jail."

"Will you press an assault charge on him, make him have to go before the circuit court judge?" Sam asked, thinking he already knew the answer.

"Why go through all that?" said Gale. "We both know the railroad can afford to buy off anything a town sheriff like me can try to do to him." He glanced down the hall toward the jail cell, where Skimmer's hands rested around the bars. "I'll hold him here as long as I can, let him go as soon as I have to." He shook his head and said with regret, "That's all the *justice* we get from big business these days."

"I don't envy you, Sheriff," Sam said, "having to put up with the colonel and his bunch."

Giving a thin, wry smile, Gale pushed his fingers back through his hair, nodded down at the badge on his chest, and said, "Hell, it's all a part of being pinned to a star, I reckon."

Leading his big Appaloosa and the weakened horse he'd brought along from the hitch rail, Sam walked into the open front doors of the livery barn, out of the afternoon sunlight. At a feed bin, he saw the blind man straighten up and turn toward him. On the ground sat Little Dog only a few inches away, watching Clay's feet, poised to hop out of their way at any second. "The livery manager ain't here, but I help him some," said Clay, holding a feed scoop in his hand, his big revolver shoved down behind a length of hemp rope that served as his belt. "What can I do for you?"

"I've got one here that needs graining and watering bad," Sam said. He stepped over and hitched the dusty black gelding to a stall rail. "He's been left too long at a hitch rail."

"I'll say he has," Curtis said, tapping the side of his shoe out gently until he found Little Dog. He followed the dog toward the ranger, his walking stick in hand. "That horse has been sweated and dried so many times, he smells like *ten* sweaty horses."

"Yes," said the ranger, "and that's not the worst of it."

"It never is," Clay commented, shaking his head as he walked up to the horse. His outstretched hand located it, yet his other senses had sought it out. *"Whooie,"* he said, running a scrutinizing hand along the emaciated horse's side. "I'm going to have to feed and water him a little at a time, else it'll kill him." He took his hand from the horse's side but held it close. "Who does this black horse belong to, anyway?"

His observation stunned Sam, and caused him to look closer at Clay's clouded eyes.

"How do you know he's black?"

"This time of day, this kind of weather, only a dark horse gets this hot in the sun."

"I see," Sam said, curiously skeptical. "But you didn't say he's dark, you said *black.*"

Clay grinned. "The darker the horse, the hotter he gets. I can tell it by the palm of my hand." His grin broadened. "But *you* can't, can you, mister?"

"No, I can't," Sam replied. "It stands to reason that a dark horse left in the sun might feel warmer."

"But you don't know if you believe I can tell a dark horse from a black horse, now, do you?" Clay grinned.

"No offense," Sam said, "but it is a little hard to believe."

Clay tapped himself on the forehead. "You think maybe I can tell it's dark and just play the odds on it being black?"

"Maybe," Sam replied, wondering where this was going.

Clay stepped closer and ran a hand along the Appaloosa's side. "Suppose I told you I could tell you what color this horse was, for a dollar? Would you bet with me?"

"No," Sam said. "I would say either you're not blind, or else you've got some kind of trick up your sleeve."

Clay chuckled. "I'm Curtis Clay, mister. I

see I can't interest you in anything."

"I don't gamble much," said the ranger. "I'm Arizona Ranger Sam Burrack."

"Are you sure enough?" Clay said, impressed without appearing impressed. "I have *heard* of you, Ranger." He stepped back from the Appaloosa. "Tell me now, what was those two shots in the air about a while ago?"

Again, his words surprised Sam. But this time Sam wouldn't comment on it. "Sheriff Gale broke up a fight with a couple of warning shots."

"I see," said Clay. He drifted back to the black gelding, ran his hand down its reins, and unhitched them as he spoke. "Being a lawman, you're right handy with a gun, I know."

Sam didn't answer; his silence spoke for him.

"No, I don't mean fast *using one*," said Clay. "I'd never ask a man something like that. I mean *handy,* putting one together that's laid out in pieces before you."

Sam looked at the shiny clean revolver in Clay's waist and said, "Not as handy as you are, I'm going to guess."

Clay shook his head and laughed. "You don't give a man a chance, Ranger."

Sam smiled. "I bet you don't either, Mr.

Clay." Without pause, he asked as he looked toward Beck's dun standing in a stall, "How's the dun with the stone bruise doing?"

"He's going to be all right," Clay said. "Do you know the owner?"

"We've met," said Sam, never one to release much information. He took a gold coin from his pocket and held it out. "Here's some money for taking care of the horse. The sheriff's office will pay anything else it costs. Obliged, Mr. Clay," he added.

Hearing the ranger turn with the Appaloosa to leave, Clay said, "It's chestnut-colored, Ranger."

Sam stopped. "What?" he asked.

"That horse of yours. He's a chestnut with dark stockings," said Clay. "That's what I say he is."

"Then you're wrong, Mr. Clay," said Sam, before turning and leaving. "He's an Appaloosa."

"Ah, see?" Clay pointed out. "I was wrong. You would have won, had you bet with me."

"I get the feeling you wouldn't have been *wrong* if I had bet with you," Sam replied.

Clay laughed again and shook his head. "You sure don't give a man a chance, Ranger."

"Good evening to you, Mr. Clay," Sam

said respectfully, touching the brim of his sombrero in spite of Clay's blindness.

"And to you, Ranger," Clay replied.

Outside the livery barn, Sam stepped up into his saddle and nudged the big Appaloosa toward a trail leading out of town.

■ ■ ■ ■

PART 2

■ ■ ■ ■

CHAPTER 10

Memphis Beck had taken caution and stayed well outside town until after dark. Knowing the three detectives were there and that the rest of the posse wouldn't be far behind, he slipped into the town along the same shadowy alleyway behind Emma's cottage. In the cover of the same white oak where he'd stood earlier, he stepped down from the roan and looked all around Emma's yard in the darkness, noting that the sheriff's horse and the pack mule were gone.

Inside the kitchen in the dim light of an oil lamp, Emma had finished washing herself in a pan of tepid water. She had dried herself, pulled on her nightshirt, and put on her robe when she heard a faint tapping at the back door.

"Emma, it's me, Memphis," she heard Beck whisper outside the door.

"Memphis, this is a bad time for me," she whispered in reply, even as she opened the door a crack and looked into his face in the darkness.

"I know," Memphis Beck said quietly, forcing the door open enough to slip inside, "it's not the best of time for me either." Judging from her reluctance to allow him inside, Beck asked as his eyes searched out along the hallway through the darkened house, "You are alone, aren't you?"

"Yes, I'm alone now, but I won't be for long," Emma said. "Sheriff Gale will be here before long."

"Yes, I know," said Beck. "I saw him here earlier, and decided to wait until his horse was gone before coming to the door." He looked in her eyes. "Why did you lie to me, Emma?"

"Lie to you?" It took her a moment to catch up to what she'd said earlier.

"I asked you if Sheriff Gale was the man you were seeing. You told me no," Beck said. "You didn't have to do that."

"Oh." Emma stalled, then said, "I know I shouldn't have lied to you about the sheriff . . . I don't know why I did. But Vince and I have talked things over, and I've decided not to stop seeing him after all."

"I see," Beck said, not hiding the disappointment in his face. "Then, I suppose that's all there is to say about it."

She cupped his cheek. "I'm sorry, Memphis," she said, meaning it. "I've gotten too comfortable living inside the law those years with Dillard. I don't think I can step back outside it." She meant that too. She didn't know what would have happened if she hadn't played up to Gale and gotten him on her side. She could have been sitting in jail tonight. Now that Gale was on her side, she wasn't about to do anything that might turn him against her. She knew that the deeper Gale involved himself in covering up the killing, the less likely he would ever be to turn her in.

Seeing a look of regret that she was unable to mask, Memphis tipped her chin up gently and looked deep into her eyes. "Emma, are you telling me everything now?" he asked softly.

"Yes, I'm — I'm being honest with you, Memphis," she said with a sigh. "For both our sakes, it's better that we leave things as they are."

"I feel like there's something you're not telling me," Beck persisted, his eyes searching hers. "Is he good to you . . . I mean, you're not afraid of him, are you? Because if you are —"

"No, Memphis, please," Emma said, stopping him. "I'm with him of my own choosing." Thinking of Omar sprawled on his back in the kitchen chair with his brains blown out, she added, "Believe me, I wouldn't take any abuse."

"Yes, I know you were never that kind of woman," said Beck, relenting. He still thought there was something she wasn't telling him, but he decided he couldn't pursue the matter any further. "If you ever need me . . . if you ever need anything at all . . ."

She smiled. "We've had this conversation before, Memphis, remember?" she said, a hand on his chest.

"Yes," he said in a lighter tone, "I remember having it the last time you left and took up with a lawman." He smiled at her. "What is it about outlaws and lawmen that keeps you coming back for more?"

"I don't know," she said softly, feeling tears well up in her eyes. "Crazy, I guess."

He took a half step back from her. "I mean it, Emma, if you —"

"Stop it," she whispered, afraid that at any second she might break down and tell him everything. She knew he would insist on protecting her if he knew. But she also knew how risky that would be for both of them. She was right, she'd been too long inside the law and didn't want to step outside and have the law hounding her.

"The truth is, Memphis, you've got to get out of Little Aces," she said. "Vince told me there are three detectives in Little Aces, scouts for some big posse on its way here."

He was glad to hear her tip him off even though he already knew about the detectives. "Obliged that you're concerned enough to tell me, Emma," he said. He stepped back to the door, not wanting to leave her, but knowing he had to. "I hate leaving the dun behind, but I've got to cover some ground."

She followed him onto the back porch and watched him slip out across the dark backyard. Ignoring the gate, Beck leaped easily over the picket fence and disappeared into the deeper darkness. She touched the sleeve of her robe to her eyes and wondered briefly if she would ever see him again. Then she turned and walked back inside.

In the silent dark, Curtis Clay waited a full five minutes before standing up from behind a row of cactus and brush along the side of Emma's yard. He had stepped out of his shack and walked along the fence line at the first sound of the roan's quiet hooves in the alleyway. He'd followed Little Dog into the brush no sooner than he'd heard the soft footsteps and the slight creak of wood as

Beck stepped over the picket fence. With his pistol in his waist he'd waited in the dark, listening to the door open and close, then open and close again moments later.

"The woman's all right, Little Dog," he whispered, his ears searching the darkness surrounding him. "Walk me to the saloon." He fingered the money in his pocket that he'd won from the cowboy a few days earlier. "It's time I get me a long drink of whiskey, find out what's been going on around here."

Inside the Little Aces Saloon, Curly Bryant, the bartender, filled two frothy mugs of beer and set them in front of the detectives, along with a fresh bottle of rye whiskey. Drinkers on either side had left plenty of space between themselves and the detectives. Roundhead's pistol-grip shotgun lay on the bar top beside his forearm. The bartender stood expectantly, awaiting one of the two to pay for the new round of drinks. They'd had been drinking heavily for the past hour. The more they'd drunk, the more prickly and quarrelsome they'd become.

"Tell me something, *Mr. Bartender . . . ,*" Bobby Vane said in a slurred voice, hooking his fingers into the handle on the beer mug. He stopped and made the bartender wait while he took a long drink of beer. Then, wiping a streak of foam from his upper lip before finishing his words, he asked, "How does a man with a head slicker than a damn billiard ball get a name like *Curly?*"

"My father started calling me Curly when I was small," Bryant said somberly. Without missing a beat, he said, "That will be six bits."

The two stared blurry-eyed at him. They'd also gotten tighter and more belligerent each time the bartender asked them to pay. "Damn, did the price just go up?" Vane asked sharply.

"No, it's the same as it has been," said Curly Bryant. "There's the prices." He pointed at a sign on the wall behind the bar.

The two stared at the sign. "I see it, damn it," Vane said. He reached into his pocket, came up with some coins, and slapped them down hard on the bar. "Get your dice and cup up here, we'll roll you for the drinks, double or nothing."

Curly considered it for a second. "All right, one time, double or nothing." He reached under the bar and pulled up a leather dice cup with six dice in it. But as he set the dice cup on the bar, he looked up and saw Little Dog walk in beneath the batwing doors, followed by Curtis Clay tapping the floor with his walking stick. "One minute," Byrant said to the two detectives, "let me get the man his bottle."

"I'm not waiting," Vane demanded, "I'm hot right now. I don't want my luck to cool."

"I won't be long," Bryant assured him. He stepped to the side and picked up a bottle of cheaper whiskey that he kept beneath the bar.

The two detectives watched as Clay tapped his way to the bar and stopped when his walking stick rang softly against the brass rail. Little Dog veered to the side and sat down close to his feet. "I've got your bottle ready and waiting, Curtis," said Bryant, standing the bottle on the bar top in front of Clay.

"Obliged, Mr. Bryant." Curtis felt around until he located the bottle and closed a hand around it, then propped his elbows on the bar. "Say, I heard all sorts of commotion from the street today," he said, laying his money on the bar top. He referred to the fight the ranger had mentioned to him.

"Yes, but it was all settled quickly, with no harm done," said Bryant, keeping his conversation short on the matter since it had involved the detectives, who stood staring at Clay. Anger showed in their glaring whiskey-lit eyes. "You come back now, Curtis,"

Bryant added quickly, sliding the money off the bar top.

"Yes, sir, I will," Clay said. He could tell by the tightness in the bartender's voice that there was good reason not to talk about the incident right now. He nodded and started to drop the bottle into his coat pocket. But beside him, Bobby Vane caught his wrist and said with a cold stare, "What's your big hurry, blind man? We're a real sociable bunch here, ain't we, Roundhead?"

"To a fault," said Roundhead, looking Clay up and down.

"Sit that bottle right down here and let's have us a friendly drink together," said Vane.

"Sorry, fellows, Curtis never drinks his whiskey at the bar," said Bryant.

"Oh? Now, pray tell, why is that?" Roundhead asked indignantly.

"Because he's colored, I bet," said Vane, reaching over, picking up Clay's bottle, and pulling the cork from it. He shook his head. "My, my, it saddens the heart to think how little we've learned since the great civil conflict." His voice sounded insincere. He dropped the cork onto the bar top and swirled the bottle.

"His color has nothing to do with it," Bryant added quickly. "Curtis always takes his whiskey home with him. Don't you,

Curtis?" He looked at Clay, who stood listening intently, his hand on the bar top, his fingers seeming to probe for his missing bottle.

"I do at that," said Curtis, realizing he was being taken by the detectives.

"Not tonight, my sightless friend," said Vane with a dark chuckle.

Gesturing at the whiskey bottle in Vane's hand, Bryant grimaced and shook his head, trying to signal the drunken detective against drinking it. But Vane didn't catch the signal. He raised the bottle, took a long sip, and tried handing it to Roundhead.

"Damn, that whiskey tastes like it's made its way through a horse or two before it got here," Vane commented, wiping a hand across his lips.

Roundhead had caught the bartender's signal and he nudged Vane's hand away from him. "None for me, I've still got some here," he said.

"What? You're turning down the man's whiskey?" said Vane as if shocked by his behavior. "If I was him I'd take offense." He looked at Clay and asked, "Did you hear that, blind man? He won't drink your whiskey!" He laughed and added, "But I will."

Curly Bryant looked back and forth with

a concerned expression, like a man feeling a trap close slowly around him.

"Can I kindly have my whiskey back, sir?" Clay said, humbly yet firmly. He reached out in the direction of Vane's voice for the bottle as he spoke.

But Vane swept his hand away. "Easy now, don't go forgetting your manners, blind man. If it was my bottle, I would share it with you. Wouldn't I, Roundhead?"

Roundhead didn't answer. Instead he said in a sobering voice, "Why don't you give him his bottle back? We've got to get out of here anyway. We've been here too long as it is."

"One more drink," said Vane. "I don't want to be unsociable to our blind friend here." He raised the bottle as if in a toast.

"Let me pour you one on the house," Bryant cut in. "Give Curtis his bottle so he can get on home."

As Vane looked at the bartender, Curtis' searching hand found the bottle and jerked it from Vane's hand, sloshing whiskey from the bottle. His free hand searched the bar top through spilled whiskey and found the cork. He quickly corked the bottle and put it in his pocket, this time keeping his hand over it. Vane cut the blind man an angry glance, but only for a second before being distracted by Bryant pouring a shot glass full to the brim in front of him. "There you are, Detective . . . drink up, on the house, like I said!" Bryant called out in a jovial tone. "Curtis, you go on now."

"Wait," Vane said to Clay as he raised the shot glass halfway to his lips. "What's a blind man doing carrying a big shiny gun like that?" He nodded at the Remington shoved down in Clay's waist. "You're not one of them *cold-blooded gunslingers* I keep hearing about, are you, blind man?"

"I'm faster than anybody at —"

"Curtis here has a trick he pulls on folks," Bryant cut in, trying to keep down any trouble.

"A blind Negro, fast with a gun?" Vane gave a look of disbelief.

"No, no," said Bryant before Clay could speak for himself. "Curtis is *fast* at assembling that Remington of his."

"I take on all comers," Curtis said, going into his pitch.

"Only, not tonight, right, Curtis?" Bryant stared hard at Clay as if the blind man could see him.

But Vane shrugged, showing no interest in who could assemble a gun the fastest. "How fast are you at drawing and shooting? is what I want to know."

"Faster than most, Clay said matter-of-factly.

"Come on, Curtis, stop joking," Bryant said, seeing trouble ahead. "He's *blind,* fellows!"

"Let's see what you've got, blind man," Vane said, straightening up from the bar. "Just for fun, let's see how fast you can skin that shooter and aim it at me."

"Mister, he's blind," a voice called out from down the bar. Vane responded with a silencing stare.

"I don't do nothing with my Remington for *fun,*" said Curtis. "You want to see who's best, I'll do it for a dollar."

"Stop it, Curtis, this is not what you do!" said Bryant. "You're not even wearing a holster!"

"But I *can* draw as good and aim as straight as the next man," Curtis said. He'd felt how much lighter the bottle had become after Vane had drunk from it, and he resented it.

"I don't care about drawing," said Vane. "Are you saying you'll bet a dollar that you'll point that Remington right at me . . . *straight* at me?" he queried. As he spoke he gave Roundhead a wink.

"Right at your belly, sir," Clay said confidently.

"Come on, Detective, let's roll double or nothing for some drinks," Bryant tried to cut in.

But Vane would have none of it. He laid a dollar on the bar. "You count to three for us, bartender," he said. Then he silently took two steps away from the bar and said nothing more, knowing the blind man could only aim by the sound of his voice.

"I don't like this," said Bryant. But seeing the look on the two detectives' faces, he said, "One!"

Clay poised his hand above the butt of his Remington. At his feet Little Dog stood up, walked a few inches away, and sat back down.

"Two!" said the bartender.

Vane grinned, his hand also poised near his gun butt.

But before the bartender could finish the count, Colonel Dan Elgin burst through the batwing doors and shouted, "Stand down, Detective Vane, or I'll have you horse-whipped in the public street!"

"Colonel Elgin!" Fear came into Vane's eyes. He sobered, his hands coming up chest high as if the colonel held a gun on him. "Sir, this is not what it looks like, I swear it's not!"

Behind the colonel the rest of the posse

crowded through the doors and spread out. Clay turned toward the rumble of boots as they came to a halt on the plank floor. Little Dog scooted closer to Clay's foot.

"Oh, it isn't?" the colonel said to Vane with sarcasm, looking at Clay's clouded eyes. "Let's see how well I can guess. Apparently I've walked in just in time to find one of my scouts, *drunk,* getting ready to shoot a blind man?" He asked the man standing nearest to him, "How accurately did I call that, Pale Lee?"

"You nailed it, Colonel," Pale Lee Hodges said with a grim expression. "A public horsewhipping sounds mild to me."

CHAPTER 11

Bobby Vane and Roundhead Mitchell sweated out most of their whiskey explaining to the colonel everything that had happened since their arrival in Little Aces. While they talked, nobody took notice of Clay when he'd followed Little Dog to a small table out of the glow of lantern light where he sat down and listened as he drank his whiskey. Little Dog sat at his feet.

"Colonel, that is the gospel truth," Vane said. "Frank was red-eyed crazy over finding his brother's horse but not finding his brother." He'd finishing his story about the ranger, the sheriff, and Frank Skimmer facing off in the street. "If we'd have thought it would help Frank, and our image as representatives of you and the posse, we would have gone at it tooth and nail. I just fig—"

"Shut up, Vane!" said the colonel, his face red, with a vein standing tight on his forehead. "You didn't do anything because you were both scared, that's the short and simple truth of it." He calmed himself and added as he looked all around the saloon, "I'm terribly disappointed in both of you."

Most of the regular drinking crowd had left as the posse men began filing along the bar, laying their rifles up alongside the bar top. "As it turns out, you two did the best thing," said Elgin. "We want to kill outlaws, not lawmen."

Pale Lee Hodges walked back in through the batwing doors, having left moments ago to go to the sheriff's office. "He's telling the truth, Colonel. Skimmer is in jail," he said, looking Vane up and down in disdain.

"Damn right I'm telling the truth," Vane growled, giving Hodges a threatening stare, but not taking things any further with the colonel standing there.

"The sheriff's not there, though," Hodges added, ignoring Vane's stare.

"Not there?" the colonel asked.

"No, he's not, Colonel, Skimmer is there all alone and madder than a kicked rattlesnake."

"What kind of tinhorn sheriff leaves a prisoner unattended?" the colonel asked toward the ceiling, gripping the edge of the bar in anger.

"We've got a good sheriff here in Little

Aces," Bland Woolard cut in from the far end of the bar where he'd been standing watching in silence.

The colonel wheeled around toward the sound of his voice. The posse men all turned and stared. "Who the devil are you, then?" Colonel Elgin demanded.

"I'm — I'm Town Councilman Bland Woolard," came Woolard's unsteady reply. "I'm sure if Sheriff Gale left a prisoner alone for a few minutes, he had good reason, sir."

"Councilman, eh?" Elgin said with contempt. "What else do you do around here?" He eyed Woolard closely as the councilman walked along the bar past the posse men, his hat in hand.

"I manage the Little Aces livery barn," said Woolard. He gestured a hand toward the bar. "I keep books for the Little Aces Saloon. I trade in horses —"

The colonel cut him off gruffly, saying, "Since you do so much for Little Aces anyway, you're just the man to help us find the *Little Aces sheriff*."

Woolard started to protest, but a shove from a posse man behind him sent him stumbling toward the door behind the colonel, who had already turned on his heel and left.

No sooner had the colonel, his posse, and Woolard gone out the batwing doors than Curly Bryant let out a sigh of relief and spoke to Clay, who sat quietly sipping from his bottle of whiskey. "I'm glad to see the last of those two," he said, referring to Roundhead and Vane. "You didn't realize what a tight spot you were in there for a minute."

"Oh, I realized it rightly enough," said Clay. "I'm blind, not simpleminded."

"If you realized what kind of men they were, why on earth did you agree to a drawing contest?" Bryant asked, a little irritated, considering the trouble it could have caused inside the saloon.

"For a dollar," Clay said with a shrug. "A man don't always get to choose who he does business with. He drank up some of my whiskey, I needed to get it back."

Bryant shook his head, glad it was over. "How is that whiskey tonight, Curtis?" he asked.

"It's good, same as always, Mr. Bryant." He held the bottle up in his hand toward the sound of Curly's voice. "You're welcome to drink."

"Obliged, Curtis, but no," Curly said with a smug half smile.

Curtis nodded, then lowered the bottle

and corked it. He knew that Curly Bryant poured leftovers from shot glasses into empty bottles and saved them to sell to him. But Clay never acted any the wiser, knowing this was the only whiskey he could afford. He was sure other people realized it too, since up until tonight he'd never had to share drinking it with anybody.

"Then I expect Little Dog better take me on home," Clay said to the bartender. As he stood up, and his walking stick felt around gently for Little Dog and found him standing in front of him, he asked, "What do you suppose happened to the detective's brother, Curly?"

"I couldn't guess," Curly replied. "These cowboys come and go, get drunk, knock their brains out on a low-hanging tree limb, who knows?"

"But his horse is still here," said Curtis.

"Yeah, that's right," said Curly, giving it only a second of consideration. "So maybe he's laid up with a woman. He could still come staggering in."

"Yeah, a woman," Clay mused, his expression and his cloudy eyes revealing nothing. "That's what I think too." He tapped the walking stick on the floor and said, "Come on, Little Dog, take us home."

■ ■ ■ ■

Outside on the dark street, the colonel and his men walked straight to the sheriff's office and shoved the door open. Inside the empty office, Colonel Elgin walked to the cell where Frank Skimmer stood with his hands wrapped around the bars. Skimmer looked down in shame under the colonel's gaze.

"I was relying on you to keep Mitchell and Vane in line. You disappointed me," Elgin said.

Skimmer looked up and said in his own defense, "I had things under control until that damned Ranger Burrack showed up with a scattergun."

"Burrack again," the colonel said, his fists clenching at his sides. "It appears our entire mission is going to be plagued by him, if we don't do something about it."

"Get me out of here, I'll do something about it, Colonel," said Skimmer. "You can count on that."

"Yes, and that's the same thing Strap and Bloody Vlak said," the colonel replied. "They're still trying to catch up to us after he took their horses out from under them and left them afoot."

"There's no cause to compare me to them two, Colonel," said Skimmer. "What happened to me could've happened to anybody. Besides, I was mindful of how it would look on our posse, me burning down a couple of lawmen right in the street." He gave the colonel a dark look. "If you don't think I could've handled them both, you had no business ever hiring me."

The colonel shook the barred door with both hands, then called out to the posse men milling about the sheriff's office, "Where is that blasted cell key, Woolard?"

"I don't know, Colonel, we're all looking," Woolard called back to him. His defense of the sheriff had changed now that he'd found himself surrounded by railroad detectives. "Gale is going to get a piece of my mind over this!"

Turning back to Skimmer, Elgin finally answered him, saying bluntly, "I hired you to get a job done. You won't get it done from inside a jail cell." He considered things, then said, "As for the ranger, I have yet to meet him face-to-face. Once I do, we might just find out that for a price he'll willingly shake the stone from my boot and get the hell out of our way."

"He ain't that kind of lawman, Colonel," Skimmer warned. "The only way he'll get out of our way is for us to kill him."

"We'll see." Elgin shook the cell door again in frustration. "Where's that key, blast it!" he bellowed out to the posse men as they continued ransacking the sheriff's office.

"We're looking for it, Colonel," Pale Lee shouted in reply.

Sheriff Gale stepped in through the open doorway, a cloth-covered basket in his hand. He looked all around at the posse men, then at Woolard, who had gotten down on his hands and knees to look up under the desktop. "I can save all of you some time," Gale said quietly, a shotgun hanging over the crook of his arm. "You won't find a key in here anywhere. I hid it." He stepped over and set the basket on the rummaged desktop.

"You hid it?" Woolard said in astonishment. "That's the craziest thing I ever heard of, hiding a cell key! Why on earth would you do something like that? This is Colonel Elgin and his posse."

Gale tipped his hat; then he took his time, looked all around again, and answered Woolard quietly. "I was concerned somebody might come in *looking* for it, maybe try to set the prisoner free while I was out." He stared pointedly at Woolard.

Woolard looked away, red-faced in embarrassment; but only for a moment. "There!" he said. "What were you doing leaving a prisoner alone anyway? Where's Lloyd the blacksmith?"

"I don't always send for Lloyd. I often leave a prisoner alone when I go to supper," Gale said. He nodded toward the basket on the desk. "I bring back supper for the prisoner, keeps anybody else from having to — sort of a two-birds-with-one-stone deal, Councilman."

Woolard looked defeated in his attempt to lay any blame on the sheriff. His attitude shifted again, back into the sheriff's defense. "There, Colonel, you see?" he said. "I told you the sheriff would have good reason if he left for a few minutes."

Looking suspicious, the colonel stepped over, stuck his hand down inside the basket, and felt the warmth of the food. Gale had hurried to Emma's and picked up the basket of food on his way back from dropping Omar's body off high up in the hills north of town. "Whatever," he grumbled under his breath. Looking at Gale, he said, "I'll pay my man's fine and get him out of here now."

"Not tonight, Colonel Elgin," said Gale. "Last I checked he was still killing mad at everybody. I won't turn him lose until morning."

"What? Do you realize who you are talking to, Sheriff?" Elgin said heatedly. "I said I want this man released, and I want him released tonight, right now! This instant!"

"And I said, *in the morning,* Colonel," Gale repeated firmly, "after the man has cooled down some. Not one minute before."

"Let me out of here and give me my gun! I'll show you *cooled down!*" Skimmer called out from his cell, not helping his case any.

"See what I mean, Colonel?" Gale said. "I can't turn that kind of attitude loose tonight."

The colonel gritted his teeth behind his handlebar mustache. He saw that the sheriff was stubborn enough to not reveal where the key was hidden, no matter what. "Blast it all!" he growled. He turned and stomped down the hallway to Skimmer's cell. "Frank, your temper has just cost you a night in jail! If you can keep from exploding again, we'll be back to get you in the morning."

Frank reached through the bars and grabbed the colonel by his shirt. "This sheriff knows something about my brother, Colonel! I can feel it down deep inside my bones!"

"Unhand me, Skimmer!" Elgin said in no

uncertain tone. "You forget yourself, sir!" He stood rigid, not about to jerk his shirt free of Skimmer's hand.

"I'm sorry, Colonel Elgin," Skimmer said, turning loose and smoothing the front of the colonel's shirt. "Please, forgive me. You're right, I'm in no condition to walk the streets tonight. I'd kill this sheriff or the ranger one, that's a plain fact." He searched the colonel's eyes. "You will be back for me come morning, won't you?"

"Of course I'll be back for you in the morning," said the colonel. He also smoothed his shirt. "Forget about this heated incident. You're still my top gun-man."

"I heard Pale Lee Hodges' voice out there, didn't I, Colonel?" Skimmer asked.

"Yes, Pale Lee and some others joined us along the trail. But that doesn't change anything." The colonel gave a smug grin. "We just have more guns to our advantage." He turned and walked away, saying over his shoulder, "Get yourself some supper and a good night's sleep, Frank. Tomorrow our hunt will continue on in earnest."

At the sheriff's desk, the colonel said, "I leave my man in your care, Sheriff. I trust nothing will happen to him."

"Not so long as he minds his manners,

like any other prisoner," Gale said.

When the last of the posse men had left, taking Woolard with them, Gale picked up the basket and walked to Skimmer's cell. He opened the cloth covering the food and handed Skimmer a plate of beans and pork through the food slot. Skimmer stepped over and laid the warm plate on his bunk, then came back and watched Gale closely as he handed him bread and an empty tin coffee cup.

"You know something about my brother, don't you, Sheriff?" Skimmer asked.

"I'll bring in the coffeepot and pour you some hot coffee," Gale said instead of answering him.

"Answer me, damn it!" Skimmer demanded.

Gale stopped and turned, facing him with a troubled expression on his face. "Nothing is going to make you turn loose of this, is it?"

"Hell no," said Skimmer. "Would you turn loose if it was your brother missing, his horse left standing at a hitch rail?"

Gale stepped back closer to the cell and said, "Just suppose I told you your brother was killed by a man whose horse he stole? Would you look for vengeance?"

Skimmer stared at him. "My brother is no

horse thief."

Gale nodded and went on. "Then, say he was killed by a woman while he was in the midst of forcing his way on her? Would that matter to you?"

"That would be a lie," Skimmer said flatly. "My brother never had to force his way on a woman. He had women falling down to give themselves to him." He paused, then asked, "Is that what you're saying happened to him? It is, isn't it?" He dropped the tin cup and bread and gripped the bars.

"I said *'Just suppose'* that was what happened," Gale said. "For all we know he could be wandering around drunk somewhere." He turned and walked out to the coffeepot atop the wood stove in the corner.

"You're lying, Sheriff, that is what happened!" Skimmer shouted from the hallway. "Who's the woman? Tell me! I'll kill her!"

Instead of picking up the coffeepot, Gale walked to his desk, rummaged through an assortment of small pistols in the bottom drawer, then walked down the hallway with one of them in his left hand, his Colt out of his holster and cocked, hanging down at his side.

Staring at him through the bars, Skimmer didn't back an inch as Gale raised the Colt and took aim. "Now you're going to shoot me, Sheriff? Make it look like somebody gave me a gun and I was trying to make a break?"

Gale braced himself, clenched his teeth, and tried to make himself pull the trigger. But he couldn't. Skimmer only stared. Finally, Gale let out a tight breath and lowered the Colt. "Damn you to hell, Skimmer," he said. "You're leaving here come morning. I want you out of my town. Don't you ever come back."

CHAPTER 12

In the middle of the night, Sheriff Gale eased quietly through the door of his office and walked to Emma's house, staying in the darkened shadows out of the moonlight. When he tapped softly on her back door, she answered it immediately.

"My goodness, what took you so long?" Emma whispered anxiously. She hurried him inside, then looked back and forth as if to make sure no one was watching. "I've been waiting, listening for a gunshot."

"I came back here as quick as I could, Emma," Gale said, slipping his arms around her, "and I have to get right back over there."

"Well? Did you get it done?" she asked, squeezing his arm in anticipation.

"No," said Gale, "I didn't kill him, I just couldn't do it."

"What?" She looked stunned. "You mean you haven't had a chance to set it up?"

Gale let out a breath. "I had the opportunity, Emma. But I'm a lawman, not an assassin. I tried as hard as I could to do it. But I can't kill a man in cold blood."

"Even a man like Frank Skimmer?" Emma said. "He's a hired gun and man killer, Vince! We both agreed this had to be done! I killed his brother. He'll kill me if he ever finds out."

"I know that," said Gale. "He as much as said so himself."

"He said *what?*" Again his words stunned her. "You two were talking about it?"

"No," said Gale. "But I asked him what if his brother had been killed by a woman in an act of —"

"Oh my God, you didn't?" Emma said.

Gale saw the terror in her eyes and held her firmly by her forearms. "Your name was never mentioned. I asked him about a couple of possibilities. That was just one of them. Besides, there's no way for him to know for sure that his brother is dead. Anyway, I wanted to see if he was a man who'd listen to reason, if his brother died committing a crime."

"And his answer was . . . ?" She left her question hanging.

Gale looked troubled. "He said if his brother is dead, he'll find whoever killed him and have his vengeance. He didn't seem to think it possible his brother would force a woman against her will." He searched her eyes, but only for a second. It really didn't matter now if she'd told him the truth or not. He'd gone this far, helping her cover up a crime.

"Oh, my God, you asked him that?" Emma gasped, her hand going to her mouth. "Why in the world did you tell him that?"

"I told you why," said Gale. "I wanted to see if he was a man who would listen —"

"Is Lloyd at the jail?" Emma asked with determination, cutting him off.

"No, he's not. I thought it best to not bring Lloyd into this," Gale replied. "The less people involved the better."

"Good. Give me your gun, Vince," Emma said in the same determined voice.

"Settle down, Emma," Gale insisted, still holding her arms, giving her a bit of a shake. "We're all right. I'm not going to let anything happen to you. Didn't I give you my word?"

"But you agreed you'd kill him," Emma returned. "He's the only thing left to take care of in this mess. If he's dead nobody will ever care what happened to Omar. He's got to die."

Gale looked into her eyes. "You're scared, and I don't blame you, Emma," he said. "But you've got to trust me. I'm a lawman. I can see us both through this. Stay calm and keep your wits about you. You've got the law taking care of you."

Keep your wits . . . ? Emma only stared at him. He had no idea who he was talking to, where she'd been, what she'd been through. But he was right, this was no time to do something rash. Keeping the sheriff on her side was important, for now anyway. She thought about Memphis Beck. Maybe she should have trusted him instead. She could have packed a bag and left, let the people of Little Aces decide for themselves what a dead man was doing lying backward in her kitchen chair. *All right, stay calm. . . .*

"You're right," she said with a submissive sigh. "What do we do now, Vince?"

"Colonel Elgin will want to get out of here come morning. Frank Skimmer is one of his top guns. I'll turn Skimmer loose only under the condition that he leaves Little Aces and never comes back."

"But will Skimmer agree to that?" Emma asked, playing naïve, realizing that it made no difference to Skimmer what he agreed to.

Gale smiled confidently. "He'll do what

the colonel tells him to do. If he does come back later on . . ." Gale shrugged. "Who knows, maybe you and I will be long gone by then."

There it is, Emma thought, feeling the world tightening around her. Gale would take her over. At the end of this, she would belong to him with no way out. "If you say so, I suppose that's the best way to look at it," she forced herself to reply.

"I *do* say so." Gale gave her a smile, tilting her face up to his. "In a few days this will all blow over. We'll have the rest of our lives to spend together."

Emma almost cringed at the thought. Avoiding his attempt to kiss her, she said, "You never told me what you did with Omar."

"That's something else you don't have to worry your pretty head over," Gale said. "I took him to the highest point in the hills and dropped him off of a trail down a steep ravine." His smile widened. "He could be still falling for all I know."

"A ravine?" she asked. "I thought you said you would bury him."

"I started to, but I needed to get back to town if I was to make it look like I was only gone for supper." He shrugged. "It makes no difference, though, he'll never be found."

"Are there any trails in and out of the ravine?" Emma asked.

"None," Gale said with firm conviction. "He's lying somewhere alongside a stream where every critter in the wilds goes for water of a night. Odds are, by morning he'll be nothing but rags and bones."

Odds are . . . ? This was her life they were talking about! Emma didn't like it. But she made herself remain silent on the matter.

Memphis Beck had traveled north up into the hill country most of the night. He hadn't pushed the red roan hard, but he'd kept a steady pace, riding one of the meandering trails that lay halfway up the steep hillsides. In the blue light of morning, he stepped down from the saddle and led the roan to a small waterfall that spilled from a rock cliff three feet above his head and splashed off over the side of the narrow trail.

Beck had stooped to fill a canteen when suddenly a sound above him caused him to instinctively snatch his Colt from its holster as he looked toward what he took to be the sound of someone running quickly downhill toward the edge of the cliff above him. Beside Beck the roan also heard the sound and shied sidelong, spooked, just as Beck saw a man spring from the edge of the cliff, arms spread wide, and descend upon him.

Beck's reflexes sent him falling away just in time. A streak of fire split the grainy morning light as his shot hit the man squarely in the chest. Beck came to his feet, his Colt cocked and ready to fire again, the half-filled canteen still in hand. But there was no need to fire again. The man lay facedown in the mud, the water from above splashing onto his lifeless back.

"Close call . . . ," Beck whispered, crouched, looking all around for any signs of other ambushers. They were everywhere, these detectives, he reminded himself. The roan had backed away with a loud whinny, and stood shaking itself off. Beck backed a few wary steps, gathered the frightened animal's reins, led it forward, and rolled the body over with the toe of his boot.

"What's this?" he asked, puzzled, staring down at the cut and battered corpse of Omar Wills. The corpse stared blankly up at him, Omar's mouth and eyes still wide open, a long twig of juniper jammed up his nose. Bits of small rock and splinters of downfall pine and juniper had embedded itself in the corpse's face, hands, and bare chest. The shirt and trousers lay in shreds. One boot had been washed away, Beck guessed.

"Man, oh man!" he said, letting the hammer down on his Colt. Seeing the black gaping bullet hole in the corpse's forehead, he knew that this man had been dead long before he came hurling out over the cliff above.

Looking up cautiously and taking a step back in case more dead came swooping down on him, Beck turned and tied the roan's reins to a pine sapling. "I won't be drinking this," he murmured, turning the canteen up and pouring the water from it.

Walking back to the corpse, he reached into the downpour of water and dragged it a few feet, onto drier ground. He propped the body onto his knee and searched through the pockets, both shirt and trousers. But he found nothing that revealed the man's identity. In the noise of the waterfall, Beck did not hear the two horses trotting at a brisk clip until the animals had rounded a turn in the trail and were almost upon him.

"It's Beck, kill him!" shouted Jack Strap. His horse reared; so did Vlaktor Blesko's beside him.

Dropping the corpse from his knee, Beck fired wildly as he ran to the roan, unhitched it, and jumped into the saddle. The two detectives also fired wildly, having come upon Beck so quickly. But as Beck batted his heels to the roan's sides and sent it racing away, he felt the sharp hot pain of a bullet slice deep into his side.

But the side wound didn't prevent him from turning half around in the saddle and firing back at the detectives, hard enough to cause them to pull back after only chasing him a few hundred feet along the treacherous winding trail. "Hold it, Vlak!" Strap shouted, reining his horse down and pressing a hand to a bullet graze along the side of his head.

"But I hit him!" Vlak shouted in reply. "He'll fall soon!"

"I'm not riding off this damned mountainside for nobody!" Strap said with finality. His head throbbed from the bullet grazing it. "How does this look?" He sidled his horse over to the Romanian and took his hand from his bloody head.

"Not so bad," Vlaktor said impatiently. "I hit him. Ve should stay on him, press him until he falls!"

"No, we're going to follow orders!" said Strap. "We were told to catch up to the posse as soon as we got to our horses. It's bad enough we made a wrong turn and spent the night lost! This will save face for us, if we play it just right."

"But if ve finished him off now and took

his body to the colonel —"

"Listen to me, Vlak," said Strap, cutting him off. "I wasn't looking forward to explaining how the blazes two *seasoned trail scouts* get themselves lost. That's what the colonel was going to want to know." He shook his head in self-disgust. "That would have looked bad on us, especially after having our horses taken from us by the ranger."

"But Beck is vounded; let's kill him!" Vlaktor insisted.

"I'm bleeding, in case you haven't noticed," said Strap. He took out a wadded handkerchief and pressed it to his head. "We're going on into Little Aces and tell the colonel what happened. We'll take credit for being the ones that killed Beck, don't worry about that. It makes no difference if we find his body, or if the whole posse finds it. We're still the ones who did the killing. Filo Heath will take our photograph . . . us standing with our rifles up, holding the body between us." He grinned thinking about it. "This is going to make up for a whole lot of things, Bloody Vlak. Oh yes, indeed. . . ."

A mile along the trail, Beck slowed the roan and looked back over his shoulder. The pain in his side throbbed mercilessly, so much so that upon seeing no one close behind him, he slumped in the saddle, pressed a hand to his wounded side, and let the horse walk along at its own pace. At a place where a narrow path led down along a steep ridge below, he reined the horse off the trail and let it pick its footing until he could look up and see nothing above him but towering rock.

Pointing the roan south, back in the direction of town, he murmured in pain, "Sorry, Emma . . . it looks like I'm bringing . . . my trouble to you."

CHAPTER 13

The ranger sat atop Black Pot in the morning sunlight, looking down at the wide dirt street of Nickels, New Mexico. At a hitch rail out in front of a ragged saloon tent stood the horses of the three men he'd spotted on the high ridges the day before. Two of the animals had saddlebags strapped down behind their saddles; one did not. Sam took note of it and understood right away.

Once he'd realized where the three were headed, he'd made a camp for himself on a hillside of towering pine and fallen asleep gazing at the starlit heavens. Now, with a good night's sleep behind him and a hot breakfast of jerked elk and coffee, he nudged the Appaloosa forward down the path, his rifle standing from his thigh.

Inside the ragged tent, Bennie Drew and Tom Cat Weaver stood at a makeshift bar still tossing back shot upon shot of whiskey.

A bottle of cloudy white mescal stood between them. Beside the mescal a rawhide bag lay open on its side, exposing a streak of fine brown powder that had spilled from inside it. Beside Bennie Drew, a young prostitute stood slumped against his side, her head hanging limply on his chest.

Tom Cat Weaver spooned up a mound of brown powder on the tip of his boot knife blade and snorted it up his nostril. "Whoa!" he said, his red-rimmed eyes snapping open even wider. Sniffing and plucking at his nose with his thumb and finger, he looked all around the tent, nudged Drew, and said between the two of them, "Look at this *loco* dandy. There is an unnatural sight if I ever saw one."

Bennie Drew looked around at Collin Hedgepeth, who sat at a table a few yards away, still drinking from the same bottle of rye he'd started out with the night before. At his feet sat his saddlebags. On the tabletop in front of him, a deck of cards lay spread out in a half-played game of solitaire.

"Damned shame, ain't it?" said Tom Cat.

"Watch this," Drew said. He called out to Hedgepeth, "Hey, English. You better get over here and stick your nose into some of this before it gets all worn out."

English Collin Hedgepeth turned a glance

toward the two men and saw them grinning at him like wild-eyed lunatics, brown residue smeared on their mustaches and cheeks. "I'll pass," Hedgepeth commented, uncertain if Bennie Drew was referring to the Mexican cocaine or the slumbering prostitute. He picked up a thin black cigar from an ash tin, puffed on it, and blew out a long stream of smoke.

"All I ever see you do is play that damned card game against yourself, English," said Tom Cat. "What I want to know is, do you ever *win?*"

"Yeah, and if you do win," said Bennie Drew, "how *much?*" The two drunken outlaws roared with laughter.

English Collin only gave them a curious look and said calmly, "One who challenges himself and never wins is a fool. One who challenges himself and never loses is a cheat." He gave them a brief trace of a smile and said almost under his breath, "As in any game, what one wins is a matter of what one wagers." He turned his attention back to the cards. "Thus far I have always managed to break even."

Drew and Tom Cat looked at one another blankly for a moment. "Did you understand any of that?" Bennie Drew asked.

"Not a word, *thus far,*" Tom Cat said

mockingly. "But I'll give it some more thought." He laughingly tossed back another shot of whiskey and took a long gurgling drink of mescal.

The two laughed and turned back to the bar. As they talked between themselves, neither saw the old white-haired Mexican *joyero* slip in through the rear fly of the tent and bend down to Hedgepeth's ear.

When the old Mexican finished whispering, Hedgepeth nodded and whispered, *"Gracias,"* in reply. Taking a gold coin from inside his dapper brocaded vest pocket, he handed it to the old man. "For your watchfulness," he said.

"Mí gracias a usted!" the old Mexican replied, examining the coin. "In my country I make rings and necklaces." He smiled and whispered, "But here I make money many ways." He closed his weathered hand over the gold coin and slipped away as quietly as a ghost.

At the bar, Drew shoved his little finger into the rawhide bag, brought out a mound of brown powder, and snorted it deeply. Wiping his nose back and forth on his shirtsleeve, he poured both his and Tom Cat's shot glasses full of whiskey and said, "Cat, the only game I like to play is the one where *I win*. Maybe that makes me a *cheat,*

I don't know. But it damn sure makes me a winner!" As he spoke he raised his glass as if making a toast.

"*Saludos, mí amigos!*" said Tom Cat. "And the only thing to win is *big money!*"

"Damned right!" Drew laughed with his glass still raised. "To *bank* money!"

"To *stagecoach* money!" Tom Cat Weaver shouted joyously.

"To *railroad* money!" came Drew's response. "Ain't that right, English?" he called out. But when the two of them turned and looked, Hedgepeth had left the tent. His thin cigar lay in the ash tin, smoke curling upward from it. In the center of the table lay the deck of cards, neatly stacked as if to say *game over.*

"Where the hell . . . ?" Drew looked back and forth. So did Tom Cat.

"He must've had to go something awful," said Tom Cat, lowering his upraised glass and putting it to his lips.

Drew only shrugged. He shoved his little finger back into the bag, brought it out, and held it over to the young sleeping prostitute. "Breakfast time, darling, wake up, wake up," he said playfully.

Out in back of the tent, Hedgepeth had not stopped for a second. Saddlebags over his shoulder, he'd walked quickly from the rear of the tent without looking back. The old jeweler stood at the open gate of a small corral, holding the reins to a rested, saddled, trail-ready silver-gray barb. He handed Hedgepeth the reins.

Hedgepeth swung his saddlebags to the old man, who in turn swung them up behind the ornate silver-trimmed Mexican saddle and tied them down. "You will like this horse, senor," the old Mexican jeweler said, turning, as Hedgepeth swung up into the saddle.

"Yes, I already do," Hedgepeth said, tightening his expensive derby hat down onto his forehead. "Good day to you, sir," he said, heeling the big horse away toward a thick stretch of woodlands lining the hillsides behind Nickels.

"Adios, mí amigo," said the old Mexican. He watched the barb horse jump up into a fast trot before he'd finished speaking.

Out in front of the tent, the ranger stepped down from his saddle and wrapped the Appaloosa's reins loosely around the empty hitch rail next to the rail where the three horses stood. With his rifle in hand, he stepped sidelong around the tent and quietly peeped in through a raised ventilation flap. Looking around, he saw no sign of the bartender, only the two outlaws and the woman.

Sam saw the bag of brown powder spilled out onto the bar and, knowing its powerful effect, realized the danger the woman could be in if he called the pair outside for a showdown. Taking a breath and letting it out slowly, he walked calmly to the open rear tent fly and stepped inside.

At the bar, the two stood with their heads bowed over the brown powder as if judging how much longer the supply should last. Neither of them noticed the ranger stepping silently toward them across the soft dirt floor, his rifle up, cocked and ready. He held the Winchester aimed at Bennie Drew.

When Tom Cat Weaver finally caught a glimpse of the ranger, it was too late and he knew it. "Damn it," he said, seeing the badge on Sam's chest. His reflex had been to reach for his Colt, but he caught himself, stopped, and raised his hands in submission.

Drew, with his arm draped loosely around the young woman's shoulders, tried to jerk her over in front of himself as a shield while he reached for his gun. But the young woman's limp figure seemed to melt to the ground as he tried to hold on to her, her falling causing him to fumble in his attempt to arm himself.

"Don't try it, Drew," the ranger warned, seeing the outlaw hang on to the woman by her limp flopping arm.

The outlaw cursed as the unconscious woman slipped the rest of the way out of his grip. "Hellfire! You got me, Ranger," he said regretfully.

"Lean back against the bar, raise your hands away from your guns," Sam ordered.

Both men obeyed. Looking all around the empty tent and at the thin cigar in the ash tin, Tom Cat said, "You've let the real outlaw get away, Ranger."

"Yeah, here we are just small-time thieves," said Drew, shaking his head at the injustice of it. "We go to jail. A big-time operator like English Collin gets off free as a bird."

"Ain't you going after him, Ranger?" Tom Cat asked drunkenly. "He's the one every lawman ought to be chasing down."

"You're the two I'm after," Sam said. He stepped forward and lifted each man's gun from its holster respectively. "Hold them out," he said. "You know how it works, behave yourselves I cuff your hands out front. Give me any trouble I cuff them behind you."

"You got us cold, Ranger," said Drew

drunkenly. "No need in us causing you any trouble."

"Yeah," said Tom Cat, equally drunk. "No use in us being poor sports, is there?"

"I'm glad you both look at it that way," said Sam. He knew it was the whiskey and cocaine that made them suddenly turn compliant. He also realized their mood could change at any second.

As he snapped a pair of handcuffs on each of their wrists, Drew said, "I expect you realize I'll be out inside of a year. So will Tom Cat. All we did was rob a mine payroll, a few other places." He shrugged, his eyes wide, red, and shiny from the cocaine.

"You're murderers," Sam said flatly. "Whatever you've got to say, you best save it for the judge. My job is just to bring you both in. He's the one who'll decide whether or not you'll hang."

"Oh yeah, murder," said Tom Cat in his whiskey and cocaine stupor. "I almost forgot."

Three miles out of Nickels, Collin Hedgepeth brought the big silver-gray to a halt and sat for a moment, looking back toward the small town and patting the horse on its withers. "The Mexican was right about you, fellow," he said aloud. Then he

207

turned the horse off the main trail at a walk and disappeared effortlessly into an endless rolling terrain of thick forest.

By late afternoon he could have emerged onto a stretch of grasslands and continued southerly, but he preferred the cover of the heavy woodlands. He made an early camp and grained and watered the barb. Then he lay down and slept until after dark. When he awakened he dined on hardtack, cold jerky, and tepid canteen water.

Near midnight he stood up, saddled the barb, and rode quietly all the way across the dark grasslands in the cover of night. He gave no thought to Bennie Drew and Thomas Weaver. They were never a part of his people, he told himself. They would have fallen soon enough with or without the ranger catching up to them. What little time he'd worked with them he'd found them to be crude, loud, and stupid — some of the worst possible traits for men in his profession.

Near morning, Hedgepeth stepped down from his saddle and led the barb the last few hundred yards through a valley flanked by upturned boulders and rough broken rock shelves until he spotted a dark outline of a cabin where smoke drifted lazily from a stone chimney. No sooner had he stopped and stood looking at the cabin than a voice spoke out quietly from among a spill of boulders to his left, "Keep your hands up where I can see them."

Hedgepeth did so in a relaxed manner. He waited until he heard the man step closer through loose gravel. "Top of the morning, to you, Cap."

The man, Earl Caplan, recognized Hedgepeth's voice and said with relief, "English, you don't know how glad I am it's you. We've had detectives breathing down our necks from every direction the past two weeks."

Now that he knew Caplan recognized him, Hedgepeth lowered his hands and faced him. "I've had the same problem. Drew and Weaver won't be with us, I'm afraid. A ranger rode into Nickels looking for them."

"Did he kill them?" Caplan asked.

"I don't know," Hedgepeth said, as if trying to recall. "I didn't hear any gunshots."

Caplan nodded. "It's just as well, as far as I'm concerned. They never struck me as much anyway."

"Nor I, Earl," said Hedgepeth, with a firm smile. He gestured a nod toward the cabin. "Now then, who have we here?"

"Just about everybody," said Caplan. "The

only ones we've been waiting on is you and Memphis. We're ready to ride."

"Memphis Beck isn't here yet?" Hedgepeth seemed surprised. "Strange, I thought he left for here before I did. I hope all is well with him."

"Aw, you know Memphis," said Caplan. "Nothing ever happens to him. He'll be showing up most any time, is my guess."

"Yes, you're absolutely right of course," said Hedgepeth. "Memphis will be here. It only concerned me for a moment because he is usually so prompt."

■ ■ ■ ■

PART 3

■ ■ ■ ■

CHAPTER 14

Frank Skimmer stared in silence as Sheriff Gale stuck the brass key inside the lock and twisted it. Looking up from the key and into Skimmer's eyes, he said to the colonel and Skimmer as well, "I hope this is not a mistake, letting you go."

Skimmer refused to say a word, but Gale realized what the angry gunman had running through his mind. Maybe Emma had been right; maybe he should have killed Skimmer last night while he had the opportunity. Knowing it was too late to second-guess himself now, he pulled the barred door open and stepped back, allowing the prisoner to walk out.

"I can assure you this is not a mistake, Sheriff," the colonel said. He led the way along the hall to the sheriff's desk, Skimmer right behind him, followed by the sheriff. On the desk lay a stack of dollar bills that the colonel had laid down for Skimmer's fine. "I would not be spending this kind of money on a man if I thought him untrustworthy." He looked Skimmer up and down as he spoke, making sure the angry gunman heard him.

Sheriff Gale watched Skimmer pick up his unloaded Colt from the desktop where the sheriff had laid it for him. Skimmer checked the gun over closely, still not saying a word. "Here's his ammunition, Colonel," Gale said, holding out his hand. "See to it he doesn't get these until he's out on the trail."

"Yes, I will do that," said the colonel, holding out his palm and receiving six rounds of .45-caliber bullets from the sheriff. "At any rate, we'll be leaving here in a few minutes. Unless circumstances demand differently, you won't be seeing us again."

"I hope that's true," Gale said to the colonel, but making it clear who he meant the words for as he returned Skimmer's cold stare.

Skimmer's expression didn't change, even as the colonel gave him a slight nudge toward the door.

Once the two were outside, Gale watched from the dusty front window as Colonel Elgin, Skimmer, and the rest of the colonel's men stood gathered at their horses, ready to mount and ride out of town.

"He knows all about my brother, Colonel," Skimmer said stiffly in a lowered tone just between the two of them.

Elgin's face reddened in anger. "You gave me your word, Frank."

"I know I did, Colonel, and I'm keeping it," Skimmer replied. "But he came within a hair of telling me that my brother, Omar, is dead." As he spoke he stepped over to his waiting horse that a gunman named Carlos Richards had brought over from the livery barn for him. "He even come close to telling me who killed him," Skimmer added. He threw open the flap on his saddlebags and took out a pouch of ammunition.

Seeing what he intended to do, the colonel said in a harsh tone, "Do not load that gun, Frank." He pointed a rigid finger. "You are testing me sorely."

Inside the sheriff's office, Gale saw Skimmer open the saddlebags. No sooner had he seen the colonel point at the gunman than he stepped away from the window and picked up a sawed-off shotgun from a gun rack, checked it, and made sure it was loaded. He closed it and cocked it on his way back to the window. Emma was right, it had been a mistake not killing this man, Gale thought. What it came down to was, which did he care more about, the woman or the badge?

He pushed the question from his mind. It didn't matter now. . . . He raised the shotgun and took aim through the dusty closed window. He'd gone as far as he could. Badge or no badge, woman or no woman, he wasn't going to take a bullet from Frank Skimmer.

At the hitch rail Pale Lee Hodges, who stood beside his horse, looked out along the street and saw the rising dust of two riders racing into town. Recognizing them, he said to the colonel and the others, "Here comes our two *lost forward scouts.* Reckon we ought to do them and ourselves a favor and kill them both before they get here?"

A ripple of dark laughter arose from the men. All eyes, including the colonel's and Skimmer's, turned to Jack Strap's and Vlaktor Blesko's galloping horses.

"Wait, what have we here?" the colonel asked. He craned his neck curiously, seeing the body lying across the rear of Strap's horse.

Upon seeing the body, Skimmer also stared closer as the two drew near. He stepped forward ahead of the colonel and the others as they brought their horses to halt. "Colonel, we shot Memphis Beck . . . caught him in the midst of robbing and killing this poor bastard!" Strap said quickly, not wanting to give anyone a chance to ask why it had taken them so long to get to Little Aces.

Bloody Vlak jumped down from his saddle, quickly untied the body, and pulled it until it flopped to the ground.

"Oh no, it's Omar!" said Skimmer, stepping forward. His brother's bloodless gray face stared blankly up at him.

"Who's Omar?" Jack Strap asked, looking back and forth in bewilderment.

"Frank's brother is missing," Colonel Elgin said, stepping forward beside Skimmer. "Are you sure that's him, Frank?" he asked, seeing the battered condition of the corpse.

"Yeah, that's him." Skimmer clenched his fist at the sight of the gaping black bullet hole in Omar's forehead. He stood trying to tie anything the sheriff had said last night to the body lying at his feet. "I don't understand it," he said under his breath, puzzled, shaking his head slowly.

Looking up at Strap, Colonel Elgin asked, "You say you two rode upon Warren Beck in the midst of this heinous crime?"

"That's the long and short of it, Colonel," Strap said, starting to wonder if this had been a good idea or not. "We heard the shot that killed this poor bas—" He caught himself, seeing the look on Skimmer's face. "This *poor man,* that is. When we rounded the turn, he still had his smoking gun out and was going through this poor man's pockets. It was a terrible thing to see, Colonel," he said in a mournful tone. "Made even more so now that I know he's kin to one of our own." Looking at Skimmer, he took off his hat in respect.

"Ve chasted Beck," Vlak cut in. "I shot him. He is dead by now."

"The fact is we were both blazing away at Beck," said Strap, "seeing what he'd done to this poor man. One of us shot him pretty bad. We'll find his body up there, if we all go searching for it."

"It vas I vat shoot him!" Vlak said, thumbing himself hard on the chest.

"All right, I'm not going to argue," Strap said gallantly. "Let's just say that we got our man, Colonel. That's the main thing, isn't it?" He looked all around at the watching eyes.

Skimmer looked up pointedly at Strap. "So, you didn't see Beck pull the trigger, you just rode up and saw —"

"What does he want from us?" Strap asked the colonel, put out with Skimmer's questioning him. "We heard the shot, we rode in, this man is dead, and Beck is robbing his body!"

Sheriff Gale walked into their midst, the shotgun uncocked now, but in his right hand, ready for use if need be. He looked down at the body, stunned, and stood in silence for a moment trying to piece together what had happened. "My goodness," he managed to say. He looked up at Skimmer, who stood staring coldly at him.

Seeing the looks on the two men's faces, Colonel Elgin said, "Well, fortunately we now have witnesses to Beck's criminal behavior, Sheriff. If he's alive I hope this means we can count on New Mexico Territory's support now in capturing this murderer."

"Beck is dead!" Strap interjected.

Ignoring Strap, Sheriff Gale said, "Yes, Colonel, this makes all the difference in the world." He stared back down at the corpse with mixed and baffled feelings.

Also staring at the body, the twigs and gravel rock stuck in its gray battered skin, Skimmer said, "It looks more like my poor brother has been thrown down a logging chute, or off a mountainside."

Out of patience, Strap said, "Damn it, we saw Beck kill your brother, Frank! We shot him in the act!" He spun toward the colonel.

"Are we going to go get Beck's body or not?"

"Yes, we are!" the colonel said aloud. Under his breath he said, "Beck, I've got you now, you son of a bitch." Having given the matter deep consideration, he realized that dead or alive, Beck being wanted for murder was a tremendous boost for him and his posse. "If he's dead, we'll bring him in and put his body on display and have Filo take some photographs, before going after the rest of the gang. If he's alive, we'll string his sorry hide up for robbery and murder!" He looked around and called out, "Filo! Do you have everything you need for photographs? Plenty of that *fer-ric, furric,* whatever you call it?"

"*Ferric salts,* Colonel!" Filo Heath, a short man wearing a black suit, shiny red vest, and battered derby hat, ran forward with bulky leather satchels of various sizes strapped over his shoulders. "Yes, I'm well supplied and ready when you are!" he said, out of breath.

"What's the stuff you ran out of a while back?" the colonel asked.

"Sodium thiosulfate," Filo said quickly.

"Yes, that stuff." The colonel grinned at Pale Lee Hodges. "I love hearing him say that." Then he turned back to the photographer and said solemnly, "I want some good likenesses this time, Filo, do you understand me?"

"Explicitly, Colonel," Heath responded to the colonel's intimidating tone of voice.

While the colonel spoke, Carlos Richards had stepped down from his saddle and walked over to where Frank Skimmer stood staring down at his brother's corpse.

"This ain't right, Carlos," Frank said, still shaking his head slowly. "I don't know what this all means, but it ain't right. I saw something in that sheriff's eyes. I can't let this go."

"Come on, Frank, I'll help you get your brother off the street," Carlos said quietly.

Memphis Beck knew he'd lost a lot of blood, but with the New Mexico hill country crawling with detectives he had no choice but to keep riding. Keeping to the shelter of woodlands, he made it to a high stand of brush across the alleyway from Emma's house without being seen. There, he slipped down from his blood-soaked saddle and rested against the trunk of a wild mountain ash. He knew he'd have to gather his strength before attempting to cross the alleyway and climb the picket fence. . . .

Inside Emma's kitchen door, Sheriff Gale

stood with a mystified yet relieved look on his face, his arms outspread. "Well, Emma, you can stop worrying about Frank Skimmer. It looks like we're going to get through this with no one the wiser!"

"Oh? What's happened to make you think that?" Emma asked. She looked at him, seeing the calm peaceful look on his face.

"Two of the colonel's men rode in a while ago carrying Omar's body, that's what." He gestured with his hands for her to come into his open arms. "They found him along the trail —"

"Oh my God!" Emma swooned and pressed the back of her hand to her forehead.

"No, wait," said the sheriff. "These two swear they saw Omar being murdered and robbed."

"They do?" Emma's hand came down from her forehead. The same look of bemused relief came to her face.

"Yes, they do," said Gale, his open arms drooping a bit since she had not come to him. "Now, here's the part that gets me." His mystified look deepened. "They say that Omar's murderer is none other than Warren Beck, alias, Memphis Beck!"

Emma felt as if the room had spun in a circle. She groped and stalled for something to say. Finally, all she could come up with was "Memphis Beck who rode into the town with the ranger the other day?" *It has to be a mistake,* she thought.

"Yes," said Gale, "it was that same scoundrel." He shook his head at the irony of it.

Emma's troubled look returned to her face. "Memphis Beck is wanted for murder?"

"Yep," said Gale, still dumbfounded by it. "The posse is gone to find his body right now."

Emma caught herself gasping. "His body?"

"The two detectives shot him," said Gale. "He was wounded bad, they say. Seems like all they need to do now is find where he holed up to die. If he's not dead it doesn't matter. They've said they would string him up. With witnesses, it would stand up in court."

Emma stood in silence, picturing Memphis Beck dying alone on some lonely hillside. Worse yet, she pictured him wounded and helpless, being pushed up into a saddle with a rope around his neck.

"I don't know how in the world this come about," said Gale. "But it sure gets us both off the hook, them thinking they saw Beck killed Omar. Skimmer didn't seem real happy with the idea. But I expect he'll come around after a while. He has to."

"You said you dropped Omar down a deep ravine," Emma said, confronting him. "How did he wind up along the trail?"

"I did drop him down a ravine," said Gale. "The only thing I can figure is he must've rolled down into the stream and it washed him downhill." He looked away reflectively. "What are the odds of him and Warren Beck ever ending up together?"

Emma lowered her head and closed her eyes for a moment. As strange as this was, it cleared up everything for her.

"So that's *that,* I reckon," said Gale. "Now I've got to go make some rounds. But I'll be back tonight. Maybe before this full moon ends, we can take a stroll in the moonlight. Wouldn't that be nice? Just the two of us out for the evening?"

"Yes, it would," Emma replied, deep in thought, hardly realizing she'd answered him.

"Well, all right, then, it's a date?" Gale asked, elated that she'd agreed to something so personal between the two of them.

"Yes," Emma answered absently, so absorbed in thought she barely heard him close the kitchen door behind himself and walk across the back porch and around the side of the house.

Even in her grief for Memphis Beck, she realized that this bizarre turn of events ended any hold the sheriff might have had on her. There were credible witnesses saying they saw Omar Wills Skimmer murdered out along the trail. That separated her from ever having had anything to do with the man.

"Good-bye, Sheriff," she murmured to herself.

Taking off her apron, she tossed it aside and walked to her bedroom. She flipped back a corner of a rug, kneeled down to a small square panel in the wood floor, and lifted it open.

CHAPTER 15

Curtis Clay smelled blood in the air. He'd first caught a scent of it when he stepped out a half hour earlier and followed Little Dog to the barn to check on the dun's stone bruise. It came to him again on a calm drift of air through the open window of his shack when he'd returned from the barn. This time it came stronger; it was a scent of human blood, he determined, his nostrils flaring a bit in recognition.

He walked over and closed the window, Little Dog right in front of him. Then he stopped for a moment and reopened the window. "Not smelling it don't mean it's not there, Little Dog," he said toward the dog at his feet, as if closing the window had been Little Dog's idea. "No, sir," he affirmed to himself on his way back to his chair.

There were times he wondered if his blindness had heightened his sense of smell, or if this was indeed his having the *gift,* that elusive supernatural insight he'd heard people talk about when he was a child growing up on the harsh Kansas plains. *Curtis' gift,* his mother and grandmother would say. *God felt so bad 'bout what he done to Curtis that he gave him the "gift."*

His *gift . . . ?* He didn't know about that. He had lived too long with whatever fueled and informed him to see it as a gift. He had never considered his blindness a curse, but he would never think of it as a gift. Whatever voids his blindness had left in him, his remaining senses had rallied together and filled from within their own resource. *Gift? Curse?* He didn't know. But there was blood on the still air today. He knew it. Yet he tilted back his head, noting some other, more pleasant scent coming to him.

Was it her? *The widow woman?* Yes, it most certainly was. There was no mistaking it.

At his feet he felt Little Dog stand up toward the door with a quiet whimper. Arising from his wooden chair, Curtis hurried to the door, arriving almost tripping over the dog who had to race to stay in front of him.

Man and dog arrived just as Curtis Clay heard the quiet knock of Emma's hand. "Mr. Clay? Hello, Mr. Clay. Are you in there?" she asked through the door.

Clay smiled to himself and clumsily ran his hands over his tangled hair. "Yes, ma'am, I'm here," he said, opening the door, feeling Little Dog crowd forward against his ankle.

"Oh, thank goodness," said Emma. "I went to the barn and didn't find Mr. Woolard there. I — I hope you can help me."

"Yes, ma'am, any way I can," Clay offered. Even as he spoke he caught the scent of blood again. But he ignored it, knowing that the woman did not smell it, and knowing that mentioning such things to people with sight served no purpose.

"I need to hire a buggy, Mr. Clay," she said, sounding harried. "I need it right away. Can you help me?"

"Yes, ma'am. I can fix you up with a rig, sure enough," said Clay. He felt his hand beside the door and picked up his walking stick. He stepped out of his shack, feeling Little Dog move away from his ankle and out in front of him.

In the barn, Emma felt a stab of sorrow when she saw Beck's big dun standing in its stall. But she looked away and tried to put Memphis Beck and his horse out of her mind. One thing she'd learned riding with Beck and the Hole-in-the-wall Gang, it was that no matter what happened, you kept on going.

Go until it all stops around you, she recalled Beck himself telling her a long time ago.

That was what he'd tell her today too, if he could; and that was exactly what she intended to do. *Go until you drop,* she told herself, following Clay out back and watching him walk into the corral and tap his way forward, following the elderly stiff-walking canine.

When Clay finished preparing the horse and buggy right in the open front doors of the livery barn, Emma took money from her dress pocket and paid him. "I'll have the buggy for the next two days," she said, knowing full well that once out of Little Aces she was never coming back.

The tone of her voice told Clay that she didn't mean what she'd said. But he only nodded and held out his hand to assist her up onto the buggy step. "Yes, ma'am, you keep it as long as you need it."

Clay felt an unsteadiness in her hand as she took his and climbed up into the buggy seat. In spite of her calm voice and determined bearing, she was afraid of something, he thought. What he felt coming from her was what he would expect to feel from someone racing to keep from being caught.

A fox ahead of the hounds, he thought; only this fox still needed to widen the distance.

"Is everything all right, Mrs. Vertrees?" Clay ventured, knowing it was not an appropriate thing for him to ask.

"What? Oh yes, Mr. Clay," Emma said, a bit taken aback, not so much by the inappropriateness of his question, but rather by the fact that he had noticed her state of mind. She took a deep breath, calmed herself, and kept careful control of her voice. "I just have so many things I need to do today. Thank you so much for your help."

"You're welcome, ma'am, and good day to you," Clay said. Everything was *not all right.* But how could he tell her he knew that? And if he could tell her he knew it, what then? He stepped back in silence, Little Dog right beside him, and gestured her forward. "If I can ever do anything for you . . ." He let his words trail.

"You are too kind, Mr. Clay," Emma said, "and good day to you too."

There, she thought, chucking the buggy reins and sending the horse forward. Had she played it calmly enough? Had she sounded like a woman with nothing more on her mind than her usual household chores or the cost of a bolt of gingham? She drove the buggy the short distance to the picket fence behind her yard, stepped down, and walked through the gate.

At the porch step she noted a half of a boot print streaked with dark blood, but her first thought was that she or the sheriff had failed to clean it up earlier. It was only when she stepped inside the kitchen and saw another identical boot print that she realized this was not Omar's blood.

Instinctively she turned back toward the door, ready to bolt through it. But she stopped when she heard Memphis Beck step into the hallway behind her and say in a weak voice, "Emma, please, help me . . . I'm shot."

She turned in time to see Beck stagger and catch himself against the wall. "Oh, Memphis!" she said, hurrying to him, steadying him. "I heard you were shot! Two of the railroad detectives said they shot you. They said you were dead!"

"I might well be . . . if we don't get this bleeding to stop," Beck said with much effort.

She helped him into her bedroom and seated him on the side of her bed. While he sat there unsteadily, she hurried to a drawer and took out her deceased husband's yellow riding duster and laid it on the mattress without unfolding it. She gave Beck a nudge and guided him backward onto the bed, keeping his bloody wound from lying on the clean white bedsheet.

"Lie still here," she said, hurriedly taking off his boots and dropping them to the floor. "I'll get a pan of water and some strips of cloth for bandages."

"I didn't know . . . where else to go," Beck said apologetically. "I know how you always hated . . . dressing gunshot wounds."

"Nonsense," Emma said wryly, "I always preferred it over dancing." Suddenly she felt like her old self again, ignoring the blood, for the moment ignoring the danger of having a wanted man lying wounded in her bed. "Did the bullet go all the way through?" she asked. As she spoke she unbuttoned his shirt for a closer look.

"Yes . . . it did," Beck said, groggy from the loss of blood.

"Thank God for that," she said, letting out a sigh of relief. "It's cutting a bullet out that I always dreaded doing."

Beck managed a weak smile. "I'm sorry, Emma."

"It's all right." She patted his forearm and said, "I'll be right back." She turned and left the room, going about her task swiftly, calmly, holding her bloody hands out in front of her.

"I'm glad . . . I made it . . . back here," Beck said, his voice failing him as he drifted into unconsciousness.

After a full day of searching all over the hillsides in vain for Memphis Beck's body, Jack Strap and Vlak Blesko stepped down from their saddles and looked back toward the rest of the posse riding a hundred yards behind them. "We better find him soon, Vlak," Strap said, "before the colonel starts getting testy with us."

Leaving their horses standing a few feet back from the edge of a cliff, the pair eased over for a look down onto the winding trail below. As soon as Strap spotted three horsemen, he jerked back quickly and gave the Romanian an excited look. "Stay back out of sight, Vlak!"

"Is it him?" The Romanian started to ease forward for a peep of his own, but Strap pulled him back.

"No," Strap whispered, "it's the ranger and two prisoners." He took out a field lens and opened it. "You stay back. I want to get a good look at them. This might be our chance to put a bullet in Sam Burrack for what he did to us."

The Romanian stood back and watched Strap stoop down and move forward in a crouch. "Who are de prisoners?"

"As soon as I find out, Vlak, I will be sure to let you know," Strap said in an irritated tone. He held the field lens to his right eye and focused on the prisoners riding in front of the ranger. As if on cue, Tom Cat Weaver took off his hat with his cuffed hands and ran a bandanna across his forehead. *"Whoa!"* Strap said over his shoulder. "One of them is Thomas Weaver."

"Tom Cat Weaver," Vlak said with a tight smile. He turned to his horse and yanked his rifle from its saddle boot.

Hearing the Romanian lever a round into the rifle chamber, Strap said, "That's right, if we can't give the colonel Beck, we'll hand him Tom Cat Weaver." He looked back to the riders as he said, "Bring my rifle too."

With both rifles in hand, the Romanian crept forward in a crouch and laid Strap's Winchester down on the ground beside him. "Who is de other prisoner?" he asked.

"I can't see his face from this angle," said Strap, "but if he's riding with Tom Cat, you can bet he's Hole-in-the-wall too."

"Ve are going to shoot them both, vithout telling the colonel first?" Blesko asked.

"Oh no, Vlak, we're not going to shoot the ranger's prisoners. We'll feed them to the colonel's rope," Strap said with a slight chuckle, reaching around and picking up his rifle. "I'm going to shoot the ranger, right now, while I've got him in my sights."

"Vithout asking the colonel?" Blesko said.

"If I ask him, he might say no," Strap said with a sly grin.

"I don't like doing this," Blesko said.

"All right, don't do it," said Strap. He levered a round into his rifle chamber and checked the sights. "In fact, why don't you ride back there and tell the colonel to get his men down onto the trail? Don't mention the ranger, just tell him that I'm about to drop two of the Hole-in-the-wall Gang right into his lap." He turned back to the trail below, this time looking at the ranger down the barrel of his Winchester instead of through a field lens.

Shaking his head in doubt, the Romanian turned to his horse, climbed into the saddle, and batted his heels to the horse's side. . . .

On the trail below, the ranger rode along behind the prisoners at a walk, watching them, yet having seen nothing in their behavior so far that made him think they might attempt an escape. In the dimming afternoon sunlight, he had just pushed his sombrero brim up, when suddenly he caught a flash of sunlight on the cliff ledge ahead of them, over a hundred feet up the hillside.

"Ambush!" he shouted in reflex. On instinct he jerked Black Pot sharply to the side to disrupt any aim that might already have been taken on him. Then before the stallion had settled, Sam swung down from his saddle and yanked his rifle from its boot on his way.

From the cliff edge, Jack Strap triggered his shot as the ranger raised his rife toward the flash of sunlight he'd seen only a second earlier. No sooner had Strap's shot hit the ground near the ranger's feet than the ranger's return shot whistled past Strap's head.

"Damn you, Ranger!" said Strap. Levering another round, he fired just as the ranger slipped over the edge of the trail and out of sight.

Hearing Sam's warning, followed by the first rifle shot from above them, Drew and Weaver had batted their horses forward along the winding trail. As the ranger's stallion raced past them, Bennie Drew even with his hands cuffed, managed to sidle close enough to the big Appaloosa to grab it by its loose reins and keep it running alongside him.

Off the edge of the trail, Sam rolled onto

his back and levered another round into his rifle chamber. Crawling back up to the edge, he lay quietly for the next few minutes, searching back and forth along the ridgeline for any sign of the rifleman. When he did venture up onto the trail, he picked up his sombrero from the dirt and slapped it against his thigh.

He looked out along the trail for the stallion as he stepped off the trail, down far enough to not make himself an easy target from the cliff line, and started walking. This late in the afternoon, on foot, he'd be lucky to make it to Little Aces before morning.

But Sam wasn't going to stay afoot for long. Two hours later, when the sunlight had gone below the crest of the hill line, he heard a horse walking toward him around a turn in the trail. Crouching, his rifle up and ready, Sam kept out of sight until he saw his big stallion walk into sight. "Black Pot . . ." he said with relief, stepping up onto the trail.

He looked the big stallion over good before stepping into the saddle. Once under way, keeping the stallion checked down to a brisk walk on the shadowy darkening trail, he found Bennie Drew's horse walking along with its reins hanging to the ground. *A bad sign . . .*

Looking the horse over curiously, he picked up the dangling reins and led the animal alongside him. Twenty yards ahead Sam spotted Tom Cat's horse standing off the edge of the trail nibbling on a clump of wild grass. *An even worse sign,* he told himself, nudging Black Pot forward until he reached the horse and picked up its dangling reins.

Leading the two horses, he looked as deep into the woods along the trail as the waning evening sunlight would allow. He'd had a hunch that whoever had shot at him was not one of the Hole-in-the-wall Gang. His hunch had grown stronger as he'd gathered the horses and ridden on. But the matter wasn't cinched for him until he saw the two outlaws' bodies drift slowly back and forth in the dim light.

Nudging his stallion off the trail and over to where the two men hung from ropes thrown over the limb of a mountain ash, Sam took out his knife from his boot well and rode in close enough to cut their bodies loose. "I expect hanging came as no big surprise to either one of you," he said, looking at the swollen faces.

He stepped down from his saddle long enough to pull the bodies up onto their horses' backs. He sniffed the air, noting the lingering smell of flash powder where photographs had been taken of the executed men. He shook his head at the thought of men posing beside corpses as if they were trophies of a hunt. Then he stepped back up into his saddle and rode on toward Little Aces, the dead lying close behind him.

CHAPTER 16

Sheriff Gale decided he'd never met a woman who could change her mind as suddenly as Emma Vertrees. Earlier she had said yes when he'd invited her for a stroll in the moonlight. Now, upon his return, clean shirt, string tie, and all, she acted as if the two of them had never even discussed it. "I'm too tired tonight, Sheriff," she'd said coldly, at the back door, acting as if she didn't want him inside her house.

Now it's "Sheriff," Gale noted to himself, dumbstruck by this manner of treatment. Yet, in spite of his disappointment, Gale took a patient breath and said, "I understand, Emma. We'll just have to make it some other time, when the moon is full again." He paused there on her back porch, his freshly brushed Stetson clenched in his hands. "Are you all right?" he queried. "I mean, it's not something I did or said, is it?"

"No, Sheriff," Emma said, giving him a tolerant smile. She reached out through the barely opened door and cupped his cheek. "Thank you for being such a patient gentleman. These past few days have been a whirlwind for me. So much has happened . . . and so fast. I just need some time to collect myself and do some thinking."

Gale cupped his strong hand over hers on his cheek and said, "Some thinking about us, I hope?"

"Yes, about us," Emma said, sounding sincere, "and about the future we both want." She pulled her hand gently away from his.

"If I can say anything to persuade you, just let me know." Gale grinned.

"I'm certain I won't need any persuasion," Emma said softly. "Good night, Sheriff." She kept her eyes on his, warm and suggestive, as she eased the door closed in his face.

For a moment Gale stood facing the door. Inside, Emma stepped over and peeped guardedly out the window at him. Seeing him from the side, standing there blankly in the dark, she shook her head. He seemed to have no idea she had just skillfully brushed him off. Well, she'd had to get rid of him, and she didn't want him suspecting that she had another man in her house. She breathed in relief when he finally turned and walked down off the porch and around the house toward the street.

Walking into the bedroom, she looked at Memphis Beck, who had only just awakened and propped himself up on a pillow when they'd heard the knock on her kitchen door. "He's gone," she said, closing the bedroom door behind herself.

"Good." Beck nodded. He took his Colt from under the blanket and slipped it behind the pillow. "I don't want to put you on a spot with your beau, Emma. Soon as I get some strength up, I'll cut out of here." He looked at the half-packed carpetbag sitting on the floor beside the dresser. But he wasn't going to ask her where she was going. When he'd been awake earlier, she'd told him she had to go move a rental buggy. If she wanted him to know, she'd tell him, he thought.

"There are some important things I need to tell you, Memphis," Emma said, reaching into the pocket of his coat hanging from a chair back and taking out a bag of tobacco and rolling papers. "Sheriff Gale is not my beau. The fact is he never really was." She sat down in the chair with a sigh.

"Oh?" Memphis watched her pause as if in reflection, the rolling paper in her fingertips formed into a trough. At length she shook a line of chopped tobacco into the trough and continued, saying, "I suppose he should have been my most natural choice after Dillard." Whatever she'd been thinking she let go of with a shrug. "Anyway, Gale wanted to be a suitor." She rolled a smoke and struck a match to it.

"But you weren't interested?" he asked.

Emma stood up, carried the cigarette to him, and placed it in his lips. "No," she said quietly, sitting down on the side of the bed.

"Then what was he doing —"

"Please listen, there's a lot to this," she said, bowing her forehead in her hand. "The day before you arrived in Little Aces, I had spent the night with a young cowboy named Omar Wills. . . ."

Beck smoked the cigarette and listened intently as she told him everything. When she'd finished, he blew a stream of smoke toward the ceiling and said, "So I'm wanted for murder now, for killing the man *you* killed and the sheriff helped you get rid of?"

"Yes, as it turns out." Emma studied his face, but saw no anger or even harsh judgment. "Doesn't that upset you, Memphis?"

"What? Being wanted for murder?" He took another draw on the cigarette. "Yes, a little, I suppose." Now it was his turn to

243

shrug. "But you didn't do it to me, at least not on purpose, right?"

"No, of course not on purpose," Emma replied. She took his hand, raised the cigarette to her lips, and took a draw for herself.

"Then I have no cause to complain," Beck said. "It's not like you and the sheriff jack-potted me. It's just that neither of you told anybody any different when those two detectives blamed me."

"For all I knew you were dead," Emma replied. "Besides, I don't think it would have mattered what either the sheriff or I said. According to him, the colonel was pleased to have a charge against you with living witnesses to make it stick."

Beck offered a weak smile, still needing time for his blood to replenish itself. "I spoiled everything for everybody, not dying out there when I should have."

"Don't talk like that," Emma said. "Besides, had I known things were going to turn out this way, I would have left with you. We would have put this place behind us and never looked back." She leaned down beside him, careful of his wounded side.

"Just like the old days, eh?" Beck whispered. He wrapped his arm around her shoulders. "The two of us, sleeping under the stars, hand to mouth, taking whatever we want, to hell with the rest of the world? We can still do that, you know."

"I know we can," Emma said, "and that's what I want. I wanted it the minute I saw you ride into Little Aces. Now that there's nothing stopping us, I want to go with you, Memphis Beck. Wherever it takes us, I'm ready for it." She took the cigarette from his fingers, took a long draw for herself, then turned and snubbed it out in an ash tin on the nightstand.

"Then let's do it," said Beck. "I have a big job set up with the rest of the gang. They're waiting for me right now. My cut will be enough to take us anywhere we want to go from now on."

"That's perfect." As she spoke she rested her face on his bare chest. "Because I wouldn't want to go back to living hand to mouth, saying to hell with the rest of the world," she whispered. "But the rest sure sounds good." She closed her eyes dreamily.

"Yes, it does sound good, my *outlaw's lady*," Beck whispered. He reached down and brushed a loose strand of hair from across her forehead and studied her face in the soft circling glow of an oil lamp. "Better than anything I've known for a long, long time."

■ ■ ■ ■

Instead of riding into Little Aces in the middle of the night, Sam had made a camp and spent the night five miles from town. Before turning, he'd eaten some jerked elk and drunk some hot coffee while he cleaned and inspected his Colt, his repeating rifle, and the sawed-off shotgun he carried beneath his sleeping roll.

In the light of morning, he rode into Little Aces leading the two horses with the bodies of Tom Cat Weaver and Bennie Drew lying across the saddles. From the front porch of the Little Aces Hotel, Pale Lee Hodges took the cigar from his mouth and said to the colonel, who sat in a large rocking chair beside him, "Speak of the devil. . . ."

Colonel Elgin turned from having the hotel clerk refill his coffee mug and looked toward the ranger. With a thin smile of satisfaction, the colonel watched the early street traffic spread apart and give plenty of room for the ranger and his grizzly procession. "Tell me, Pale Lee," he asked curiously, "did you have the telegraph wires cut and taken care of, like I ordered?"

"I did," Pale Lee answered, sipping from his coffee cup and leaning his straight-backed chair against the clapboard hotel front.

After a moment of muse, the colonel asked, "Do you suppose a ranger like Burrack ever gets tired of the dead always following him around, the flies, the smell?" He made a sour face.

Pale Lee deftly adjusted the butt of his revolver that stood in the long holster tied to his thigh. "I like our new way better, take their photo and leave the rest to the buzzards," he chuckled.

"Speaking of buzzards and photographs, where's Filo this morning?" the colonel asked, watching the ranger intently as he stopped out in front of the telegraph office, stepped down, and walked inside.

"He's at the livery barn, doing whatever he does in the dark to make sure the photos come out clear," said Pale Lee.

The colonel nodded and said to Jack Strap, who sat leaned back on the other side of him, "I hope this was the right thing, just firing a couple of shots to scare the ranger away, yesterday. He looks as if he awakened with his bark on this morning."

Pale Lee stifled a sarcastic laugh. "It takes more than a couple of shots to scare a ranger off the job. Strap, I think you meant to shoot him dry-gulch style, but missed."

He looked across the colonel at Strap, who sat glaring at him. "What say you to that?"

"If I meant to kill him, he'd be dead," Strap said flatly. "As dry-gulch style goes, I say the element of surprise is the only advantage a man gets out here when it comes to who lives and who dies."

"Ordinarily, I would agree," Pale Lee said, giving a sly grin and pointing his finger at Strap and clicking his thumb as if it were a pistol. "But as we see, even dry-gulch style, Burrack is still alive."

Responding in the same pistollike gesture, Strap said stiffly, "Only because I knew the colonel didn't want me to kill him. I knew the colonel would want those two Hole-in-the-wallers, which Vlak and I handed to him on a platter." He let his thumb drop with finality.

"But we still don't have Memphis Warren Beck, now, do we?" said Pale Lee, his thumb falling too, both men shooting it out finger to finger, the colonel in the middle.

"Stop it, both of you," said Colonel Elgin. As he spoke the ranger walked out of the telegraph office. He watched Burrack step into his saddle and lead the bodies toward the hotel. The colonel did not like the dark look on the ranger's face as he watched him draw nearer. "Where is Frank Skimmer?"

Elgin asked. "Has anyone seen him?"

"I saw him at breakfast," said Pale Lee, smoothing down his shirtfront with his hand, and flicking a bit of cigar ash from it. "He's still smarting over his brother's death."

"One of you go find him, bring him here right now," the colonel said, sounding urgent, as the ranger veered toward the hitch rail in front of them. But as Jack Strap started to stand up, Elgin said, "No, wait. I may need you right here beside me. Get the rest of the men out of the lobby. Quickly now."

The ranger saw the detectives step out onto the front porch as he slowed to a halt out in front of the hotel. He pushed up the brim of his pearl gray sombrero and stared at Colonel Elgin knowingly for what the colonel considered an uncomfortably long time. Not wanting to squirm and look worried in front of the ranger, Elgin broke the awkward silence and called out, "Top of the morning, Ranger Burrack." He gestured at the two bodies. "It appears you've had a productive trip since last we met."

Sam only stared, knowing how much it troubled a man, especially one who knew why he was being stared at so intently.

Unable to simply sit still and stare back in

silence, the colonel called out, "Will you step down and take breakfast at the hotel this morning? I — that is, *we,* all of us here, will vouch for its fine quality." He spread a hand toward the rest of the posse, to make sure Sam saw how many guns were facing him, the ranger figured.

"I'm particular about who I eat with," Sam said flatly with no attempt at courtesy. "I cut these bodies down from a tree last night. I've never believed in a lynching. I always call it the work of cowards."

"Who the hell are you to call —" Pale Lee started to say before he caught himself. On the colonel's left and right, both Lee and Strap leaned the chairs forward off the front of the hotel and rose halfway before Elgin's arms spread in each direction, stopping them.

"Easy, gentlemen," said the colonel. "He wasn't calling us cowards, since none of us had anything to do with ambushing him or hanging these men."

"Who mentioned an ambush?" Sam asked, his cold stare fixed like spearheads on the colonel. He swung down from the saddle and stepped sidelong from in front of his stallion, letting the reins of the other two horses fall from his hand. Without making any fast move, he lifted the Colt matter-of-factly from his holster, cocked it, and tilted the barrel up until it pointed at the colonel.

Elgin's face reddened. "I must have assumed there had been some sort of —"

"Save your breath, Colonel," said Sam, cutting him off. "You're a liar, and you and your men are craven cowards." He looked back and forth along the men facing him, seeing that they wanted to spread out, but had been caught so quickly by surprise that they didn't know quite how to go about it now.

"Easy, Detectives," Elgin said, his arms still spread as he stood up from the big rocking chair. "The ranger here is only goading us. He obviously has a mad-on over someone hanging his prisoners. We happen to be the closest targets." He gave a smug grin. "Sorry, Ranger, we're not going to fall for your crude invitation to a gunfight."

As the colonel stood talking, Filo Heath came hurrying along the street from the livery barn, sheets of heavy photograph paper in his hand. "Colonel, I have them, they're stunning!" he said.

"Not now, Filo," Elgin said, his breath turning tight in his chest.

The photographer slowed to a halt, seeing the look on everybody's faces. But where he stopped was close enough to the ranger that all Sam had to do was take a step sideways and grab the stiff photos from his hand. Without lowering the barrel of his Colt, Sam looked at the top photo, seeing Tom Cat Weaver and Bennie hanging dead from the tree limb.

"All right, Ranger," said Elgin. "Yes, we did hang those felons! But we were within our rights to do so. But we had nothing to do with ambushing you. If you feel we did, prove it. Otherwise, that's all I'll say on the matter. We work for the railroads, we don't answer to you or anybody else!"

"I just came from the telegraph office," said the ranger. "You don't even answer to the railroads if you can keep from it."

"Are you implying we cut the lines, Ranger?" Elgin asked indignantly.

"I'm not implying, I'm accusing," Sam said bluntly. He held the photographs out and let them fall from his hand into the dirt. "I intend to let the railroads know what you've done up here." He rubbed his hand up and down his shirt as if to clean it. "Even the rail barons went beneath themselves, hiring a bunch of gutless thugs like you," he said brazenly, looking back and forth along the porch. Finally he centered his stare on Pale Lee Hodges, the one who had taken the greatest offense. "We all know who I'm talking to when I say *craven cowards.*"

The colonel held his men in check with a raised hand as the ranger walked away.

Beside the colonel Pale Lee said, "He's not interested in telegraphing the railroads. He just knows that saying so will make us have to kill him."

"Then he's about to get what he's pushing for," the colonel growled.

CHAPTER 17

Inside the sheriff's office, the ranger stood at the window and looked out toward the hotel porch a block away across the street. Colonel Elgin and his detectives were all on their feet now, crowded onto the hotel's porch, looking toward the sheriff's office. Sam watched them huddle together in conversation.

"My goodness, Ranger," Gale said behind him, pouring them both a cup of coffee from a blackened pot sitting atop a potbellied stove. "It looked like you were trying your best to strike up a gunfight! I have to agree with the colonel on that." He looked closely at the ranger and asked, "What come over you anyway?" He stepped over from the stove and set the steaming cups on his battered desktop.

"They tried to kill me, Sheriff, and they took my prisoners and lynched them," Sam said firmly, not thinking that anything beyond that needed explaining. He turned from the window with a hard, sharp look in his eyes and stared at Sheriff Gale.

Gale nodded his head. "I understand," he said, almost withering under the ranger's smoldering gaze. "But this Colonel Elgin is just smug enough and shrewd enough that him and his bunch can get by with it. What was those photos all about?" He had come upon the ranger and the colonel's men and diverted Sam away, to his office, for a cup of coffee and some *law talk,* as he'd put it.

"Those were photos of my two prisoners hanging from a tree limb," Sam said, keeping the bitterness in his voice from showing. Had he been trying to provoke the colonel and his men into a gunfight? That was for him to know, he told himself. Gale struck him as a good sheriff, but he wasn't telling him what his plans might be. Plans were best kept a mystery until time to carry them out, he'd learned.

"I don't know what to say, Ranger," Sheriff Gale said sincerely. "If there is something I can legally do, tell me, and I'll do it."

"There's nothing right now," Sam replied, seeming to ease down a little. He realized that what he'd done was put the colonel and his detectives on notice. Now he could only wait and see how the colonel would handle it. There was a fight coming, he knew it.

Returning the ranger's stare, but with less intensity, Gale pushed one of the cups of coffee across his desk to the ranger. "Here, drink this while we have ourselves some *law talk.*"

"Obliged." Sam peeled off his riding gloves and picked up the cup. He blew on the hot coffee out of habit and sipped it still steaming.

"The fact is, I've got a problem with one of the colonel's men myself," Gale said, trying not to sound disturbed by it.

"Which one?" Sam asked

"The gunman, Frank Skimmer," said Gale. "Ever heard of him?"

"More times than I cared to," Sam replied. "He's nothing but a killer carrying a gun . . . and these days a railroad security badge."

"These days there's lots of killers carrying railroad security badges," Gale added grimly. He cupped his big hands around the coffee mug. Sam saw the troubled look on his face.

"What kind of problem?" he asked.

Sheriff Gale gave a half shrug, but Sam knew it wasn't a matter the sheriff took lightly. "He thinks I had something to do with his brother's death. His brother had been missing a few days, his horse stood starving out front of the saloon. Two of Elgin's trail scouts brought the brother's body into town, swore they shot Memphis Beck when they caught him robbing and killing the man out on the trail. Still, Frank Skimmer has it set in his head that I either killed him or had something to do with it. I keep hoping he'll turn the notion loose. But so far he hasn't done it."

"They're saying they caught Beck robbing and killing the man?" Sam asked curiously.

"They're swearing to it," said Gale. "I don't know what else Skimmer needs to hear to convince him I had no hand in it."

"If they shot Beck, where is he?" Sam asked. "Why didn't they bring him in?"

"In my opinion they were scared to track him down, the way some men won't track down a wounded mountain cat," said Gale. "They came back here to get the rest of the posse, and their photographer, of course," he added with a tone of contempt. "The colonel wanted to string Beck up and get a photo for the railroads."

"So hunting Beck is what they were doing up there yesterday," said Sam, putting it together. "They didn't find Beck, so they decided to stampede my prisoners instead."

"This is a bad, dangerous bunch, Ranger," Gale said, shaking his head. "I ain't sure you threatening to contact the railroad is the wise thing to do."

Sam just stared at him for a moment until the sheriff got the idea. "Oh, I see," Gale said, "you're not concerned with contacting the railroads right now."

"They hanged my prisoners," Sam repeated, this time in a stronger tone.

Gale nodded. "I'd feel the same way. The colonel's posse has to spill enough blood to keep the railroads happy. I reckon at a point it doesn't matter whose blood it is."

"My prisoners were Hole-in-the-wall men," said Sam. "But they'd only ridden with the gang a short while. They were wanted for murder in Arizona Territory. That was my only interest in them. Had I taken them back for trial, they would've more than likely swung for murder. But it would have all been done proper. They would have had a fair trial. The colonel hanged them for robbery . . . most likely for robberies he couldn't ever have proven in a court of law. I take a man prisoner he's under my protection until I turn him over to the circuit court. I can't abide men getting killed under my watch."

"Me neither," Gale agreed. "These tin

badges get heavier every day, don't they?" he offered, thinking about what Sam had said. "Sometimes I think mine is going to rip my shirt pocket off." He gave a tired smile.

Sam nodded in agreement. After a sip of coffee and a moment of consideration, he went on to say, "Robbing and killing a man doesn't sound like Memphis Beck's kind of work. It sounds more like something Colonel Elgin and his detectives set up just to get New Mexico Territory after Memphis Beck."

Gale seemed to consider it, but Sam could tell by the look in his eyes that he knew more about the situation than he was telling. "I don't know," said Gale, "but whatever the case, if Skimmer doesn't ease up I'll be having to face him again in the street. And Frank Skimmer is not the kind of man I want to face *again* in the street."

Sam knew this was as close as the sheriff could come to asking him for help. He also knew that Gale didn't want to hear him say he'd stand up with him against Frank Skimmer. Lawmen didn't have to say the words, Sam reminded himself. "I have a hunch we'll both be hearing from the colonel's men shortly," he said. "Frank Skimmer is just one gun on their side. If he stands with the posse, he falls with them."

"I understand," Gale said with resolve, realizing that whatever the situation, from here on, the ranger had just told him they'd stand together. As for who killed Omar, he and Emma were free and clear. But Frank Skimmer was another matter. If he had to face the man, he at least had a better chance with the ranger on his side.

"When are you going after him?" Sam asked, catching Gale by surprise.

"Who?" said Gale.

"Memphis Beck," said Sam. "If he killed someone inside your jurisdiction, I figure you'll be wanting to bring him in." He'd only asked in order to hear what kind of response Gale would give him.

"I — I don't know that I will," said Gale. "At least not any time soon." He nodded toward the window. "Not with the trouble we've got brewing here."

Good enough answer, the ranger thought, still feeing the sheriff knew more than he was telling.

Out in front of the hotel, surrounded by his men, his coffee cup and cigar still in hand, Colonel Elgin saw Frank Skimmer walking toward them from the Little Aces Saloon. When Skimmer drew close enough, the colonel said stiffly, "So glad you could join us today, Frank. We just about had a shoot-out with your friend and mine, Ranger Sam Burrack."

"I had some things to take care of," Skimmer said.

"Oh, I see. . . ." Colonel Elgin stared coldly at Skimmer and said, "I suppose all is well at the saloon this morning?"

Frank's face reddened. "I wasn't at the saloon," he said, his voice also testy and stiff. "Not to drink, anyway."

"Oh? Why, then?" the colonel asked, already knowing it had something to do with finding out more about his dead brother.

"The bartender there told me that the sheriff is stuck on a woman who lives in a house across the street back there." He thumbed over his shoulder. "It's the little white house that sits back off the street. She's the widow of the man who used to be sheriff here."

The colonel stared at him. "I thought I told you to let it go. This thing the sheriff told you about your brother might have been just what he said it was, an *example* . . . a *just suppose* . . . a *what-if!*"

"He's hiding something, Colonel," said Skimmer. "I've got to find out, for my dead brother's sake."

"Look at me, Frank," said the colonel. "I'm not hiding anything." He stepped in closer. "If you're going to ride with this posse, you're going to have to put everything else away and give us your best."

"You're getting my best, Colonel," Skimmer said firmly without giving an inch. "I'm here now, what is it you want me to do?"

The colonel put the matter aside and took a deep breath. To the rest of the men gathered around he said in a raised voice, "All of you go back inside, have another cup of coffee."

The men looked at one another and began drifting back in through the hotel door. But the colonel stopped Pale Lee, Jack Strap, and Bobby Vane. "You three, come here. We all need to talk."

When the three gathered around the colonel and Frank Skimmer, the colonel said in a lowered voice to Vane, Strap, and Hodges, "You three saw what happened here. The ranger is getting in our way too damn much." He glanced at Frank and said to all four of them, "Burrack has to be *stopped,* else we're going to stumble over him and his judgment every move we make out here. Do I make myself plain enough on that?"

The four men nodded.

"You four are my best gunmen," he said, "so you're the only ones I'm telling this to. Burrack just laid it out clearly for us. He's spoiling for a fight, over us hanging those two vermin. The only way we're ever going to quit having his nose in our business is to kill him."

"Now you're talking," said Skimmer.

The colonel looked at Frank. "I want you to get your mind on business. I'm offering a thousand dollars to the man who takes the ranger down, and five hundred dollars to whoever helps him do it."

"What about the sheriff, if he gets in our way, or sides with Burrack?" Skimmer asked.

The colonel saw that Skimmer still had vengeance in mind. "You better listen to me closely, Frank. I want this town to fall under a bad plague of violence. When it does, these folk will quit caring what happens to their sheriff. They'll be glad to get rid of him when he fails to keep the peace. We've got to press this town hard enough that everybody will keep off the streets and out of the way for a while. We don't need a town full of do-gooders witnessing what we do, now, do we?"

"The less witnesses the better, I always

say," Jack Strap put in.

"In other words, you want us to hurrah Little Aces every way we can think of?" Bobby Vane asked.

"No, Bobby, not in *other words*," said the colonel, his smile widening, "but in those words *exactly.*"

Jack Strap grinned. "This is starting to sound like Statler all over again. I don't know about the rest of you fellows, but I can stand some more of that kind of excitement."

"Turn this town on its ear the way we all did in Statler," said the colonel, "and I promise additional bonuses for all of you."

"I'll tell Roundhead, right away," said Bobby Vane. "He loves a lively gathering. He's always happy to roast up a pig or two, open-pit style!" He smiled, his hand on his gun butt, his fingers tapping nervously.

"Yes, do that, Bobby," said the colonel. To the others he said, "Have some of the men start making rounds to the businesses. Tell them to find some reasons to bust up a couple of places. Get everybody worried, make them want to close their doors and duck down."

"And stay down until this *big bad* ole railroad posse leaves town," Skimmer said, thinking about the sheriff, the ranger, his dead brother, and the vengeance he felt he had coming.

"Yes, that's the spirit." Colonel Elgin tossed the rest of his coffee from the mug and turned toward the hotel door. "Start a tab for us at the saloon, run it up high . . . tell them the railroads are paying for everything." He stopped long enough to look over his shoulder at the four men still standing in the dirt street. "Well, gentlemen, what are all of you waiting for? Turn hell loose on Little Aces."

CHAPTER 18

Curtis Clay had spent the night in a troubled sleep and awakened with a troubled mind. By noon he still had not shaken off the feeling of something bad looming ahead, either something directed at him, or someone near him . . . or even at the town itself, he'd decided.

The feeling seemed to have started coming upon him at about the time he'd caught the scent of blood the day before. He wasn't sure that the scent had anything to do with it, but whatever it was, he'd felt troubled enough that he'd turned away two cowboys who'd ridden into Little Aces at daybreak just to try their hand at beating him in assembling their range Colts.

As badly as he'd hated to turn down the money, Clay had refused to even answer their knock on the door of his shack. When they'd given up and left, he'd even taken his big Remington from behind his rope belt and left it on the table inside the shack, before walking to the saloon. A bad feeling was cause enough to not carry a gun, he'd thought.

Feeling edgy and anxious, he'd picked up his walking stick and followed Little Dog out and along the alleyway behind Emma's cottage. In the stretch of alleyway along the weathered picket fence, he once again caught the scent of blood on the air. This time it was not the crisp scent of fresh blood he smelled. This time it was the faint rank and coppery smell of old blood.

Healing blood, he thought, not turning his face toward the cottage, although it would have made no difference if he had. Instead he walked on, wishing that his troubled feeling had nothing to do with the woman, in spite of a wary voice inside that told him it did.

"I know what you're thinking," Clay said to the small stiffly walking canine. He tapped his walking stick close behind the purposeful animal. "You're thinking a nosy old fool ought to mind his own business. But I said we'd look after her, and we will, Little Dog, so long as she needs us to."

Clay walked on, taking the long way around, past the Vertrees cottage before turning out to the main street, counting each step with deft familiarity, hearing the dog's small, soft footsteps in front of him. . . .

On the boardwalk out in front of the mercantile store on the wide main street, two of the newer detectives, a Montana gunman named Joe Graft and a wild-eyed young Texas hired killer named Fletus Belton, lounged in boredom on a long wooden bench. Roundhead Mitchell and another more seasoned detective named Mike "the Fist" Holland had gone inside with a surly, demanding attitude, following the colonel's orders to set the town on its ear.

The mercantile owner, Woodrow Hayes, had seen a marked change in the detectives' demeanors as soon as they stepped through his door. Only three days ago the same two had been at the counter purchasing ammunition. They had courteously paid him and left. Today was different. Seeing the way the two eyed his wife hungrily, he'd immediately given her a nod gesturing her to the stockroom.

"Will that be all, gentlemen?" Woodrow asked, keeping his voice steady in spite of seeing these men appear to be looking for trouble of some sort.

"More pepper," Roundhead said coldly, a tin of pepper sitting on the counter in front of him. "I told you I needed lots of pepper, you gave me one damn tin?" He appeared irritated.

"My apologies, sir!" Woodrow hurriedly turned and reached onto a shelf behind the counter. He took down two more tins of pepper and stood them beside the first. Smiling nervously, he said in an attempt at civility, "My, but that's a lot of pepper. What are you preparing, if I might ask."

"No, you may not," Roundhead said, his eyes going from the counter to a glass-encased display of handguns.

"He's roasting us up a damn pig," Mike the Fist answered, giving him a hard stare. He leaned over the polished counter toward Woodrow. "Be careful it don't wind up being you."

"Oh my," said Woodrow, trying to keep his smile and play the words off as a joke.

But the Fist would have none of it. "Did I say something funny?" he asked bristly, leering at the nervous store owner.

"Oh no, sir, that is —" Woodrow didn't know what to say. His smile vanished quickly.

"Hand me that gun," Roundhead demanded, his thick finger pointing down atop the glass case at a finely engraved Colt with shiny white ivory handles. "How much is it?" he asked impatiently as Woodrow scrambled to open the case.

"Well, it's —" Woodrow stopped and tried to regain his rattled composure. "The thing is, I haven't really priced this one. As you see it's quite ornate, and, well, frankly, more of a showpiece. It's not the most practical gun for carrying holstered. It's more the sort of gun a store owner like myself —"

"Hand me the damned gun!" Roundhead demanded in an abusive tone, rudely cutting the worried-looking store owner off.

"Yes, of course," said Woodrow. He reached into the case, took out the big Colt, and handed it over. "But like I said, I really haven't priced it. I didn't really think anyone would be —"

"How much?" Roundhead said, jerking the cylinder open as he inspected the gun.

"Sir, if you would like to look at one of the other guns. Perhaps you'd —"

"He doesn't want to sell you the gun, Roundhead," Mike the Fist chuckled darkly.

Thumbing bullets from his belt and shoving them into the open cylinder, Roundhead asked as he clicked the cylinder shut, spun it, stopped it, and cocked it in the general direction of the store owner. "How much?" he demanded with finality.

"How about sixty-five dollars, because of

its engraving, the ivory handles —"

"Too much," Roundhead said, still cutting him off rudely.

"It's quite a showpiece," Woodrow said, still trying to maintain a businesslike manner.

"How much are the others?" Roundhead asked, letting the hammer down by pulling the trigger recklessly and catching the hammer with his thumb.

"From sev— seventeen dollars to twenty-eight dollars," he managed to say, his nerves shattered by Roundhead's careless gun handling.

"I'll take it, for seventeen," Roundhead said, giving a him threatening stare.

"Oh, sir, I couldn't possibly —" This time Roundhead didn't cut him off. But seeing the big detective get set to cock the hammer again, he stopped short.

"You know if you're one of the good customers here, Roundhead," the Fist said, grinning cruelly, "you wouldn't have to pay for it today. He'd keep it on a bill for you, right, storekeeper?"

Before Woodrow could answer, Roundhead said in a bullying tone, "What? I'm not a *good* customer? I was here the other day. I'm the one who bought all that ammunition. Now you're telling me I'm not a good customer?" He cocked the gun again.

"Please, gentlemen," Woodrow pleaded with his hands spread, "I don't want any trouble."

"Do you hear that? Now he says he doesn't want any trouble," Roundhead said flatly, "after insulting me that way."

"Yeah, he says it," said the Fist, "but I'm not sure he means it, are you?"

Out in front of the mercantile store, Joe Graft looked toward the end of the boardwalk where Curtis Clay stepped up from the alleyway, tapping the dirt-crusted oak planks with his walking stick.

"What the hell have we got coming here?" Graft laughed, drawing Fletus' attention away from twirling his Colt Thunderer on his trigger finger.

Fletus Belton stopped twirling his gun and pushed up his battered hat brim. "That old dog looks like he's been dead longer than most dogs have been alive."

Curtis heard their voices but gave no sign of it as he tapped forward. "Watch this," Graft whispered sidelong to Belton. He stretched his legs out and crossed his boots in the path of the dog and the blind man.

Trip a blind man . . . ? Belton gave him a disbelieving look, but watched without saying a word.

Having heard the boots slide out on the boardwalk, Clay stopped short, then followed the sound of Little Dog's tapping nails as the elderly dog swung wide around the boots and continued on.

Belton laughed at Graft under his breath, watching the blind man and the dog pass them by. "What the hell?" Belton said, embarrassed that his crude nasty trick hadn't worked. "That old turd's not blind!" he said, coming up from the bench and hurrying over alongside Clay. "Hey, you!" he said, fanning his hand back and forth in front of Clay's eyes.

Clay, seeing the darker image move back and forth in front of his face and feeling the air stirred by Graft's hand, ducked his head slightly. On the boardwalk, Little Dog, frightened by the boots having hurried over toward them, turned and growled low.

"Aha!" said Graft. "I told you he ain't blind, he saw my hand!" Grabbing Clay's coat sleeve, he said, "This old Negro is a phony. He's no more blind than I am."

"I wish it was true," Clay murmured, tapping his walking stick around gently, probing toward the sound of Little Dog's growl. "Easy, Little Dog," he said, trying to quiet the frightened animal.

"Yeah, you better settle the old mutt up," Graft warned, "before I feed him the toe of my boot." As he spoke he stamped his foot toward the shaking animal. But instead of the gesture settling the dog, it made him worse. He growled louder and crouched as if ready to charge Graft's boot.

"Leave the old dog alone, Joe," said Belton. "Send the old Negro on his way. He can't see nothing, just shadows is all."

"Huh-uh, he's faking for sure, and I'll prove it," said Graft.

"Oh yeah? Just how are you going to do that?" Belton asked.

"How? I'll show you how," said Graft, slipping his gun from its holster. "I bet he'll dance when he sees a bullet shot at his feet. Won't you, old man?"

On the boardwalk Little Dog growled louder, seeing Graft as a threat to his master. "Get out of here, you old mutt!" said Graft, again stamping his boot at the dog. This time Little Dog took a dive at the threatening boot even though Clay called out trying to stop him.

"Bite me, you little son of a bitch?" Graft snarled, swinging his gun toward Little Dog.

Sensing what was going on by hearing the gun cock, Clay shouted, "No! Don't shoot him! This poor dog is just old, and scared!

He thought you were hurting me!"

"Come on, Joe, the old dog's not worth a bullet," said Belton, chuckling, sounding bored by it all.

"You're right," said Graft. Instead of firing the gun, he gave the old dog a swift, vicious kick in its brittle ribs, sending it rolling across the boardwalk and onto the dirt street. Clay, hearing the kick and the dog's sharp yelp of pain, swung the walking stick without hesitation and broke it in half across the gunman's nose. Graft staggered backward and crumbled to his knees. Blood flew.

"My God, Graft!" Belton shouted, stunned by the blow. He stared at the walking stick broken in two, half lying on the boardwalk, half flying out into the street. "This old blind Negro has put you down on your knees!" He gave a short startled laugh.

Clay had dropped onto his hands and knees and searched frantically and clumsily for the edge of the boardwalk, calling out to Little Dog.

"He's down there, Negro," said Belton. He stood and gave Clay a shove with his boot, sending the man sprawling into the dirt, where his hands found the small dog whining pitifully, gasping for breath.

"He's broken my nose! Shoot him!" Graft

shouted. His own gun had flown from his hand and skidded along the boardwalk.

"You want him shot? Here, you shoot him," said Belton. He bent over to pick up Graft's gun, but a boot seemed to come from out of nowhere and clamp down on it. "Take your hand away from the gun," the ranger said quietly but firmly, his free hand already grasping Belton's Colt and slipping it from its holster.

Belton straightened, raising his hands. "I wasn't going to shoot him, Ranger."

"No," said the ranger, "you were going to let this other snake do it." His gun barrel swung fast and merciless and cracked Belton across the side of his head, sending him to the boardwalk.

Graft scrambled to his feet quickly, a hand cupping his bleeding nose. He held out his free hand at arm's length to keep from getting the same thing he'd seen Belton get. "I'm hurt, Ranger!" he said. "Look at me!"

"Not enough," said the ranger, taking a step toward him. Graft stumbled backward and once again found himself on the boardwalk.

In the dirt, Clay gathered the gasping dog into his arms and stood up. "My dog is hurt bad, Mr. Ranger! I got to get him home! He's scared to death out here in the street!"

Sam stepped down from the boardwalk, keeping his eyes on Graft. "Come on, Mr. Clay, I'll get you home."

"Ranger, what about our guns?" Graft called out as Sam led Clay away toward the alley leading back to his shack.

"Come and get them anytime," Sam said menacingly. He looked back at the bloody gunman as he and Clay walked out of sight around the corner of the building.

No sooner had Clay and the ranger gotten out of sight than Mike the Fist and Roundhead stepped out of the mercantile store, Roundhead holding a bag of supplies up under his arm. The ornate ivory-handled Colt stood in a new slim-jim holster. The Fist wore a brand-new Stetson stockman's-style hat.

"What the hell's going on out here?" Roundhead asked, seeing one detective knocked cold and the other on the board-walk bleeding from his nose. He looked at the broken walking stick lying in two pieces. "That old blind man did all this?" he asked.

"Hell no, he didn't do all this!" Graft denied, standing up from the rough plank boardwalk. "But I'm going to kill that old blind son of a bitch, you better mark my words!"

Inside the mercantile store, Woodrow hurried to the door, slipped the latch into place, and turned to his wife, who had started walking out of the stockroom. "What are you doing, Woodrow?" she asked. "We're not closing because of them!"

"Oh yes, indeed we are," said Woodrow with determination. "There's trouble brewing. I want no part of it. We're taking the afternoon off, letting whatever this is blow over."

"You're talking crazy," said Ethel Hayes.

"Have you ever seen a bunch of gunmen hurrah a town, Ethel?" Woodrow asked. Not waiting for her to reply, he said, "Well, I have. And I don't want to ever see it again." As he spoke he opened the cash drawer beneath the counter, jerked out a handful of bills and coins, and stuffed them into a canvas bag.

CHAPTER 19

The ranger stood beside Clay as the blind man laid the injured dog on a saddle blanket at the foot of the small bed the two shared. Even without benefit of his walking stick or Little Dog in front of him, Clay moved with efficiency inside his familiar habitat. Sam watched, noting the dog's labored breathing.

"This dog is too old to take a kicking," Clay commented, reaching down, finding the dog, and rubbing its head gently. Little Dog raised his muzzle weakly and licked Clay's hand. "But I know horses and dogs. He'll be all right," Clay offered, in order to ease his grave concern for the animal.

The ranger looked at the Remington laying on the table. "What about you, Mr. Clay? Are you going to be all right?" Sam asked.

"I'm good, Ranger," Clay replied without hesitation. He felt around for a chair at the table. Finding it, he sat down, his hands flat on the tabletop, on either side of the big gun. "I woke up this morning feeling like something bad was about to happen. Something told me not to take this Remington with me to the saloon. It's a good thing I didn't. Somebody would have died."

The ranger recognized his seriousness, even though he couldn't help but question the man's capability. "Your feelings were right on target this morning, Mr. Clay," he said. "This would be a good time to stay indoors the next couple of days, if you can."

Clay turned his face to the ranger. "There's trouble brewing? Law trouble?"

"Yes, law trouble," said the ranger. He did not want to get into any more details than necessary, yet he felt as though he should warn the man.

"You and Sheriff Gale together?" Clay ventured, without pressing. "Against the railroad posse, I'm guessing?"

It was more than the ranger wanted to reveal, but he saw no harm. "Yes, we've had some trouble between us and the posse, Mr. Clay. I hope you'll heed what I'm saying and stay off the streets."

"I would," said Clay, "but I'm afraid you and the sheriff will need my help. I'll have to get me a new walking stick." His hand moved sidelong, found the Remington, and patted it. "But this is my town. I want to do my part like the rest of the town."

"I'm obliged, Mr. Clay, and I know Sheriff Gale is too," said Sam, meaning it. "But we'd both feel better if townsmen like yourself would stay back and give us room to do our job."

"I see," Clay said, bowing his head slightly in thought for a moment. "This trouble you and the sheriff have with the posse . . . it's all private trouble between you?"

The ranger gave him a curious look, impressed by his perception. "As a matter of fact, it is," he said, not wanting to go any further talking about it.

Clay detected the ranger's reluctance by the slightest tightness that came into his voice. "Don't tell me if you don't want to, Ranger. I won't ask you nothing more about it."

"Obliged," Sam said, realizing Clay was a hard man to keep anything from.

"But let me ask you this," Clay said. "Has the moon been on the wan these past nights?"

"Yes," said Sam, finding his question peculiar. "Why do you ask?"

"Just checking, so I can keep up with it," said Clay with a shrug. "I always like knowing where the moon is, don't you, Ranger?"

"I haven't given it much thought lately," Sam replied. This man clearly had a reason behind everything he did or said. "I hope you'll stay in tonight and look after your pard there," he said, nodding toward the dog even though Clay couldn't see his gesture.

"I will take care of him, sure enough. And if I hear shooting, I'll keep my curiosity to myself," Clay anticipated.

"The sheriff and I would both appreciate it," said the ranger.

Clay nodded, then stood up and felt his way to the bed and sat back down, reaching out to the dog and rubbing its muzzle. "I've got plenty to do looking after this old dog and finding myself a new walking stick, Ranger," he said sincerely. "I won't be out there." He paused as he heard the ranger step toward the door and turn the handle. Then, letting his words trail, he said, "But if there's anything I can do for you . . ."

On his way to the street, the ranger didn't realize that Emma Vertrees had seen him as she carried a feed bag of oats and a pail of water to the buggy horse she'd hitched in the shade, out of sight in a grown-over lot across the alley. She ducked behind the cover of a rickety abandoned chicken coop until the ranger disappeared around the corner. Then she moved quickly and quietly and continued on with her chore.

When she finished she walked back to the house, put away the feed bag and water bucket, and walked inside. Hearing her at the door, Memphis Beck had slipped the Colt from under his pillow; but upon hearing her call out to him from the kitchen, he put the gun back and sat on the side of the bed, his strength returning steadily.

"Well, it's good to see you up and around," Emma said, walking into the room, seeing he had gotten up and dressed himself.

"I had the best of care," Beck said as she came over to him and he put his arms around her. "Much obliged, ma'am, for everything," he said, thinking about the two of them beneath the warm quilt in the night when she'd spread open her robe and drawn him against her, her warmth infusing him.

She nestled his head to her stomach. "The buggy horse is fine. I grained and watered him. Are you going to be able to ride tonight?" she asked.

"I can ride right now," said Beck. "But since I'm not all the way up to my game just yet, we better wait and leave under the cover of darkness. Besides, I want to take the rented roan back and get my dun out of the livery. His bruise ought to be healed up enough for him to tag along behind the buggy."

"I can't wait to get out of here," Emma said. "I don't care where we go, or what we do. I just want to get going."

"We will, Emma," said Beck. "It won't be much longer now. We'll be together just like before."

On the street out in front of the saloon, Sam met Sheriff Gale, who had started carrying a sawed-off double-barreled shotgun in the crook of his arm. From inside the saloon came loud quarrelsome voices above the sound of tinny piano music. Two townsmen who drank regularly at the Little Aces Saloon came through the batwing doors and walked briskly away with scared looks on their faces. They didn't even notice the sheriff when he spoke and touched his hat brim toward them.

"Hear that, Ranger?" Gale said, nodding toward the loud voices beyond the batwing doors. "They're just loud enough to run away the regulars."

"I figure they'll get worse between now and dark," Sam said, noting the sun had already started descending in the western sky.

"The colonel's men must've started knuckling everybody down right after you confronted them at the hotel this morning." Gale's eyes moved all around the town as he spoke. "I've had complaints all day. The colonel's men are on the prod. A desk clerk said they're roasting two pigs in the yard behind the hotel."

"Where do you suppose they got the two pigs?" Sam asked.

"Oh, I'm certain they lassoed them out of a backyard near here," said Gale. "Either the owner hasn't noticed they've been stolen yet, or else he's afraid to say anything."

"A pig roast and an old-fashioned town hazing," the ranger commented. "I ran into some trouble out front of the mercantile store. Only in this case two of his men met their match with Curtis Clay. He broke his walking stick over one of their noses."

"Good for him," said Gale.

"But one of them kicked his dog and hurt it," the ranger added.

"The sons a' bitches," said Gale. Together they watched Woodrow and Ethel Hayes walk toward them along the boardwalk at an excited pace. "Looks like another complaint coming," Gale said, adjusting the shotgun in the crook of his arm.

"I'm wondering if Clay is going to cause

us a problem once the colonel's men make their move," Sam said. "He feels like it's his civic duty to help us out."

"You told him what's going on?" Gale asked, seeming surprised.

"Just what I thought he needed to know, enough to keep him off the streets tonight," the ranger replied.

"I never know what to make of Curtis Clay," said the sheriff. "He's a blind man all alone in a blind man's world." He shook his head slightly. "I don't know what things are like in there."

"Sheriff Gale! There you are," Woodrow Hayes called out as he and Ethel drew closer. "I want to report two of the railroad detectives coming into my store and bullying me out of fourteen dollars' worth of stock and dry goods . . . and a sixty-dollar engraved Colt pistol, with ivory grips."

"What else did they take, Woodrow?" Gale asked with no sign of surprise in his tone of voice.

"They took a two-pound bag of salt, three tins of ground black pepper, three air-tights of apples, and a black Stetson hat, the stockman's model — the hat and Colt are two of the most costly items in the store."

"They shouldn't be hard to spot," Gale said, "wearing a stockman's hat and carrying an engraved ivory-handled Colt. If we see them we'll get your items back for you, Woodrow. Meanwhile, I'd like for the two of you to get off the street for the rest of the evening."

"Oh, I get it," said Woodrow, "so there is trouble here with that railroad bunch. I told Ethel that's what I thought." He looked all around the near empty street. "Don't worry, we're getting out of town for the evening, Sheriff." He paused, then added hesitantly, "That is, unless you need for me to load a bear rifle and come help you."

"Obliged, Woodrow," said Sheriff Gale, "but the ranger and I have things under control. You two go enjoy the evening off."

Woodrow looked at his wife and said as he guided her away from the two lawmen, "I told you, didn't I?"

"That's how it's been," Gale said. "Earlier, the barber come and told me a detective walked in, got a shave and haircut, had his hat blocked and his boots cleaned. Told the barber to put it on his tab."

Sam started to reply, but just as he did, a rifle shot hammered into the dirt only inches from his boots, causing him and Gale to dive for cover. Sam's Colt came out of his holster as he hit the ground and came up in a crouch behind the cover of a water trough. In the open upper window of an unoccupied building across the street, he saw rifle smoke drift sidelong on the air. He waited, poised, ready to fire. But he saw no movement in the window.

"Do you see anybody?" Gale asked, crouched in the alleyway, near the corner of the clapboard saloon building.

"Nothing," said the ranger. Still watching the window, he cut a sidelong glance along the empty street, seeing no one run out to see what had happened.

"They're starting early," Gale said.

"No," said Sam, "this was just to make sure everybody in town has gotten the message to stay off the streets."

Nodding toward the building, Gale said, "The place used to be the land title building. It's sat empty for the past three months."

"Good place for an ambush," Sam said, still watching the window. He noted that someone had opened it while they were talking to the mercantile store owners.

"Which do you want, the front door or the rear?" Gale asked.

"I'll go straight in," said Sam, already figuring whoever had made the shot was gone, but knowing they needed to use caution all the same. "You take the scattergun around back, see what I can send out to you."

The ranger ran across the empty street, his Colt in hand, and ducked inside the empty building. Covering the ranger, Gale waited until he saw him slip inside. Then he ran across the street and around the building to the rear door. Noting that it stood wide open, he let out a breath, knowing the rifleman was gone. Yet he waited, keeping a watchful eye inside the shadowy building until he saw the ranger come back down the stairs and walk toward him, lowering his Colt on his way.

"He's gone, just what we thought," said Sam, holstering his Colt as he stepped out the door. The two of them walked back around to the empty street.

On the street, the two lawmen stood for a moment looking toward the hotel porch a block away where Colonel Elgin and three of his men had walked out and stood looking toward them. The colonel smiled knowingly and took a seat in the big rocking chair, like a man settling himself to watch a parade. He held a thick cigar in his fingers and gave the lawmen a courteous tip of his hand.

"Sometimes I have more respect for the cutthroats and trash we deal with day to day," Gale said quietly to the ranger as they stared at the colonel and his men.

"Yes, I know," said Sam. "With the outlaws you know where you stand. You throw down and get it over with. Men like these step around the law every way they can. When it's time to do their killing, they have every last detail worked down to their advantage."

"They're bigger than the government, these railroads and their *rail barons*," said Gale, gripping the stock of his shotgun.

"These rail barons *are* the government, Sheriff," Sam replied. His gaze was fixed on the colonel and his men. "Their money makes all the laws. Elgin and his thugs are the ones who enforce them." He paused in grim consideration, then said, "That's why men like them and us are bound to butt heads anytime we get too close."

CHAPTER 20

Clay had checked on Little Dog by laying a hand gently on the small animal's side and feeling it rise and fall slowly, *painfully,* Clay thought. "You're going to be sore, but at least you're alive," he said down to the half-sleeping dog. "You live through this I don't want you ever jumping on anybody again, no matter what you think they're fixing to do to me," he scolded quietly. "You hear me, old dog? You're too old to be doing something like that."

Little Dog raised his head stiffly and licked the blind man's hand. Clay felt his cloudy eyes well up and said in a soft voice, "You always did think you was tougher than you are." He wiped an eye. "That's what makes you special to me. So don't go getting yourself killed."

Little Dog laid his head back down and drifted back to sleep. When Clay turned from the bed, he caught the sweet familiar scent of Emma Vertrees through the open window and stopped cold. Yes, it was her scent all right, no mistaking it, he told himself. Yet he found her scent wrapped within another scent. This other scent was only recently familiar to him, the smell of wood smoke from campfires, of leather, and whiskey and . . . *dried blood.* He paused. This was the scent of the man who'd left the stone-bruised dun under his care. The man hadn't smelled of blood before, nor had he carried the scent of Emma Vertrees. But he did now, Clay told himself.

Clay walked to the door and opened it just as Memphis Beck raised his hand to knock. Beck looked surprised, his right hand resting on the Colt holstered on his hip. "What can I do for you?" Clay asked out of habit, already knowing why the man stood at his door.

"I'm here about my dun horse," Beck asked. "How's he doing?"

Hearing the volume of Beck's voice change slightly as he'd spoken, Clay realized the man had been looking back and forth checking the alleyway. "He's doing real good," said Clay. "I expect he's most fit to travel if you need him to."

"Yes, I do need him," Beck said, still cutting a glance back and forth along the alleyway. "I need him tonight."

"Tonight?" said Clay. "You're going to be traveling on this dark moonless night?" He realized he was being nosy, asking, but he did so anyway.

"I'm afraid so," said Beck, only wondering mildly how the man knew there was no moon. "I have the rental horse I took. He's standing at the hitch rail out here."

"I know he is," said Clay, not only having scented the animal but also having heard the roan's deep steady breath less than fifteen feet away. "If you need a lantern, there's one we can light for you in the barn." He stepped out of the dark shack into the greater darkness of night.

"That will be good," said Beck.

"So, you follow me," said Clay, stepping over to the horse at the hitch rail.

"Where is your dog?" Beck asked, noting the absence of both Little Dog and Clay's walking stick.

"The dog is hurt," said Clay. "One of the posse detectives kicked him . . . caused me to break my walking stick too." Unhitching the roan, Clay stopped and said, "Say, you're not one of them posse detectives, are you?"

"No," said Beck, "I didn't even know there were any in town."

Clay believed the first part — this man didn't strike him as a detective, or as a lawman of any sort. The second part was a lie, Clay could tell by the slightest shift in the man's voice. This man knew the detectives were in Little Aces. Why did he lie about something like that?

Being familiar with the path to the barn even without Little Dog and his walking stick, Clay led the roan and asked when he knew they were halfway through the darkness to the barn doors, "You're acquainted with Sheriff Dillard Vertrees' widow, aren't you?"

"Yes, I am acquainted with Mrs. Vertrees," Beck replied, wondering what he might have said to reveal such information to this man.

Clay caught the curiousness in Beck's tone of voice, but he only smiled to himself without explaining that he had smelled the woman on him. Yes, Clay thought, he knew that the man and the woman were *acquainted,* and now that he'd weighed the content of the man's voice when he'd answered, Clay also knew just *how well.*

"Stand still while I drop this saddle. Then I'll get the lantern and strike it for you," Clay said when he'd guided Beck into the pitch-darkness of the barn.

"Obliged," said Beck, at the blind man's

mercy and knowing it.

Clay left him standing until he'd stripped the roan of saddle and bridle and given it a slap into its empty stall.

A moment later Beck heard a match scratch along the barn wall and saw the small streak of fire follow it. He watched the glow of light grow wide and brighten inside the lantern globe, reflecting in Clay's cloudy sightless eyes.

"There, is that better for you?" Clay asked, catching a dim shadowy image for only a moment before it faded. He turned, holding the lantern out toward Beck, listening for the sound of his voice.

"Much better," Beck replied.

"I say your dun horse is all right, but you're the one riding him. You best take a look for yourself," Clay offered, stepping in the direction of Beck's voice.

Beck took the lantern, walked into the stall where the dun horse stood looking at them, and hung the lantern on a wall peg. In spite of the pain in his wounded side, Beck bent down, raised the dun's healing foreleg, and inspected it closely. "He looks good," he said, "and he doesn't flinch a nerve when I press on him. You've taken good care of him, Mr. Clay. I'm obliged."

"I wouldn't put him to hard testing for a

few more days if you can keep from it," Clay cautioned.

"I won't," said Beck, dusting his hands together as he straightened up and lifted the lantern from the peg. Before Beck walked out of the stall, Clay heard two sounds at the same instant. He heard the front barn door open and from within the dun's stall, the sound of Beck's Colt slide up across the leather holster and cock.

"Hello, in there, Curtis?" Councilman Woolard called out as he stepped inside the barn and closed the door behind him. "What are you doing in here? Where is your pesky little mutt?"

"The man came for his dun horse, and brought back the roan he rented, Mr. Woolard," Clay called out, ignoring the remark about Little Dog.

"Oh, good! I've been keeping a sharp eye out for you, sir," said Woolard, stepping over and seeing only the upper half of Beck from over the stall gate. Clay knew a gun had been drawn and was now pointed at Woolard. But sensing Beck's intensity, he decided it prudent not to say anything just now.

"Oh? Why's that?" Beck asked, sounding wary and a bit dangerous, in Clay's perceptive opinion.

"I like that dun horse, sir," said Woolard.

"I told Curtis to let you know that I'm interested in trading for him. I suppose it slipped Curtis' mind, like most things I ask him to do." To Clay he said, "I don't know why I put up with you, Curtis."

Hearing the disrespect in Woolard's voice, Beck lied quickly, "Mr. Clay mentioned it. But I have to tell you the same thing I told him, I'm not interested."

"Oh, I see," said the councilman. "Well, perhaps another time, that is if you're going to be in Little Aces very long, Mr. . . . ?" He let his question troll for an answer.

"Conrad, sir," Beck said, recalling the name of an attorney he'd once known in Chicago. But he went no further, saying nothing about how long he planned to be in Little Aces.

After an awkward second, Woolard cleard his throat and said, "I must say, Mr. Conrad, you look familiar. Have we met before?"

"No, I don't think so," Beck said flatly.

"Oh, well then." Woolard dismissed the matter with the toss of a hand. *Conrad indeed!* Yes, he looked familiar, Woolard thought. He'd seen him arrive the other day in handcuffs! "Should you ever change your mind, I hope you'll consider me. I'm always on the lookout out for good horses."

"Yes, I will," Beck said, seeing the man

already back away and head for the door. "Curtis, I seem to owe you an apology this time," Woolard said over his shoulder. "For *once* you did as you were told." He gave a short chuckle and walked out the door.

"Yes, sir, Mr. Woolard," Clay called out to the closing door. He'd noted the change and the tension in Woolard's voice right after he'd asked if he and this man had ever met. *What was that . . . ?* Clay asked himself.

Frank Skimmer stood in the dark beneath an overhang out in front of an apothecary shop across the street from Emma Vertrees' cottage. He'd been on his way to the hotel to meet the colonel and the rest of the men for roast pork before going after the two lawmen. But vengeance mattered more to him than food. He decided to check on the cottage one more time, hoping to get a look at the widow who the bartender told him lived there.

Yesterday he'd followed the sheriff and watched him go around the side of the house and into the back door. He was becoming more convinced that this was the woman the sheriff had been referring to the night he watched the lawman wrestle with whether or not to kill him inside his cell and call it an attempted jailbreak.

Forced himself on her . . . ? That was a damned lie, he thought, thinking back on what the sheriff had said. Ha! Not his brother, Omar. Skimmer spat and stared closely at the lamplight in the cottage window. All he needed was a little proof of any sort. He had no qualms about killing a woman, not if he knew she'd killed his brother.

When he saw Councilman Woolard hurrying along the dark street beneath the dim glow of streetlamps, he stepped out and said, "Whoa, Councilman. Where are you headed in such a hurry?"

Woolard gasped like a woman and halted. "My goodness, but you gave me a start, Mr. Skimmer!" he said. "I'm on my way to the saloon, to tell your colonel that I saw the man you're all looking for! He's right here, in Little Aces . . . under your noses!"

"Easy, now," said Skimmer. "The colonel and the men are not at the saloon. They're roasting pigs behind the hotel. What man are you talking about anyway?"

"The Hole-in-the-wall outlaw who rode in the other day with the ranger!" Woolard said. "I just saw him at the livery barn! I came running to tell the colonel. I always try to help the railroad any way I can!"

"That's thoughtful of you." Skimmer

grinned. "I expect you also wouldn't mind collecting some reward money if the colonel feels you deserve it?"

"I wouldn't rule it out," said Woolard. He started to continue on, but Skimmer caught him by the forearm.

"Memphis Beck is dead, two of our detectives shot him!"

"I dare to differ," said Woolard. "I'm afraid they are mistaken!"

"Those lying dogs," Skimmer growled, wondering, if they'd lied about shooting Beck, what else they had lied about. About his brother, maybe? "How long ago did you see him at the livery barn?"

"Please, unhand me, I need to see the colonel!" said Woolard.

"You're seeing me, that's the same thing," said Skimmer. He gave the councilman a hard shake, his hand resting on his Colt. "How long ago, damn it! Don't make me twist an ear off!"

"Only moments ago!" Woolard answered quickly, raising a protective hand. He had no doubt that this man would twist his ear until it ripped from his head. "I just left there and came running! Please see to it the colonel knows I delivered the information to him straightaway."

"You bet I will," said Skimmer, already

shoving Woolard toward the livery barn in front of him. "Let's go."

"No, not me!" said Woolard. "I don't want to face a man like Beck! That's too dangerous!" He stalled in the street, but Skimmer gave him a harder shove forward.

"So is being out here on the street tonight, you idiot," said Skimmer. "All hell is about to break loose out here."

"It is?" Woolard looked terrified and began running along in front of the bullying gunman.

"You damn well bet it is," said Skimmer. "Lucky for you I stopped you when I did. You'd never have made it to the saloon before somebody blew your fool head off."

"Oh my God!" said Woolard, running in the eerie glow of streetlamps, looking back over his shoulder in terror.

At the corner where a street ran back to the livery barn, the gunman shoved him on toward the far end of town and said harshly, "Get on home, Councilman! Don't let me catch you out tonight, or I'll turn you into a steer!"

Chuckling to himself, satisfied that the horrified man would not show himself anymore tonight, Skimmer drew his Colt from its holster and crept along the side street quietly until he turned into the alley leading to the barn.

Before going to the barn, he slipped silently along the side of Clay's shack, not realizing that silence wasn't silent enough for Clay's keen hearing. Inside, Clay sensed danger. He kept a hand lying gently on the dog's side, hoping it wouldn't awaken and begin to growl. When he felt the presence outside the shack had moved away in the darkness, he arose and drew the Remington from beneath his pillow. Leaning down close to Little Dog, he whispered, "Don't you worry about me. You just get some rest." He slipped out of the shack and made his way toward the weathered picket fence along the alley.

In the pitch-darkness, Frank Skimmer had almost walked into the side of the dark barn before realizing it was there. "Damn!" He couldn't remember a night ever being this dark, he thought as he felt along the rough planks and found the front door of the big barn.

Inside, he struck a match and looked all around. Seeing the lantern hanging from a wall peg, he walked over and took it down, noting how hot the globe was from having only recently been extinguished. All right, he thought, lighting the lantern and looking down at the dirt floor at the fresh set of hoof marks. Now he'd find out just which direction Memphis Beck had taken.

Once he got his hands on him, Beck would tell him the truth about his brother. He'd see to it, if he had to get the information from him with a hot branding iron and a pair of wire cutters.

Following the hoofprints along the alleyway, Skimmer put out the lantern when he found the horse hitched to a tree beside the buggy. Looking around in the dark, he saw the light in a kitchen window. It took only a second to realize he had gone in a circle and now stood at the rear of the widow's cottage.

"Well, I'll be," Skimmer said to himself. Leaning back against the tree, he pushed up his hat brim and smiled. Before helping the colonel and the rest of the posse take care of the sheriff and the ranger, he would take care of his unfinished business. He wasn't sure anymore who had killed his brother; but if he killed both Memphis Beck and the widow, who else was left? He smiled to himself.

CHAPTER 21

In the rear yard of the Little Aces Hotel, Roundhead carved a thick sizzling slab of meat from one of the roasting hogs. With a big two-tong fork he flung the steaming meat onto a tin plate that Jack Strap had brought over for the colonel. "Nothing like a good plate of roasted pig before a long night's work, eh, Roundhead?" Strap said, licking hot pork grease from his thumb.

Roundhead only grunted, absorbed in basting the sizzling pig carcass above the licking flames with one hand and twirling his engraved ivory-handled Colt with the other. In the yard several of the colonel's men sat eating from tin plates on their laps. From the rear door of the hotel, the night clerk stared out at the flames with a worried look on his face.

Walking the steaming meat over to where the colonel sat sipping whiskey straight from the bottle, Strap handed him the plate.

"Roundhead says he hopes you enjoy this, Colonel," he said.

Colonel Elgin only nodded, set the plate on his knee, and took a shot of whiskey, before capping the bottle and dropping it on the ground beside him.

Strap looked at the faces of Pale Lee, Bobby Vane, and Bloody Vlak, who sat flanking the colonel. "If you don't mind me asking, Colonel," Strap asked, "what's going to be our plan of attack?"

"Plan of attack?" The colonel took a bite of the hot roast pork and spoke as he chewed. "I count we've got sixteen men, Strap. I plan on half of us going right to the sheriff's office and calling the ranger and the sheriff out into the street. The rest of us will be strung out in the dark on both sides of the street." He swallowed the meat and took another bite.

"We'll take on some wounded that way," Strap speculated, "maybe even lose a man or two."

"That may well be," said the colonel, giving him a harsh look. "Did you suppose there would no risk involved in killing two lawmen, especially one of them being the renowned Sam Burrack? Why the hell else would I pay a thousand dollars to whoever does the killing? Why would I even pay five hundred to the second gun on the job?"

"I was just thinking out loud," said Strap, backing down quickly from what he'd said.

"Don't think with your mouth open, Strap," said the colonel. "It makes you look like an idiot."

Pale Lee chuckled out loud. "I'd think that nobody here would want to kill the ranger worse than you and our Romanian pal here." He gave a mocking nod toward Vlaktor Blesko. "The way he set you afoot . . . sent you both packing with your tails between your legs."

"I do not have de tail," Vlak growled.

"Only by luck of the draw," Pale Lee laughed tauntingly.

Jack Strap fumed. But he kept his words civil as he stood up and said, "Come on, Vlak. You and me will be the ones to collect that money . . . me for killing the ranger, you for helping."

Vlak just looked at him as he stood, dusted the seat of his wool trousers, and followed him across the yard, out of the circle of firelight.

As the two walked away, the colonel blew a chunk of gristle out into the dirt and said, "If any of yas need a *plan of action,* here it is, "Go get them and kill them both." He looked around solemnly from one face to the next. "Any questions?"

"Just one," said Pale Lee, holding up a greasy finger as he swallowed a bite of pork. "Where the hell is Frank Skimmer?"

"He's got it stuck in his head that he has to kill somebody over his brother's death." Colonel Elgin shook his head slowly. "If it were anyone but Frank, I'd be fire-pissing mad." He let out a breath. "But he is still my *top gunman*. I know how he operates in cases like this. He's off getting ready for the unexpected, the way he always does. Frank is good, make no mistake about it." He raised his eyes and looked back around at their faces. "Let me make this known to all of you. Tonight is a good night to impress me, to let me know which ones of you are good enough to go on up in the ranks after this Hole-in-the-wall job is done."

"Meaning?" Pale Lee asked.

"Meaning, a man can do a lot worse than making a career for himself *dicking* for the railroads," the colonel said. "Anybody who wants it, best be ready, willing, and able to show me something tonight." He uncapped the whiskey bottle on the ground beside him. "Now eat up, drink up, and let's get this done and over with. I'm sick of running into that ranger at every turn in the trail."

"Yeah, and the sheriff too," said Pale Lee,

raising his own bottle in a toast, "for siding with him!"

Memphis Beck looked at the large carpetbag lying on the floor beside a heavily loaded steamer trunk. Seeing the look on his face, Emma said, "I know this looks like a lot to take with me where we're headed. But I'll go through everything and get rid of most of it once we're away from here."

"It is a lot," Beck said, looking doubtful. "Maybe it's best to leave it behind to begin with? It's only going to slow us down."

"I can't leave it behind, Memphis," she said. She was in a hurry to leave while the sheriff had his hands full with the railroad detectives. "There's a lot of memories there," she said tenderly. "I need some time to sit down and go through everything."

Beck nodded, keeping quiet on the matter.

"You do understand, don't you, Memphis?" she asked, almost apologetic.

"Sure." Beck shrugged. "I understand. I just don't keep much around to remind me of anything." He tapped the side of his head. "Any memories I've kept, they had to find themselves a place up here. You know me . . . I always travel light."

"Yes, and so do I, if you'll recall," Emma

308

said. "But be patient with me, Memphis, please. It's been a while since I've been on the trail. I'll get back to my old self as soon as we're out of Little Aces."

"I'll be patient with you, Emma, I promise," Beck said reassuringly, "but right now we need to get moving before the sheriff shows up." Stiffly, without disturbing his bandaged wound, he stooped down, picked up the carpetbag, and walked through the house to the kitchen door.

Feeling harried and somehow put upon, Emma looked all around her bedroom with a hand to her forehead. All the years she'd spent here, inside this house, the only real home she'd known since childhood, were coming to a fast ending. She couldn't stop it, she didn't want to stop it. Yet she needed more time. *Time for what?* she asked herself.

"Time to say good-bye," she heard herself murmur softly, as if there were something there that could hear her.

Outside the kitchen door, Beck hefted the carpetbag to his chest and walked down into the dark yard. He didn't stop to light the small lantern hanging on the back wall of the house for just such a purpose. He wanted the starless, moonless darkness to blanket him from the world. But it wasn't to be. As he'd opened the kitchen door,

Frank Skimmer had recognized him in the light that spilled out onto the porch until Beck closed the door behind himself.

I've got you, Memphis Warren Beck! Skimmer said to himself, gripping his Colt in his gloved hand. He crouched beside the tree Beck would have to walk past to get to the rented buggy sitting thirty feet away. From the darkness, Skimmer saw the outline of Beck walking toward him in the broken light from the kitchen window.

As Beck grew closer, leaving the glow of kitchen light behind in the yard, Skimmer heard the unsuspecting outlaw open the gate and continue toward him, his footsteps coming closer and closer. Timing each step, Skimmer arose and stepped out behind Beck. Quickly he grabbed Beck by the back of his shirt. Before the man could respond, the detective made a vicious swing with his gun barrel and sent him crumbling to the ground.

"Now for your girlfriend," Skimmer whispered, still holding on to Beck's shirt. The blow had stunned Beck, but the darkness caused Skimmer to miss solidly, landing it across the back of his head. Beck lay half conscious, powerless to act, yet still knowing what had just happened to him.

He felt himself being dragged along across

the dirt by the detective until they reached the buggy. "This will have to do for now," Skimmer whispered in a raspy voice, knowing the sound of a gunshot would ruin everything. "I'd cut your throat, but I don't want to bloody my shirt."

Beck felt the detective pull his arms forward roughly and cuff his wrists through the buggy spokes. He felt a bandanna pull tight across his mouth and tie at the back of his throbbing head, keeping him from calling out and warning Emma. "Now then, we'll just wait here real quietlike until she comes to see about you." He leaned in close and said mercilessly, "I expect you and her will want to die together."

In her bedroom, Emma waited as long as she could for Beck to return. When she grew anxious she walked to the kitchen window and peeped out, not knowing what she expected to see in the darkness. This was the part of going back to her old way of life she could live without, she reminded herself, the uncertainty, the suspense of never knowing what lay in wait. . . .

She stood in deep thought about things for another five minutes. "All right," she said aloud, "what's going on out there?" Picturing Beck on the ground, his wound having reopened from struggling with the heavy carpetbag, she opened the door and stepped out onto the porch.

She wasn't about to go out there alone, posse or no posse, she told herself, taking down the lantern and lighting it before stepping down off the porch into the dark yard.

Carrying the lantern low at her side, exposing as little light as necessary, she walked warily through the yard. At one point she could have sworn she heard someone moving right along with her, tracking her footsteps along the side of the yard through the perimeter of tall unkept grass and foliage. But that was foolishness — fear of the dark, she told herself.

But her fear felt more real when she'd left the yard, crossed the alley, and, following the path toward the buggy, found the carpetbag lying abandoned in the dirt at her feet. "Memphis?" she called out in a hushed voice, her eyes searching the darkness in vain. "Where are you? Are you all right?"

"No, he's not all right, lady." Frank Skimmer suddenly appeared beside her, his hand clamping around her forearm. She felt the tip of his gun barrel jam against the side of her neck. "But why don't I just take you to him? You can see for yourself." He jerked the lantern from her hand and dragged her forward by her arm. When she gasped, he said, "Uh-uh, lady, if you try to scream I'll cut your tongue out. And I don't want to do that. You're going to need it, to tell me why you killed my brother." He shook her as he dragged her along. "That's right, I put two and two together. Now it's your turn to die . . . you and your murdering outlaw boyfriend, Memphis Beck."

"Beck had nothing to do with your brother's death, I swear he didn't!" Emma said, hoping beyond hope that saying it might make a difference.

"I don't believe you, lady," said Skimmer, stringing her along, knowing if he kept her talking and pushed hard enough, he'd find out what he wanted to hear.

At the buggy, Frank Skimmer shoved her to the ground and held the light out to get a look at both her and Memphis Beck. "She had nothing to do with killing your brother, Detective," Beck said, having come to and worked the bandanna down enough to speak in a muffled voice. "I did it, just like your detective friends told you," he lied, speaking quickly. "I shot him in the head, then in the chest. I would have shot him again if they hadn't showed up and —"

"Shut up, Beck!" said Skimmer with a swift kick to his ribs. "If I want to hear from you, I won't be bashful . . . I'll let you know."

"He's lying," said Emma. "He didn't kill your brother. I did."

"There now," said Skimmer, "we're starting to get somewhere." He pointed his Colt at her, stooping to watch her face and hear her tell him what had happened. "Start talking, lady," he demanded, "and don't even try telling me my brother forced himself on you. All that will do is make me madder."

CHAPTER 22

From the dimly lit window of the sheriff's office, the ranger looked out along the deserted street and saw the half-dozen detectives walking forward. The men had spread out, walking abreast toward them. He knew there were more moving along in the darker shadows out of the streetlamp glow. "Here they come, Sheriff," he said calmly to Gale, who stood at the desk behind him.

"Any sign of the colonel out in front?" Gale asked skeptically.

"No," said Sam, "and I'm not surprised. I figure he's farther back, out of the street-lamps. That's where we're headed." He looked around the office as if making sure they weren't forgetting something. "It's time we get out of here."

Gale slipped the strap of a canvas bag of fresh shotgun rounds over his shoulder. "I'm ready, Ranger." Before stepping to the back door, he said, "Can I ask something from you?"

"Right now?" Sam gave him a curious look.

As if not hearing the ranger's question, the sheriff said, "It's about the widow Vertrees, the woman I was with when you rode in the other day?" He let out a breath. "She means a lot to me. If things should go badly for me out there tonight . . ." He paused, as if uncertain of how to finish his request.

"I'll tell her you spoke of her," said Sam.

Gale nodded. "Obliged, Ranger." Then he added before walking to the back door, "She's a good woman. She was a good wife to Dillard Vertrees, I understand, and I believe in time she would have been a good wife to me."

"She still might," said the ranger.

"No, I get a feeling this is as far as it's going, her and me," said Gale. "I'm asking, if something happens to me, would you look after her?"

"That's an unusual request, Sheriff. We should've talked about it earlier." Sam glanced out the window, seeing the detectives walking nearer. Soon the colonel would send someone to cover the back door, if he hadn't already.

"A man could do lots worse than Emma

316

Vertrees, Ranger," Gale said. Taking the hint, he also glanced out the window, then headed to the back door.

"I'm sure you're right," said the ranger, throwing the door open wide and taking cover beside the frame for a moment before going out.

"So, what do you say, Ranger?" Gale asked. Crouched and ready to go, he searched the darkness behind the building.

"If things don't go well, I'll do what I can," said Sam. "But I can't promise anything beyond that. She might have ideas of her own."

"You're right," said Gale. "I'm just saying if there's anything —"

"Stop it, Sheriff," Sam said stiffly. "Let's go."

The ranger let Gale run on ahead of him, he himself lagging back just long enough to close the door and lock it behind them. Hurrying, Burrack catching up with Gale, they stopped inside a stretch of woods sixty feet away and looked back at the building. "Just in time," Gale whispered, watching three figures appear out of the darkness and creep toward the locked door.

"This is as good a place as any to get things started," Sam said. He raised his rifle to his shoulder. "Be ready to ride."

The sheriff hurried toward their two horses standing hitched to a sapling five yards away, where the ranger had left them earlier. By the time he'd unhitched the animals and swung up into his saddle, a shot exploded from Sam's repeating rifle, followed by a scream of pain from one of the men at the rear office door.

"They're in the woods!" a voice shouted as the ranger came running to his waiting horse and snatched the reins from Gale's hand.

Even as they turned their horses and booted them into a run, Gale saw blossoms of gunfire from the direction of the building. One man lay dead in the dirt at the rear door. The other two had begun firing as they fled and took cover behind an abandoned buckboard wagon.

Riding as hard as they dared push the horses through the tangled woods and brush, the two lawmen heard shots whistle through the air behind them. When they had flanked the town from thirty yards away, they slowed their horses and looked to their right, where gunshots exploded on the wide dirt street. Heavy gunfire pounded the small plank and adobe building front and rear.

"The fighting's commenced without us," Sheriff Gale said wryly, "just the way we like it." But the two rode on in grim silence, both knowing that the fight was far from over. . . .

Out in front of an apothecary on the main street, Colonel Elgin stood in the dark with his whiskey bottle hanging from his left hand and his big Walker Colt hanging from his right. Above him hung a streetlamp; one of his men had shinnied up the lamppost and extinguished the flame, casting a portion of the street into darkness.

"Any word yet from Skimmer?" Pale Lee asked, leaning in close for the colonel to hear above the gunfire.

"No," said Elgin, "but we'll likely hear from him. Frank is a natural manhunter. If you hear shots from where you'd least expect to, that'll be Frank getting a jump ahead of these lawmen."

A few feet away, Bobby Vane called out loudly above a cacophony of gunfire, "If they're in there, Colonel, I'm betting they're dead by now." He pointed toward the sheriff's office, watching as bullets sliced through the darkness and ripped chunks of dried earth and pine splinters from the front of the small building.

"Keep them firing, Bobby!" the colonel said, loud enough for Vane to hear. "I'll tell you when they've had enough."

No sooner had he spoken than one of the new men named Delmar Sherman ran up and said, "Colonel, they're in the woods behind the jail! They shot Leroy as we were going inside to surprise them!"

"Damn it!" said Elgin. To Vane he called out above the noise, "Well, Bobby, there we have it. They made their getaway before we arrived. Have everyone cease fire!"

"Want me to call them all back here to regroup, Colonel?"

"No, Bobby," Elgin said. "Everybody stay where they are. We'll hear from them shortly, unless they've turned tail and run out of town at the last minute."

Beside him, Pale Lee warned, "I wouldn't count on that, Colonel."

"I'm not counting on it, Pale Lee," said Elgin, looking back and forth along the dark street as the firing began to die down. "But we can't very well stand here and shoot an empty building into the ground. The next move is theirs. It won't be long, I'm certain. Get around to everyone, make sure everybody's ready."

"Yes, sir, Colonel," said Pale Lee. Before turning to leave, he said, "This is just like the good old days, you giving the orders, me passing them on, eh?"

"Yes," said the colonel, "but keep in mind

how much more it will pay when you take these two down."

"Yes, sir." Pale Lee almost saluted, but then he caught himself, turned, and hurried away.

Frank Skimmer had ignored the sound of gunfire when it began erupting from the main street. He had the ones he wanted right here in front of him. "Go on," he said, jiggling the gun in Emma's face when she'd finished talking. Above the roar of gunfire, she'd told him everything, Memphis Beck listening on the ground right beside her, having watched Skimmer closely and found no way to make a move that wouldn't get Emma killed instead of saving her.

"That's — that's all there is to tell you," Emma said, knowing what that meant to a killer like Frank Skimmer. "I am sorry I killed him, if that helps any," she added.

"Not a bit, lady," said Skimmer. "You're dead." He jiggled his gun at her. "So is this outlaw boyfriend of yours."

"But you don't have to kill *him!*" Emma said quickly, looking straight into the barrel of the gun in Skimmer's hand. "His railroad reward is still good even if he's alive!"

"He's got to hang for murder, lady," Skimmer said with a half smile. "Which do you want to do, Beck, swing from a rope, soiling yourself, your toes scratching for some ground . . . or a fast bullet in the head?"

"You know which one I want, Skimmer," Beck said in a calm voice.

"But he didn't murder anybody!" Emma insisted. "I told you. It was me!"

"Explain it to her, Beck," Skimmer said.

"He doesn't want you to hang for murder, Emma," Beck said grimly. "He wants to kill you himself." As he spoke he wondered if he could swing his legs around fast enough, wrap them around Skimmer, and hold him while Emma made a play for the gun. If only she could know that was what he had in mind and be ready to make a move.

"Go on," Skimmer instructed, still wearing his half smile of satisfaction.

Beck shrugged. "With me he wins either way. I hang for murdering his brother, he gets the railroad reward anyway. A bullet in my head, he still gets paid."

"So, you see, lady, it's pretty damn generous of me to give your boyfriend a choice. Right, Beck?"

"You're all heart, Skimmer," Beck said flatly, his mind racing, wondering if he could count on Emma if he made a move. He knew there had been a time when she would be ready, just waiting for him to make such a move, but that had been a long time ago. He wasn't sure of her now. Should he do it? *Go on, do it!* he coaxed himself. If he didn't try she was dead anyway. He felt himself tense, his legs ready. *Do it! Do it! All right, here goes!*

But before he could make his move, Skimmer stood up and took a step back, the Colt leveling down toward Emma's head.

"No!" Beck shouted, seeing that nothing he could do would save her.

"Shut up!" Frank growled at Beck. Cocking the gun slowly as if drawing everything out to his satisfaction, he said to Emma, "So long, widow woman, see you in he—"

His words stopped short as a bullet exploded through his shirt from behind. Only a few drops of Skimmer's blood hit Emma, but it sprayed Beck from head to toe.

Emma gasped. Skimmer's gun was still pointed down at her as he rocked back and forth, his hand still trying to pull the trigger. "No! No!" she shouted as she rolled away, covering Memphis Beck, as if to keep him from getting shot.

Another bullet exploded from the darkness as if triggered by the sound of her voice. This one sliced through Skimmer and exploded out of his chest six inches from the first. "Damn you . . . lady!" Skimmer managed to say in spite of his life spilling down his chest into the dirt at his feet.

Four more shots ripped through him in rapid succession. Skimmer sank straight down slowly, the bullets seeming to climb up his chest until the last one caused his head to explode.

"Oh God! Oh God! Oh God!" Emma murmured nervously as Skimmer hit his knees and toppled forward onto the burning lantern. Beneath him the oil spread quickly into a bed of fire.

Seeing the fire from the lantern oil lick up around Skimmer's lifeless body, Beck said, "Emma, get the key! Hurry!"

Upon hearing the gunshots from the main street out in front of the bullet-riddled sheriff's office, Bobby Vane shouted, "What the hell?" He looked back along the street at the other men's shadowed faces in the glow of the streetlamps.

Knowing that Skimmer was the only man not out along the main street, Colonel Elgin smiled smugly to himself and shouted, "Frank Skimmer has found them! Get back there, every one of you . . . lend him a hand!"

"Right away, Colonel," said Jack Strap,

turning to hurry toward the sound of gunfire.

"No, not you, Strap!" said Elgin. "I'm
keeping you and my best men around
me. . . ."

CHAPTER 23

At the far end of town, Sheriff Gale and the ranger had stepped down from their horses at the time the fierce shooting started in the alleyway behind Emma's house. Just out of the glow of a streetlamp, the ranger saw the worried look on Gale's face. "Oh no, Emma!" he shouted. He bolted toward the sound of gunfire and the orange fire of the broken lantern Skimmer had fallen upon. Sam tried to grab his arm and stop him, but Gale moved too quickly.

"Don't run in there, Sheriff. They'll kill you," the ranger called out to him, knowing their voices were being heard up along the street. But Gale would have none of it. He ran from the main street toward the sound of gunfire even as the gunmen who'd stayed with the colonel started firing in the ranger's direction.

"They're not in the alleys!" the colonel shouted from farther up the wide dirt street to the men who'd gone running at the sound of gunfire. "They're right here . . . on the street!"

With bullets whistling blindly past his head, Sam dived farther out of the street-lamp glow, onto a boardwalk, and ran in a crouch around the corner of a building. There was nothing he could do for the sheriff now. All he could think about was staying alive.

Fifteen yards away Jack Strap and the Romanian came to a halt beside a stack of shipping crates out in front of the Little Aces Overland Stage Company. They had hurried ahead of the colonel and surrounding top guns, remembering how the ranger had left them afoot up on the high trail.

"Here's our chance to even old scores, Vlak," Jack Strap said, hugging his back against the wooden crates. He peeped around the corner and called out to the darkness where he'd seen the ranger leap away from the outer edge of the lamplight, "It's Jack Strap and Vlak Blesko, Ranger! We haven't forgotten about you!"

Sam looked around the corner of the building without answering. Seeing the crates where the voice came from, and seeing the dark shadowy silhouettes moving from cover to cover along the street beyond, he raised his rifle to his shoulder. He knew he would have to shoot and run, to keep the gunmen from homing in on his muzzle flash.

Behind the crates, Strap asked in a whisper, "Are you ready, Vlak?"

"I'm ready," Vlak replied. Yet as the two prepared to make a run toward the spot where they'd last seen the ranger, they saw Mike the Fist Holland step out into the grainy edge of lamplight on the other side of the street. No sooner had the detective made the move than a shot from the ranger's rifle knocked him backward to the ground.

Without hesitation, the Romanian saw the flash of the ranger's gun barrel and returned fire, rapidly. But before his third shot struck the corner of the building where the ranger had fired from, a shot thumped into the wooden crate from a different position. "He has already moved!" said Vlak.

"Then move with him, damn it!" said Strap. As soon as he'd spoken, he leaned around the corner of the crates and fired wildly along the dark street.

This was how it would be, Sam told himself, levering another round into the rifle chamber as he watched a shadowy figure move along the boardwalk toward him. He could hold off his share of the colonel's men. But in the distance he heard the shots continue from the alley behind the Vertrees cottage. He hoped the sheriff could do as well. . . .

In the alley, Joe Graft lay on his back, his hands clasped to the gaping wound in his chest, breathing heavily through his recently broken nose. "Who the hell . . . shot me?" he murmured to himself, staring up at the starless sky.

Curtis Clay did not answer, although he sat only a few feet away, deftly reloading his big Remington.

Scattered throughout the alleyway on both sides, and through the empty brush-covered lots on each side of the Vertrees cottage, the detectives fired back and forth wildly. Streaks of orange-blue fire split the darkness. Clay's eyes caught glimpses of the gunfire, but only dimly, as he closed the Remington's cylinder, stood up in a crouch, and centered his hearing on his next target.

"It came from Joe, over here!" said Fletus Belton, running through brush firing as he raced toward his downed companion. But no sooner had he shouted and fired than Clay's shot slammed into his chest, picked him up, and flung him backward into the brush.

The detectives' gunfire grew heavier upon

seeing and hearing the shot that killed Belton. But Clay wasn't worried. He stooped down and walked away in a crouch, knowing by heart the thin footpath that he himself had worn into the ground through many years of him and Little Dog walking the vacant lots of a night. When he'd gone a few yards, working his way closer to the buggy, he turned and listened closely to the sound of footsteps running through the brush toward him.

In the darkness Carlos Richards cursed aloud as he ran in the direction of the bullet that had silenced Joe Graft. He saw the sudden flash and heard the explosion, yet he hardly knew what hit him when Clay stood up, unseen, only twenty feet in front of him and fired.

Clay heard the sound of Carlos' body tumble through the brush and come to a silent halt.

Shots exploded anew from the rest of the men as Clay moved away, calmly, unhurriedly inside his pitch-black world. *In the darkest night only the blind have eyes,* he told himself somberly.

As soon as Skimmer's body had fallen forward and begun burning, Emma had wasted no time reaching in quickly and getting the key from his hip pocket as the flames grew dangerously close to her hand. As shots began erupting, she'd managed to loosen the cuffs from Beck's wrists and tossed them aside as he rose to his feet, bullets whistling past them.

"Let's go!" he shouted, grabbing her arm, shoving her up into the buggy, and scrambling in right behind her. Slapping the reins to the buggy horse, Beck sent it bolting forward, his horse hurrying along behind. Looking back, she saw Sheriff Gale run into the firelight of Skimmer's burning body and look all around for her, calling out, "Emma? Emma?" He stared in the direction of the buggy as if having seen her, and now searched the darkness she'd disappeared into.

Looking back at him, she saw him suddenly bolt upright, his arms spread wide as a bullet sliced through him.

"Oh no, the sheriff's hit!" she said.

"We can't go back, Emma," Beck said, giving her only a sidelong glance in the darkness as he continued slapping the reins to the buggy horse. "He knew his risks, he took his chances."

"I know," she said, turning her face forward with determination. "That's what Dillard always told me." Behind them bullets still exploded, but the sound soon began to grow distant as the buggy rolled on, away from town where streaks of fire split back and forth across the night.

On the street, the ranger had noticed the waning of gunfire as a glow of orange flame and greasy black smoke spiraled upward from Skimmer's burning body and the surrounding dried brush, wild grass, and bracken across the alley. He'd heard the sheriff cry out for Emma Vertrees and he'd heard his voice cut short.

Sam knew what that meant, but he had no time to slow down and see about the sheriff right now. If Sheriff Gale had gotten himself wounded or killed trying to protect the woman he loved, so be it. Sam understood. But whether Gale was wounded or dead, the ranger's purpose now was to keep from joining him.

Sam knew the clock was ticking. The cover of night was his only advantage against so many men. But at the end of the night, the advantage would fall to the detectives. He needed to thin down the odds while he could, he reminded himself, raising his rifle to his shoulder, ready to fire and keep moving.

Up the street Filo Heath stood beside the colonel. He'd abandoned his photo equipment for the night and taken a rifle from his saddle boot in order to join the fight. Feeling secure in the cover of total darkness where the streetlamps had been put out, he ventured a step forward and took it upon himself to call out, "Ranger, when this is over I promise to take a nice photo of you tied to a board and mail to your fam—"

"Filo, shut up, you fool!" the colonel shouted. But his words came too late. A blossom of gunfire exploded, not from the end of the street where the ranger had been firing from, but from the mouth of the alleyway almost straight across from the colonel and his remaining top gunmen.

"Oh!" Filo said, sinking down sideways onto the ground. He caught himself with his free hand, his other hand clasping the bullet wound in his side for a moment. "I'm . . . shot," he said in disbelief. Then he turned limp in death and fell into the dirt.

"You damn fool!" the colonel raged, even as he and the others fled from Heath's body and took cover beside a building. Lowering his voice, the colonel said, "I saw the shot, it came from over there. Who the hell is it?"

"Blast whoever it is!" Pale Lee shouted, firing as he did so.

As the men fired across at the alley, Curtis Clay had already turned and hurriedly felt his way along the building, back into the alley. As the men fired on Clay, from his end of the street the ranger quickly sent round after round of rifle fire into their midst, one grazing Pale Lee's leg. The other shot hit the colonel in his left shoulder. He staggered backward, leaned against the side of the building, and caught his breath.

"All right, that's enough of this!" the colonel demanded when the impact of the rifle shot began wearing off. "I want this place lit up like a noonday sun!" He felt all around until his hand closed on Pale Lee's arm. "Get some men and build a fire, set the empty building ablaze. We can't keep stumbling around in the dark . . . it's not working!"

"Set it on fire, Colonel?" said Pale Lee. "What are the railroad owners going to say when word of it gets back to them?"

"To hell with the railroad owners!" the colonel shouted, enraged. "It won't matter if we're all dead! Set it ablaze and let any townsmen know they're to stay back and let it burn." He bowed his head and shook it closely, grateful no one could see him in the pitch-dark. "All of our detectives . . . our whole damned posse, and we haven't managed to kill two lousy lawmen. . . ."

■ ■ ■ ■

From his latest position beside the telegraph office, the ranger watched flames grow from the size of three torches into licking flames. He could have fired on the torches as the three men carried them into the building, but he wasn't ready to give up his new spot just yet. He knew the colonel had the rest of his men watching closely for him as the torch men rushed inside the empty land title building.

Besides, he told himself, he needed time to reload and let the colonel and his men wonder where he'd disappeared to. Lying still, he took a few minutes, a few deep breaths, and reloaded his rifle while he watched the flames grow and swell, reaching out the windows and up the sides of the vacant building. Then he levered a round into the rifle chamber, looked up along the roofline, which would soon be the only part of town not exposed by firelight, and moved away as quietly as a ghost.

From the vacant lot to the right of Emma's cottage, Curtis Clay stopped and stooped down long enough to sniff the smell of burning wood and listen to the crackle of the growing fire coming from the main street. He still held the big Remington in his right hand. His left hand cupped his forehead, where blood ran down freely from the gash in his forehead.

"You did well, Curtis Clay," he murmured to himself, standing in a crouch and moving along now on the familiar footpath back toward his shack. He grinned and chuckled aloud at the throbbing knot beneath the deep bloody gash. "For a blind man in a gunfight . . . you did a real *fine* job."

When he got to the shack, he slipped inside and stood for a moment listening for the sound of anyone behind him. Once satisfied that no one had followed him, he stepped across the shack toward the gentle batting sound of Little Dog's tail tapping on the bed. "Ah, I hear you there, awake," Clay said quietly. "You must be feeling better, wagging your old ragged tail."

Sitting down on the side of the bed, he laid the Remington down and said to the dog, "Well, I busted my fool head on something out there. But it'll be all right. It'll be sore for a few days, but it's worth it, Little Dog. You and I can convalesce together."

He sat slumped in silence for a few minutes, his bloody forehead in his left hand, his Remington hanging from his right, almost touching the floor. Finally he said in a more gentle, serious tone, "I saved the woman, Little Dog. Saved her just like I always knew I could when the time come."

Tears welled up in Clay's cloudy sightless eyes with pride. "I helped the lawmen too . . . I sure enough did. Nobody'll ever know it. I'll never tell. But I did my part for Little Aces . . . for *our* town, just like anybody would." The tears spilled and ran freely down his face with the fresh streaks of blood. "Lord have mercy, yes." He laid his hand on the dog's side and rubbed it gently as it licked his hand. "I sure enough did. . . ."

CHAPTER 24

The colonel's men had set the fire and left the building quickly, knowing they would make good targets amid the firelight. Once away from the fire, they'd taken cover and waited, silent, watchful, the flames reflecting in their guarded eyes. "Think maybe he gave up and left?" a new man whispered beside Bobby Vane.

Vane just gave him a look.

"Well, he *could* have," the young man said.

"Who are you?" Vane asked quietly.

"I'm Chris Denver the Third," the young man said. "I rode in the other day with Detective Hodges and the others."

"Denver . . . Oh yeah," said Vane, "you're the one whose pa is friends with one of the rail owners."

"Yes, that's correct," said the young man, his tone turning stronger now that his name had been recognized.

"Your pa wanted you to get some dirt on

your hands, so to speak, between classes?" Vane gave a smug grin.

"I suppose getting some practical experience is part of it," said the young man.

"Practical experience . . ." Vane shook his head and spat, looking along the shadowy street at the dead lying strewn in their grim twisted repose. After a silent moment of staring at the crackling, licking flames, Vane said, "How's it working out for you so far?"

"I have to admit, I find it a bit distressing," the young man said. "This ranger is willing to kill and die over two men who would have hanged anyway? That makes no sense to me." He shook his head slowly, deeply pondering the matter as firelight flickered in his wire-rimmed spectacles.

"Unless you scratch really deep for it, most things men fight and die for make no sense, especially to men who won't kill or die for anything. That's the practical experience your pa was looking for, I'm guessing."

"I suppose so." The young man gave a shrug. He didn't know.

Bobby Vane took a battered tin whiskey flask from his pocket, opened it, sipped from it, and passed it to the young man. Looking back at the dead in the street and the raging fire, Vane let out a long breath. "Let me ask you, Chris Denver *the Third.* If we sent your pa a letter telling him he'd better send us fifty thousand dollars, else we'd kill you . . . think he'd send it to us?"

The young man gave him a strange look. "Who do you mean when you say *us?*"

"Us," said Vane, "you know, you and me?" He grinned slyly. "Think he'd pay up?"

"I don't know, why?" said young Denver, considering it.

Vane looked him up and down. Seeming to have decided for himself, he said, "Never mind, I was just thinking out loud."

"I suppose if Father thought I was in immediate danger, he might consider such a transaction."

"Yeah, right." Vane nodded and took his flask back from the young man. "Do us both a favor, Denver. From now on when you're around me, just don't say anything."

Standing in the darkness of a boardwalk overhang, the colonel took a step forward and looked up the long dirt street. Holding a bloody bandanna to his shoulder wound, he said to the men gathered nearby behind what cover they could find, "Men, I'm counting on you. I'm bleeding, and I want this matter ended. There's an additional five hundred to whoever kills Burrack." He looked off along the street, not knowing how many of his men were still alive, taking cover in the darkness.

Listening from atop a roof two buildings away, Sam peeped down back and forth from one end of town to the other. The main street below lay awash in dim flickering firelight. From the rooftops the ranger still had an advantage, but he knew it couldn't last, especially with the colonel upping the ante five hundred dollars.

In a crouch, the ranger walked along the roofline quietly, keeping close to the facade, hoping to get into a better firing position. But before he'd made it halfway across the roof, Jack Strap and the Romanian stood up on a rooftop across the street and began firing.

"There he is, up there, Colonel!" Vane shouted, standing and firing, having caught a glimpse of the ranger as Sam returned fire. Hearing Vane, Sam turned to run for cover now that his whereabouts were known. But as he ran down the slanted roof to the rear of the building, he felt the boards beneath his feet grow weaker with each step.

By the time he'd reached the center of the wide roof, the boards began cracking and breaking apart. Before he could do anything to stop himself, he felt himself fall helplessly amid a cloud of splinters, broken boards, and tarpaper. As he clawed the air instinctively for something to hold on to, his rifle flew from his hands.

When he landed amid a pile of broken shipping crates, he did not lose consciousness, but the breath had been knocked out of him and he lay stunned for a moment, hearing the sound of boots running along the boardwalk toward the building. Then he heard those same boots kick the door in and come running toward him. He tried to draw his Colt, but before he could he felt Bobby Vane's boot clamp down on his gun hand.

"No, you don't, Ranger," Vane said, his gun pointed down at the ranger's face. "I got you fair and square. You just made me fifteen hundred dollars." He cocked the hammer of his big Smith & Wesson revolver and started to pull the trigger.

But from the doorway the colonel called out, "Hold it, Bobby! I want to see his face when you send him straight to hell." He walked forward, holding his bandanna to his wounded shoulder, Pale Lee limping along beside him. Behind them Roundhead Mitchell hurried in, his pistol-grip shotgun in hand, the engraved ivory-handled Colt in his belt.

Stepping in and nudging Vane aside, the colonel looked down at the ranger and held his wounded shoulder forward for Sam to see. "Look at it, you son of a bitch, this is what you did to me! This alone is reason enough to kill you."

The ranger didn't answer; he lay still, trying to collect himself, get his breath back, and look for a way to make a stand for himself. His rifle lay a few feet away, atop a pile of rooftop debris, covered with dirt and splinters, but ready to fire if he could only get his hand on it and cock the hammer.

Colonel Elgin straightened and said bitterly, "Before you *die,* tell me something, Ranger. Are you any better than my men and I? We hanged your prisoners without a trial. But you took vengeance for us hanging them when you had no proof we did it?"

"No, I'm no better than you, Elgin," Sam managed to say, regaining his breath, feeling his strength coming back. "But the railroads gave you power and put you above the law. The bigger you get the further outside the law somebody will have to go to stop you. I figured I ought to give it a try."

"Yes," said the colonel, with a smug grin of satisfaction, "and just look where it got you."

"I didn't make it," Sam said, "but I'm hoping I brought attention to it."

From outside, Jack Strap and the Romanian ran in through the open doorway, out of breath, having climbed down from the roof across the street. "Let us through, we want to see this," Strap demanded as they maneuvered their way through the few remaining men, up alongside Pale Lee and the colonel.

The colonel gave a dark chuckle at what the ranger had said. "Do you think anybody is going to give a damn that I hanged those two rogues without benefit of a trial?"

"Probably not," Sam replied. He resisted the urge to look at the rifle again, yet tried to judge how quickly he could grab it, given the opportunity. "But I couldn't turn it loose just because they were nobodies. That's not how I lived . . . it's not how I'll die."

"Well spoken, Ranger," the colonel said with sarcasm. He turned to Bobby Vane and Pale Lee and said, "It will be daylight before long. Take him out in the street. We'll kill him in the dirt where he belongs."

Sam knew if he ever made a move for the rifle, it had to be now before the two gunmen reached down to lift him to his feet. But before he could make a move, he looked through the crowd and saw a bloody figure appear in the open doorway. *Gale . . . ?*

Before he'd even fully recognized the sheriff, he saw the raised gun buck in his bloody hand and heard the blast rattle the windows on the building.

"Colonel!" Pale Lee shouted in disbelief as the colonel's blood and brain matter splattered all over the men, the wall, the debris, and the ranger. Even as the impact of the shot hurled the colonel's body past him, Sam scrambled sidelong in the rubble from the falling roof and grabbed his rifle.

Rolling into a firing position, the ranger swung the rifle first toward Roundhead Mitchell just as the detective turned his sawed-off shotgun toward the sheriff. Sam's first shot hit Roundhead in his side, causing his shotgun to jerk toward the large window when it went off. A wide spray of glass and buckshot killed one of the men who had come running when he'd seen the sheriff stagger from the alley across the street.

Hearing the ranger's rifle shot, Pale Lee swung his gun away from Sheriff Gale, but only in time to have Sam's second shot hammer him in his stomach, picking him up and flinging him backward as he jack-knifed at the waist. His gun fell from his hands as he grabbed his belly. Levering a round quickly, the ranger turned his rifle toward Strap and the Romanian as they both fired at him, their shots missing by only inches.

Amid their fire, Sam's next shot hammered Strap backward as a shot from the Romanian sliced across the ranger's forearm. The ranger's next shot silenced Blesko, sending him sliding backward in the rubble on the floor.

The wounded sheriff wobbled unsteadily in the open doorway. Sam swung his rifle toward Bobby Vane just as the sheriff and Vane traded shots. Vane's shot hit Gale in the side. The sheriff's big Starr bucked again and sent Bobby Vane spinning on his way to the floor with a gaping bullet hole in his forehead. Chris Denver the Third ran across the debris-littered floor, leaped through the window frame, and ran away into the darkness. Two other new men ran out through the rear door without firing a shot.

Sam scrambled to his feet, ran to the sheriff, and pulled him inside and down onto the floor. Then he ran back to the open doorway in time to see a gunman from across the street sliding to a halt. The man dropped his rifle and raised his hands chest high, seeing the ranger's rifle pointed at him. "Don't shoot! I'm done, Ranger! You win!"

"Tell anybody else out there that the

colonel is dead," Sam called out as the man backed away into the darkness. "Tell them to go home. There's no money on my head now."

"I'll tell them, Ranger," the man said. "It's all over. We don't want no more."

Sam listened to the sound of a bucket brigade forming out on the dirt street as he kneeled on the floor, cradling Sheriff Gale in his arm. The telegraph clerk had ventured up to the open doorway, looked all around inside, and said, "My goodness. I better go get some help."

Sam had only nodded. He loosened the bandanna from around his neck and wiped the sheriff's bloody face. He pulled the front of Gale's shirt open for a look at the chest wound. He felt a little relieved not seeing any foamy blood. "Looks like it missed your lungs, Sheriff," he said quietly.

Gale gave a faint ironic smile and said in a weak voice, "My . . . ain't I . . . the lucky one?"

Sam didn't answer. Instead he said, "I wasn't expecting you back. You most likely saved my life, Sheriff."

"I had to . . . come back, Ranger," he said in a halting voice. "I felt bad . . . leaving you the way I did."

"How's the woman?" Sam asked.

"She's gone, Ranger," he said. "I thought I . . . saw her leave in a buggy . . . Memphis Beck's horse behind it . . . but I'm not sure."

"The telegraph clerk went to get help," Sam said, seeing by the look in his eyes that *yes,* he was sure. "You lie still until it gets here."

"I'm sorry . . . I left you when I did, Ranger," he said, already drifting out of consciousness.

"It's all right," Sam said. "You showed up at the right time. That's the main thing." He held the sheriff for a moment with his head bowed, weariness starting to catch up to him.

He looked up moments later when he heard footsteps crossing the boardwalk from the street. He saw the telegraph clerk walk away from the open doorway. Behind the young clerk, Emma Vertrees stepped inside and stopped. "Look who I found riding into town," the clerk said.

She only gave the ranger a passing glance before looking down at the sheriff, asleep, his head resting in the crook of Sam's arm. "Is he . . . ?"Her words trailed.

"He's alive," Sam said. He watched her walk over slowly, then stop and look down at the two lawmen. "He said he saw you leaving town." Sam's eyes searched hers. He wouldn't ask why, but he wanted to know.

"Yes, I —" She started to give him a story, but she couldn't come up with any she thought he'd believe. "I *was* leaving, Ranger," she said, "but I changed my mind." Speaking over her shoulder to the clerk as she dropped her shawl and unbuttoned her dress sleeves, she said, "I need some bandages and some water. Please hurry."

No sooner had the clerk left than Sam leaned sideways a little, enough to see the big dun standing at the hitch rail out front. He recognized it at once in the flickering firelight. "That's Warren Beck's horse," he said.

"Yes, it is," Emma said flatly. "He gave it to me." She stooped down and pulled the sheriff's shirt open carefully, examining the wound. "Memphis Beck and I were once friends —" She caught herself and shook her head. "No, we were much *more* than friends, Ranger." She cut Sam a guarded glance. "I was leaving here with him when Vince saw me."

"Oh?" Sam just listened. Whatever she said was up to her.

"But we got out there, and I thought about who I am, where I am, where I've been the past few years." She paused, then said, "Anyway, I decided I couldn't leave here. I suppose I've been too long in Little Aces."

Sam watched how skillfully she attended to the wounded sheriff. "Vince is a good man, Ranger," she said.

Sam watched and listened, wondering if she was trying to convince herself that his being a *good man* was enough.

"We were young, Memphis Beck and I, when we were together," she offered softly, her fingers touching injured flesh gently, as if she understood it. "Time changes everything, especially a person's perspective." She sighed. "So, Memphis and I said good-bye, and he rode off to meet some of his friends, go off on his next adventure . . . and here I am. Right back in Little Aces. But I'll say one thing — I sure managed to snap out of mourning. Does this all sound crazy and strange to you?"

"No," said Sam, "I understand."

"Do you, Ranger?" she asked. "Do you really?"

"Yes, I believe I do," he said. "Memphis Beck belongs to a world you stepped out of. You miss it, the way a person always misses the past. You wanted to step back into it, but you know now that the past is best seen in memories."

She looked at him a bit surprised. "So you do understand?" Sam noted the tears well up in her eyes, her fingers busily at work with the bandages. "I have to tell Vincent everything . . . just like I had to tell Dillard before we married and took up our lives together." She touched the shoulder of her dress to her eyes and kept on working. "Do you suppose he'll understand?"

"Why not?" said Sam. "I did."

She looked up at him, then looked off through the front door into the dark night away from Little Aces toward the trail she'd ridden back in on. "Yes, why not?" she said. She looked at Sam with a wry smile. "After all, you're both lawmen." She shook her head. "And you lawmen are all alike."

Sam nodded and returned her smile. "I suppose that's true." He looked out through the open door, across the street where Curtis Clay stopped at a hitch rail and stood with his face toward the waning fire. A few inches in front of him, Little Dog limped to a halt and sat down in the dirt. "Maybe we're all the same in lots of ways, men and women alike," Sam said quietly. "We all need to prove to ourselves that we're alive now and then."

He watched her nod in agreement and go

back to cleaning the sheriff's wound. Gale let out a soft moan, as if he recognized her gentle touch and somehow knew he would be all right now.

I expect you are the lucky one at that . . . , Sam thought, looking down at the sheriff's sleeping face.

ABOUT THE AUTHOR

Ralph Cotton is a former ironworker, second mate on a commerical barge, teamster, horse trainer, and lay minister with the Lutheran church. Visit his Web site at www .RalphCotton.com.